**Select praise for
New York Times bestselling author
Maisey Yates**

"Her characters excel at defying the norms and
providing readers with…an emotional investment."
—*RT Book Reviews* on *Claim Me, Cowboy*
(Top Pick)

"A sassy, romantic and sexy story about two
characters whose chemistry is off the charts."
—*RT Book Reviews* on *Smooth-Talking Cowboy*
(Top Pick)

"This is an exceptional example of an opposites-
attract romance with heartfelt writing and solid
character development.… This is a must-read that will
have you believing in love."
—*RT Book Reviews* on *Seduce Me, Cowboy* (Top Pick)

"Their relationship is displayed with a quick writing
style full of double entendres, sexy sarcasm and
enough passion to melt the mountain snow!"
—*RT Book Reviews* on *Hold Me, Cowboy* (Top Pick)

Books by Maisey Yates

The Carsons of Lone Rock

Rancher's Forgotten Rival
Best Man Rancher
One Night Rancher

Gold Valley Vineyards

Rancher's Wild Secret
Claiming the Rancher's Heir
The Rancher's Wager
Rancher's Christmas Storm

Copper Ridge

Take Me, Cowboy
Hold Me, Cowboy
Seduce Me, Cowboy
Claim Me, Cowboy
Want Me, Cowboy
Need Me, Cowboy

For more books by Maisey Yates,
visit www.maiseyyates.com.

You can also find Maisey Yates on Facebook,
along with other Harlequin Desire authors,
at Facebook.com/HarlequinDesireAuthors!

MAISEY YATES

One Night Rancher
and
Need Me, Cowboy

HARLEQUIN
DESIRE

DESIRE™

Recycling programs for this product may not exist in your area.

ISBN-13: 978-1-335-67995-6

One Night Rancher & Need Me, Cowboy

Copyright © 2023 by Harlequin Enterprises ULC

One Night Rancher
Copyright © 2023 by Maisey Yates

Need Me, Cowboy
First published in 2019. This edition published in 2023.
Copyright © 2019 by Maisey Yates

For questions and comments about the quality of this book, please contact us at CustomerService@Harlequin.com.

Harlequin Enterprises ULC
22 Adelaide St. West, 41st Floor
Toronto, Ontario M5H 4E3, Canada
www.Harlequin.com

Printed in U.S.A.

CONTENTS

ONE NIGHT RANCHER

Chapter 1

"You have to spend the night in the hotel if you want to buy it. Because they had too many people back out. Isn't that completely wild, Grandpa? I mean, I'm sure that it is haunted. Nothing can be around that long and not be."

Cara Summers looked up at her grandfather. He was sitting on the shelf behind the bar. In an old Jack Daniel's bottle.

Just as he had asked.

Cara had done her very best to fulfill his last wishes. Cremated and then placed on that shelf behind the bar so he could see everything.

He didn't answer her question.

At least not audibly. She didn't expect him to. Though she often felt his presence. It wasn't anything she could really describe. But she knew he was there. It was why she talked to him. Almost as easily as she had when he was here. Hell, maybe it was even easier because he didn't interrupt.

"The bar is empty, scrap. Who are you talking to?"

She knew the voice. She didn't have to turn.

Even if she didn't recognize the tone—and of course she would, after this many years of friendship. It was the way it made her feel. Because that was the thing. Jace Carson was one of six brothers. They all sounded relatively similar. Deep, rich male voices. But not a single one of them made goose bumps break out over her arms or made a suspicious warmth spread all through her body when they spoke. No. That would be way too convenient. Kit Carson liked to flirt with her, or at least he had before he had married Shelby Sohappy. And Flint enjoyed flirting with her to rile Jace up. But she knew that none of it was serious. Well. She had a feeling that any number of the Carson brothers would've happily had a dalliance with her if she was of a mind. They weren't exactly known for their discernment when it came to women. Every one of them except for Jace. Oh, Jace wasn't discerning either. But Jace was...

He was not interested in her that way. And just the mere suggestion of it made him growl.

They were friends. Best friends. Had been since middle school. It was a funny friendship. He was protective of her. And sometimes a little bit paternalistic. Or brotherly. But that was the thing. He saw her as a younger sister. The younger sister he no longer had, she knew.

And in some ways, she was an emotional surrogate for what he had lost when he had lost Sophia. She knew that. She'd always known it.

Every so often these days it made her feel bristly and annoyed.

Because the problem with Jace was that she wanted him.

And he didn't want her.

"Just telling Grandpa about my next move."

"Right," he said looking around the bar. "Is he here now?"

"He's always here," she said, gesturing to the make-shift urn.

"Cara…"

"I know you don't believe in any of this. But I do. I believe that I can talk to him. And that he hears me."

"I'm sure that's comforting."

"I think that sounds more condescending and less accepting than you think."

"I don't mean to be condescending. But I don't really mean to be accepting either. Just… I can understand why you need to think it, I guess."

That was Jace. He just didn't have a fantastical bone in his body.

He himself was a wonder. A masculine wonder. Over six foot but with broad shoulders, a well-muscled chest and not a spare ounce of fat over his six-pack abs.

He had a square jaw and compelling mouth with the thin white scar that ran through his upper lip. His nose was straight, his eyes the color of denim. Each Carson brother was sort of the same man in a different font, a remix of very similar and very attractive features.

It seemed kind of unfair that all six of them were just there. Exposing the female populace to their overwhelming male beauty. But there they were.

The really unfair thing was that none of their particular beauty called to her the way that Jace's did.

When she had been a kid, the first time she'd met him, it was like the hollow space had opened up inside of her chest, just to make room for the sheer enormity of the feelings that he created within her.

She could still remember that moment.

She'd been so angry. And so hurt. Wearing one of her oversize T-shirts to school, her grandfather's wristwatch, a pair of secondhand sneakers and jeans with holes in the knees. She had a brand-new pink binder that her grandfather had gotten her, and she knew that it had been a big deal. There were so many years where the bar that her grandpa owned—The Thirsty Mule—barely made ends meet, particularly back then. The downtown of Lone Rock had been functionally dead in the early 2000s. All the way up until the 2010s, and there just hadn't been a whole lot of money to go around.

Most of the shops back then had signs in the window that they were for sale or rent, while they sat empty.

Not only that, her grandpa just hadn't known what to do with a young granddaughter that he had taken in a few years earlier.

He loved her. Fiercely. But he had all sons, and his wife was long gone. And the gesture of buying her the pink Trapper Keeper that she had wanted so much had been... It had meant the world to her.

But there was a group of girls at the school who lived to terrorize her. For being tall and skinny and flat chested. For not being cool at all. For the fact that half of her clothes were men's, and certainly weren't in fashion. For her long blond hair, her freckles, her horse teeth...

She was occasionally amused by those memories. Because suddenly at age sixteen her boobs had come in, and when they had come in, it had been a real boon. She was stacked now, thank you very much. And it turned her a pretty impressive amount in tips on a nightly basis at the bar.

Whatever.

She thought maybe she should feel a little bit guilty that sometimes she wore a low-cut top to collect a bit more cash. But then she thought of the girl that she had been in seventh grade. The one who'd had *president of the itty-bitty titty committee* written on the outside of her locker door. And then she pulled the tank top lower and leaned toward the patron with a big smile. Everybody had their childhood trauma.

But, her breast boon notwithstanding, she could clearly remember when that same group of girls had taken that light Trapper Keeper with its beautiful white butterflies and tossed it into the dirt.

And one of the boys on the football team had held her back while they'd made sure that it was irreparably torn and stained.

She hadn't let them see her cry. No, she turned around and punched the boy right in his face. And then she got sent to the principal's office. For fighting.

"What was I supposed to do? He was holding on to me."

"You're supposed to go and get a teacher," the principal had said, maddeningly calm.

"Why wasn't a teacher there to help?"

"They can't be everywhere at once. You can't retaliate. You have to get help."

She had decided that was bullshit. Then and there. She had burned with anger.

And in fact, had said as much to the principal. "That's bullshit."

"Young lady, we can't tolerate that language."

And that was how she had found herself suspended, because she had thrown even more language in the principal's direction. And the funny thing was, she had just been channeling her grandpa and the way he talked on any given Sunday.

But then, that was the root of the problem. Everything

about her was wrong. Wrong on some level. She said the wrong words, and more, the wrong things. She didn't know how to be a girl. Whatever that meant. Except that she knew that she wasn't even in the same species as those other girls. And not just because she wasn't a bitch. They had really been bitches. They were *still* bitches.

But she had ended up crying down by the river behind the school. Not sure how she was going to go home and tell her grandfather that she was suspended for a week.

And she was trying to wash the dirt off the binder, scrubbing at it in the water, trying to find a way out of her misery.

And that was when he'd appeared.

He'd been in eighth grade. Tall and lanky at the time, with shaggy blond hair. His family had only come to town a couple of years before, and any other family would have still been considered new. But while the Carsons hadn't lived in Lone Rock for a few years, they owned land there and were part of the original founding families, so they were considered foundational, not new.

"Hey," he said. "What's the matter?"

"Nothing," she said. "Well. Everything. First of all, middle school is bullshit."

"Right," he said. "No argument from me. Why are you crying?"

"I got suspended. Because these girls ruined my binder. And this boy was holding on to me so that I couldn't stop them. So I punched him in the face."

"Good," he said, nodding decisively.

"Then I told the principal that I thought middle school was bullshit."

"And that's why you're suspended?"

"Yes."

"It all sounds reasonable to me. Not the suspension.

*Everything you did. The question is, why didn't it seem
reasonable to the principal?"*

"I can't answer that."

"I'm Jace Carson. What's your name?"

*And she suddenly felt shy and self-conscious. Because
he was an older boy. And he was just so... Cute. And
older boys, or boys her age, or really any boys, never
talked to her.*

*"I'm Cara Summers. But I warn you. I'm not cool.
And they call me horse teeth. And if you talk to me, they
probably won't think you're cool either."*

"Seventh graders? I'm fine with that."

He had walked her home. He had helped her explain
the situation to her grandpa. And then he had helped with
some chores around the property.

He told her a couple days later, after he came by to
visit and finish some of the work, she reminded him of
his sister.

He hadn't explained any of that then.

But later, about six months into their friendship, he
told her that he had a sister who would be her age now.
One who had died when she was a little girl. "You remind me of her. Makes me want to look out for you. The
way that I looked out for her."

And that was it. They had really been best friends ever
since then. Through a whole lot of things.

She'd admired him, for years. Just looked up to him
like he was a god.

And she felt weird and possessive, and hadn't particularly liked it when he had girlfriends.

Not that he ever had them for all that long.

And she knew that when he was out riding in the rodeo
he did a lot of casual hooking up. But she just did her best
not to think about that.

It wasn't until one night at the bar, when she had been back there helping her grandpa, that she had really watched him putting the moves on a woman. He had his hand on her hip, and then he'd let it drift slowly up to her waist, and Cara had felt a physical, visceral response to it.

And that was when she'd realized.

It was when she'd realized that she wasn't just possessive. She didn't just admire him.

She was attracted to him.

She wanted him to touch her like that.

And she thought about saying something. About asking him if he would be her... It was so embarrassing. If he would be her first. Because she trusted Jace, so, it seemed like a pretty reasonable idea.

But then her grandpa had died. And that had been one of the single most devastating, destabilizing things that had ever happened. And in the four years since, she had done her level best to build herself back up. To take the bar and build it up. And handily, Lone Rock was having a bit of a boom, a resurgence. People were enjoying traveling locally, taking road trips, spending time in small towns.

There were all these posts that went up on the internet. These most charming small town posts, and Lone Rock was almost always there, as an 1800s gold rush town that still had original Western facades on a bunch of the buildings. With outlaw lore deeply embedded into the dirt all around, it was an attractive place for people to come and visit. Which was why she was now ready to invest in the hotel property. She wanted to reopen it. She wanted to get it online. It was haunted, that was the thing. And ghost stays were incredibly popular.

It was just that there had been three buyers that had backed out, and now the seller—who didn't live in Lone

Rock—was demanding that potential buyers spend at least one night there to prove that they could handle it. To prove that they knew what they were getting into.

She wasn't afraid. In fact, she loved that stuff. It was just the idea of spending the night there alone…

It didn't really appeal.

But that was future Cara's problem. Right now, she had a bar to run, and Jace was here.

"What brings you in?" she asked.

"Beer. And a burger. I figured I would try to miss the evening rush. It's too hard to talk to you when you've got all those bros crowded around the bar drooling on you."

She rolled her eyes. It was the funny thing about her relationship with Jace. It wasn't like they didn't acknowledge those kinds of things. He talked about men panting after her all the time and was often growling at his brothers when they made commentary that was specifically designed to rile him up.

And she often talked about the way women acted like fools around him.

But they didn't make it personal. It wasn't about what he thought about her. But what other men thought.

And of course she never shared any actual details about her love life.

Well. Probably because she didn't have one.

That was irrelevant.

"Nobody drools," she said. "And even if they did, I don't mind if they leave tips."

"Yeah. Well, the place has become awfully popular."

"It's definitely different than it used to be."

"Too bad Mitch never got to see it."

"Of course he sees it," she said. "Like I said. He's here all the time."

"So you're telling me that his spirit lives on, and he's still hanging out in the shitty bar?"

"That's back to what I'm telling you. Anyway, I was just telling him about the hotel."

"You still fixating on that?"

"Yes. I'm going to until I get to buy it. There's just one weird little hoop to jump through. There were a couple of other offers in, but they fell through, because when they were looking around the place, there was some stuff that was… A little disconcerting. So now the owner is demanding that somebody spend the night there before they put in an offer. So… I'm gonna spend the night."

"You're gonna spend the night in the hotel? Why?"

"Because it's haunted. That's what I mean, people keep backing out because there's all this haunting stuff. I guess he's come close to selling it twice, and they were about to sign the papers when something spooky happened. So…"

"So you have to spend the night in the place to prove that you're not going to back out on the sale?"

"Yep."

"That's the dumbest thing I've ever heard. Why is he letting people with overactive imaginations cause so much grief? And why give any credence to it?"

"It works in my favor—it gave me enough time to get all my finances together. Anyway, I *want* it to be haunted," she said. "I can get it on the national list of most haunted places in the United States. People come from all over to stay in haunted hotels. It's something they're fascinated by."

"I don't want to stay in a haunted hotel. Because that's how I know the owner is a pancake short of a full stack."

"So you think I am not playing with a full deck?"

"I think that you are a bull short of a herd."

"Rude."

He shrugged. "Sorry if you don't like it."

"I don't think you are. I think you're always far too happy to give out your opinion."

"Oh well. You keep me around. Did you put my order in with the kitchen?"

She groused, but punched his burger order in at the register, then went over to the tap to pull a draft beer for him. She knew what he liked. She didn't have to ask. She had it in the glass, and he took a seat at the bar. There were only three other patrons inside, and they were in the corner next to the jukebox, not listening to anything that was happening over at the bar, from her conversation with Jace to her earlier conversation with her grandpa.

"It would be nice not have to be at the bar all day every day. If I make some money with the hotel, I can hire more people."

"Except, it's a huge additional expense."

"I know that. I've saved up for it. I can afford it. Especially if I can get it to a certain capacity during the high tourist times. But there's just not much in the way of lodging around here. Yeah, there's vacation rentals, but the only other hotels are thirty to forty minutes away. Hotel right downtown would really be something."

"You know, if you need money…"

"I'm not taking your money. I've basically been taking your charity since eighth grade, and I have no interest in continuing to do it," Cara said.

"It's not charity. It's friendship. Anyway. When are you fixing to spend the night in the hotel?"

"Tomorrow night. I'd… I don't know. There's no real furnishings in there. It's going to be a little bit… Bracing." She wrinkled her nose.

"I don't really like the idea of you staying in a big

empty insecure place by yourself. Especially not when some people might know that you're staying there," Jace said.

"I stay at the place I *live* by myself all the time."

"I don't know. This just feels different to me. I'm not comfortable with it. I should stay there with you."

"That's fine," she said, ignoring the slight jumping in her stomach when he offered that.

She had spent the night with Jace any number of times. Mostly camping. But, what would this be if not camping? They would end up bringing sleeping bags and probably a space heater.

It would just be like all the things they'd done when they were kids.

"Yeah, all right. That sounds good. In fact, now the burger's on the house."

"Why? You don't have to pay me to stay with you. I want to keep you safe."

"You get a free burger because you're submitting yourself to going on a ghost journey with me. And I know how much you hate that stuff."

"Please don't tell me you actually think that it's haunted."

"I think it might be. It stands to reason. It's historic. There were so many gunfights in this town back in the day…"

"Why are you talking to me about ghosts like there's anything logical about them? Come on. It's ridiculous, Cara, and I think on some level you must know that."

"I do not. It is as reasonable and logical as anything else in this world, Jace. And you know what, you'll see. I think that we will have a haunting."

"I don't think so."

"If we don't, it'll be because he's scared away by all your skeptic energy."

"Well isn't that convenient. An even better reason for you to have me out. Because if you don't see a ghost, you can blame me."

"Don't be silly, Jace. I always blame you."

Chapter 2

"**S**he thinks it's haunted," Jace said, looking at his brothers that night as they sat around the table outside at the Carson family ranch.

Their mom had ordered a big spread from the barbecue place on the outskirts of town, and they were all enjoying a meal together. Well, everybody except Buck, who hadn't been home in nearly a decade. But the rest of them were there, including Chance and Kit and their wives. Callie wasn't there, because she lived in Gold Valley with her husband, but that was a different sort of absence than Buck's.

Callie wasn't home because she had a life. A happy, functional life. Buck wasn't home because he was a mess.

And what they had around the table was like a strange, evenly divided set of teams. Kit and Chance, settled with their wives, done with the rodeo. Flint and Boone, single, happy about it and definitely not done punishing their bodies on the circuit.

They were all very certain in those things.

And for some reason, more and more, Jace wasn't.

He had never been one to wallow in uncertainty. Or even entertain it. You couldn't do that as a bull rider. You needed a clear eye, a firm grip and some big balls. And he had all three, thanks. It wasn't uncertainty, more a feeling of the world shifting, and it being harder to plant one foot in Lone Rock and one in the rodeo.

A sense that he was going to have to pick.

Maybe it had to do with Cara buying the hotel. Watching her commit to this life so deeply.

"And you're spending the night with her?" Boone asked, a sly smile curving his lips.

"I spend the night with Cara all the time."

He ignored the looks that he got from all of his brothers. And he ignored the fact that it was a lie. He and Cara had camped occasionally together when they were kids and hadn't really done that as adults, but, whatever.

She was his friend.

And really, more like a sister.

He could still remember the first time he'd ever met her. Crying but angry. So angry. And he had just loved that spirit. That great fighting spirit that she had.

It had drawn him to her right away.

And it had just made him want to… Protect her. Protect her in a way that he had never been able to protect Sophia…

"Oh yeah. Adult sleepovers?" That question came from Kit, who got an elbow in the chest from his wife.

"No," he said. "Because we're friends. And unlike you assholes, I actually don't see it as a conflicting thing to have a platonic friendship with a woman. Because I see her as a whole human being and not a sex object." His sisters-in-law, Juniper and Shelby looked at each other, and then they applauded.

"Thank you," he said to them.

"Our husbands are animals," said Shelby.

"And jackasses," said Juniper.

"I know that," said Jace. "I really don't know how the two of you put up with them."

"They're hot," said Shelby.

"Well," said Jace, frowning. "That kind of bums me out. Next time, don't take it there."

"Sorry," said Shelby, grinning.

"The point of the story," said Jace, "is that she thinks the place is haunted."

"And you don't?" Flint asked.

"I don't believe in that shit. You can't tell me that… I mean, come on."

"There's a lot of things in the world that can't be explained," said Kit. "I would never presume to know whether or not there were ghosts."

"I would," said Jace. "I presume it. You can't see it, you can't measure it, you can't prove it."

"You can't disprove it," Boone pointed out.

"Oh, shut the hell up, Boone," said Jace. "That's not a valid point and you know that."

"Seems valid enough to me."

"I don't see why you're all so invested in harassing me about Cara, anyway. She's been my best friend since middle school."

"It's because it makes you mad," said Boone. "It's that simple. And you fall for it every time, little brother. It's one of my favorite things about you."

He scowled. It really was a bitch being the youngest out of these jackasses. Well, the youngest except for Callie.

Callie had come much later, her parents hoping for another girl after the loss of Sophia.

But he was the youngest boy, and often the subject of quite a bit of harassment. Which was fine. It was just that he wished he wasn't such a chronic youngest that he fell for it.

But maybe that was one reason that Cara had felt so important to him when they had first met.

She filled the gap in the family. A gap in his life.

He had that other person, right there. He loved his sister Callie. But she was a *baby* sister.

Sophia had been close in age, and Cara was more like that.

He had just… He had just missed Sophie so damn much. That dynamic they had. Then he'd met Cara.

"Well, alternatively, you could all grow up."

Boone grinned. A big, broad smile that made Jace want to punch him. "I know you are but what am I?"

So he did punch him. Just in the shoulder.

"You're the worst."

"I know," said Boone.

And the thing was, maybe nobody would ever understand his relationship with Cara. He needed it. She was maybe the single most important person in his life, as much as he loved his family.

She had needed him, and that mattered to him.

Because the rest of his family… It wasn't the same. His parents needed Callie in a particular kind of way, because she had healed them.

They had needed Buck, who would then abandon them. And their older sons had taken on a lot of the burden.

Their father was so into the rodeo, and they all rode in the rodeo. It was just there was an excess of them.

So one of them wasn't particularly more important than the other in all of that.

But as far as Cara went? She needed him.

He looked out across the table, at the barn, and saw a bright white butterfly land on the bright red wood. It fluttered its wings for a second before it lifted off again and continued on his way. That moment sort of reset his thoughts, cleared them out.

He wanted to help her and he… Dammit, he worried about her making a big business move like this without him around. There would be repairs needing done, and systems to set up…

She needed him, and he guessed on some level he needed to be needed. Which was why he was submitting himself to the ridiculous ghost thing—even though all of that made him irrationally angry—and why he wasn't going to let his brothers make him too angry with all their nonsense.

As far as they went, their nonsense didn't matter.

What mattered was Cara.

And making sure she was taken care of. So that was exactly what he would do.

The old hotel building was beautiful. It was at the very end of Main Street. A three-story building with balconies and wooden porch rails. Old Western lettering that said Lone Rock Hotel. She could imagine it repainted. The gold around the border of the letters brightened.

She could imagine it lit up bright in the night. Filled with guests.

It would be like…

Almost like a family.

She shook that intrusive thought off. She hadn't expected it. And it wasn't particularly welcome.

Then she heard the sound of an old truck pulling up to the place and she turned and saw Jace.

"Hi," she said, even though he was still in the truck. She waved, so that he knew that she had greeted him.

She immediately felt kind of silly.

She cleared her throat and tucked her hair behind her ear.

She still felt like a lanky, gangly teenage girl around Jace sometimes. And that was silly. But then… The whole thing with him was often silly. She was comfortable with him. More comfortable than any other living human being. But at the same time, there were moments of intense awkwardness. Moments where she was so deeply aware of what she felt.

And in those moments she became unbearably self-conscious. In a way she just… Never was around other men. She thought it was funny that she tended to make them self-conscious. She wasn't overly concerned with her appearance, and she didn't spend a ton of time on it. But, she liked to put on a little bit of makeup and enjoyed a little bit of cowgirl bling. Studded belts and tank tops with a little bit of rhinestone energy.

She liked the attention that got her.

She never worried one way or another if random men thought she was pretty. If they did, great. If not, she didn't care.

And yet, all that insecurity came back to her sometimes when she stood there looking at Jace. And she could never really quite reconcile all of those things. The fact that in general she was more confident than she had ever been and the fact that she was often the most comfortable around him. Then also the least.

He got out of the truck, and she shoved all of those things off to the side.

"I hope you brought a sleeping bag," she said.

"Yeah I did," he said.

"I brought a space heater too," she responded. "You know ghosts can really bring down the temperature."

She watched his facial expression as he made the clear, deliberate decision to ignore her ghost comment. "Are we meeting anybody?"

"Other than ghosts?"

"Cara."

She smiled. "No. We got sent a code to open up a lockbox on the back door. So let's go hunting for it."

She went around back and she could hear his footsteps as he followed her.

She felt unbearably self-conscious of the fact that he might be watching her.

She banished that. It was Jace. They were friends. Maybe it was the strangeness of spending the night with him, but it wasn't like they had never done that before. Of course they had.

It had just been a long time, because they were grown-ass people, and they didn't tend to have sleepovers anymore. Or camping trips.

But they had. This was hardly singular.

"How did the rest of the night go last night?" he asked.

"Just fine. Like always. I know it's a shock to you, Jace, but my world turns just fine when you aren't there."

He looked at her. And it was far too clear a look.

For some reason, her stomach went tight, and she had the vague impression that maybe he could see into what had happened last night after she had gone home. No. She refused to think that. She refused to even entertain that thought. Because, if at three in the morning she had finally stumbled home and gotten into the shower, and if, when she had started to run her hands over her body as the water had cascaded over her curves, she had had a few moments where she had let herself imagine that they were Jace's hands skimming over her skin, and then maybe she had some trouble falling asleep, and she had taken those erotic thoughts to her bed with her and let them carry her off to a natural conclusion…

She really did try not to think of him that way. Yeah, it was one thing to think that he was hot; it was quite another to have actual, full-blown sexual fantasies about him, which just felt intrusive and wrong, and she always felt quite guilty after.

And she only ever did it on nights when she was really exhausted, and good sense had deserted her and…

Whatever… She supposed that she could justify that all she wanted, and the end result would still be the same. It was sort of shitty to think about your best friend like that.

And here she was, thinking about her best friend like that. Again. While he was standing right there. She cleared her throat and aggressively undid the padlock that contained the key, typing the code in with a lot more force than was strictly necessary. And then she pushed the door open and exhaled.

It was beautiful in here. She had come inside one time when she was a kid, and her grandfather had been looking at the property. It had been a pipe dream to buy it then. There had been absolutely no way. There wasn't enough tourism in town to make it worth it, and they had been financially strapped as it was.

But it had been his dream. And ever since then, it had been hers. Other than the one time they had gone inside to look at the place, she had only ever seen it from the outside looking in, and in pictures. But even now, dusty and in a bit of disrepair, it was the most beautiful place she had ever seen.

The floors were real wood, the drapes might be full of dust and mites and God knew what else, but they were beautiful.

They would just need some cleaning.

A deep rich red, with velvet damask. The wallpaper was lovely, but would definitely need to be replaced with something authentic. It was too water-stained to be restored, she had a feeling, and anyway, it would be less expensive to simply replace it all. But the original front desk was still there, a beautiful oak that needed to be oiled—she knew all about that, because the original bar from the 1800s was still in The Thirsty Mule, and she had ample experience at taking care of it.

There was a big crystal chandelier that hung in the center of the room, and it was the thing that gave her the biggest thrill.

The entire hotel had been outfitted with electricity and indoor plumbing by the 1920s, and it was currently such a glorious mix of all the errors that had come after and the original foundation. She loved each and every layer of history.

Enough that for a moment, it had knocked her out of her Jace haze. But only for a moment.

She turned and realized that he hadn't followed her inside. And then a moment later, there he was, holding both sleeping bags, the space heater and the bag of groceries that she had brought, so that they would be able to eat something tonight.

"I like it," he said, looking inside. "Slumber party snacks."

They weren't just snacks—she had a whole charcuterie situation in there, but she couldn't find any wit rolling around in her head right now.

For some reason the words *slumber party* made her fidgety.

"You know me. I don't like to be hungry."

"Who does?"

"Well, no one I assume, but not everybody will launch a feudal war over hunger pangs. But you know I will."

"That is true."

"Anyway. This is it. Isn't it great?"

"It is a lot of space. Just this room is a lot of space. Empty space."

"I'm not destitute, Jace. I pretty obsessively squirrel money away, actually. Anyway, Grandpa had a life insurance policy, and I've got that socked away in savings too. I've been living with my belt tightened so that I can get this place. But I have it all planned."

"Yeah, and you're secretive too."

"I haven't talked to you about it because I knew that you would be… This," she said, gesturing toward him.

And then he did something that shocked her. He reached out, wrapped his hand around her wrist and made that same gesture but practically up against his chest, all over again. "What is… All this?"

The way that his calloused fingers felt against her wrists sucked all the air out of her body. She felt like she was gasping. She felt like she was losing her mind. And she couldn't remember what she had been about to say. Because he had touched her, and she hadn't been expecting it. It wasn't that they didn't touch. They did, casually enough on occasion. But there was usually a flow to it, or something that felt slightly mutual. This was combined with her fantasies last night, and the fact that they were in the hotel now…

"You're a skeptic," she said quickly, suddenly finding the words and retrieving them from deep inside of her brain. "About everything. And I needed to be able to dream about this. If I wanted skepticism, I would ask for skepticism. But I don't want skepticism. I wanted to be able to believe that something magical could happen. That I could fulfill this long-held wish that my grandfather had… And you know what, I needed to be able to believe wholly in it and in myself in order to make it happen."

"You are perilously close to sounding like one of those self-help gurus that I hate. You were practical. You worked hard. It's hardly manifesting."

"You know what, I don't see what harm manifesting does?" She was getting irritated at him, and that felt welcome. Necessary even. "You're so skeptical about everything—this is my point. There is no way that thinking negative thoughts is actually better than thinking positive ones. And I didn't need any doubt to creep in. Yes, I did have to do the work, and I acknowledged that. But I also needed to believe in order to stay motivated to do it. And you…" She decided that since he had touched her, touching him was fair game. She put her fingertips on his chest and gave him a slight shove. "You are nothing more than a Debbie Downer."

Her fingertips felt like they were burning from where they had made contact with his well-muscled chest, and she realized that it was something that had definitely punished her more than it punished him.

She folded her fingers in and rubbed them against her palm. It wasn't really a punishment, if she were honest. Touching him felt good. It was just that it led to all sorts of other thoughts that didn't have a place to go, and that was what made it all feel like torture. That was the problem.

"Right. Well. I'm sorry that you feel that way. I would've

supported you, though. I do support you. And if I try to provide a…counterweight to your buoyancy, it's only because everybody needs a ballast, right?"

"I guess," she said. "I get it. I do. But the thing is, you treat me like I'm a kid. We are like a year and a half apart, Jace. There is no call to treat me like that."

"Yeah, there is," he said, his voice suddenly going gruff. "Where should I put the stuff?"

She knew what he was thinking. She knew what he was going to say. She wasn't going to give him a chance to say it. "Well, I don't know. We have to find a bedroom. We might as well find the best one." They started to walk up the stairs. One of them creaked, but it wasn't so bad.

The carpet on the stairs was somewhat threadbare, and she wondered if it would just be the better part of valor to get rid of all of it and reveal the honey oak beneath.

But there would be a lot of expense involved in refurbishing the place. Still, it would be worth it. And she could afford it. Really, for the first time in her life, she could afford a dream, and it was brilliant and amazing.

She was not a kid.

And she was definitely not Jace's baby sister. No matter how he acted.

The hallway was long, with numbered doors facing opposite each other. Ten in total. "All right. Let's see what we have."

The first room was entirely barren, with lace curtains that barely covered the window, and she decided that unless they had to, that wasn't going to be the room.

The next room was filled with nightstands and wardrobes and other miscellaneous furniture—a dining table and some chairs, all stacked up and filled from back to front. "Well, I guess it's good to know there's some furniture left in here. Some of it is probably salvageable.

Or at least, we can use the wood for something. There's probably some local artisans that could make something great with it."

"Yeah," he said.

And she could tell that he was biting his tongue. Damn him.

He was trying—that wasn't fair.

"Let's go, so that you don't pull a muscle," she said, carrying on down the hall and opening two more doors, before deciding to open another.

And in that room, there was a bed.

A big bed that was likely full of dust and had a rich brocade bedspread on it. There were canopy curtains and matching velvet curtains over the window. It was set as if it was exactly prepared for guests. A nightstand, wardrobe, a small vanity with a bowl and a picture, which she knew would have been used as a washbasin.

"Well, here we go," she said.

"Look," he said. "I don't even believe in this haunting business, and even I know that if one of the rooms is going to have a ghost in it, it's going to be this one."

"But you don't believe in ghosts," she said. "And I want to see one, so that declaration is hardly a deterrent." She grabbed a sleeping bag out of his hand and looked around the room. "I hope you don't have allergies."

"No. Thankfully. Otherwise living on a ranch would be rough. I can deal with a little bit of dust."

"You can sleep in the bed if you want," she said, grinning at him.

"Yeah. I'll skip it."

Then suddenly, it was way too easy to imagine the two of them in a bed, and she wondered if she had miscalculated by choosing this room.

It was one thing to think about sleeping on the floor

with sleeping bags—which they were still going to do—
it was just that the fact that they were in a room with a
big bed…

She was starting to feel a little bit sweaty. She was
starting to feel a little bit shaky. Jittery. And she just
didn't have the presence of mind to figure out how to
not feel that way.

It's Jace.

This was the problem. It wasn't like this all the time. It
was just like this sometimes, and usually for set periods
of time. Like, something would happen, there would be
a touch, a little bit of something that felt out of the ordi-
nary that brushed up against her hormones, and then she
would have a fantasy about him, and then things would
feel awkward, but then they didn't usually spend the night
in the same bedroom.

"Okay," she said, desperate for a reprieve. "You lay
out the sleeping bags and get the space heater going, I'm
going to go downstairs and see what I can find in the way
of utensils and get some snacks prepared. And, I also
brought a bunch of downloaded movies."

"Awesome. See, we don't need ghosts for entertain-
ment. We can entertain ourselves."

Chapter 3

He stood there in the middle of the room, completely motionless for a good thirty seconds after Cara left. He could not quite figure out why there was something about his own words that hit him wrong. They could *entertain themselves*.

He also couldn't figure out why his chest still felt electrified where she had put her fingertips.

Things were a little bit weird. And he wasn't quite sure what to make of that. But he did as he was asked. He laid out the sleeping bags at the foot of the bed, then plugged in the space heater between them.

This kind of amused him. It was a little bit like a campfire.

He looked over at the bed. And he ignored the rising tension in his gut. There was no reason to be tense. His idiot brothers had gotten in his head was the thing. They specialized in that. That was what older brothers did, after all, but what they did not do was understand that Cara was a sacred object.

And Jace was not a man who fucked around with the divine.

No. He knew that he had no call ever taking her out of the category that he'd put her in all those years ago. His best friend. And the woman he wanted to protect more than anything in the whole world.

She'd had it so hard, and he just wanted to shield her from ever having another hard thing happen to her.

She wasn't a woman to him. Not really. She never had been.

Yeah. There had been the unfortunate moment in high school when she... Filled out a little bit and he'd been seventeen—nearly eighteen—and not as experienced as he was now, and it had been a little bit difficult to keep from marveling at the changes that had occurred. But that was teenage boy shit. Dumb shit.

He was a grown man.

He had been riding out on the rodeo circuit since then, and he had a hell of an education in the female form during those years.

He'd also learned a lot about himself.

There was something about having the miraculous beaten out of you at an early age that made it impossible to believe in lasting love and connections. Well, it did him.

His parents had clung together after Sophie had died. They'd had Callie. They'd kept on hoping. He supposed.

Callie, well, she hadn't been alive when Sophia had died, so while she knew, she didn't really know.

Chance and Kit, their love stories were gritty. More than they were miraculous, he supposed. They had both fallen for incredibly tough women, women who took every opportunity to take them to task when they needed it, and Jace found it amusing as hell.

He was happy that they could do that thing.

But then there was Buck, who had left town under a cloud when he was still in his early twenties. Buck, who clearly couldn't find anything miraculous to hold on to.

And Flint and Boone were as noncommittal as he was in the relationship department. Meaning, they didn't have them. Flint had quite famously broken up with the woman who'd gone on to be a famous country singer. And the song that she'd written about him—when it had hit the airwaves a couple of months ago it had caused a slight explosion.

Granted, she didn't use his name, but everybody knew it was about him. Everybody.

People around Lone Rock were too smart to mention it. But… Yeah, occasionally he and Boone would trawl the online forums looking for things to interrogate their brother about.

"Where is the scarf, Flint?"

"Yeah. Where is it?"

"I don't know what the hell you're talking about," he would growl.

"She claims you kept her scarf."

"Fuck you."

"That reminds me, there was a key chain…"

"There is no key chain," said Flint. *"It's not about me."*

Point being, he was the only one of them that had tried a relationship, and it hadn't gone well. Boone sure as hell wasn't stupid enough to even try.

He just didn't have it in him. He thought you had to be some kind of crazy to invest in a relationship like that.

You had to be some kind of starry-eyed, and a hell of a lot of things he just wasn't.

He would never drag a woman through that.

He had never wanted to. He had his family, he had Cara, and that was enough.

A moment later, she returned. "Well, I managed to get this all set up." She had a tray of meat and cheese, and two wineglasses, plus a bottle of...

"Rosé?"

"You got a problem with that?"

"A prissy meat and cheese tray and a bottle of girls' night out wine?"

She stared at him blandly. "Not when there's no one else here."

She sniffed as she settled onto her sleeping bag and set the tray out in front of her. "Your toxic masculinity is strangling you to death."

"No." He settled down on his own sleeping bag and reached out and took a wedge of cheese. "It would be if I refused to partake. But here in the sacred space..."

"You're an idiot," she said.

"Yeah. Probably."

"Are you going back out to the rodeo?"

He had been avoiding that direct question. Not even his brothers had asked. Boone and Flint were still at it, but Buck had left a long time ago, with Kit and Chance retiring recently.

Jace was younger than Boone and Flint, but he knew he was getting to about the age where you had to start considering how many permanent injuries you wanted to walk around with for the rest of your life all for the sake of chasing continued glory.

He liked a little glory, it was true, but he also valued the fact that he didn't walk with a limp, and the longer you stayed in the game the less likely that was to continue to be a thing.

Their father was on the verge of retirement, and he didn't know that any of them were chomping at the bit to become the next Rodeo Commissioner. Or maybe they were; they hadn't really talked about it. Jace wasn't, that was all he knew. The family was more and more settled in Lone Rock. And maybe that wasn't such a bad thing.

"Don't know," he said.

"You really don't know?"

"I really don't."

"That doesn't seem like you."

"Maybe not," he said, shoving some of his discomfort aside. "I don't know. Stuff is changing. It kind of started with Callie getting married a couple years ago, and now... I don't know. The family's more settled here. For a long time it seemed like my dad was just running. Running from everything. Running from his grief and all of that... But they've expanded the ranch here so much, and I think he's finally ready to quit moving around all the time. At his age, he probably should've done it a long time ago, but given that he's him... I think it might be kind of a big deal."

"That makes you think about change."

"It just makes me wonder what I'm doing. The thing is, we've all won the top tier of all the events that we've ever competed in. There's a point where the only way you can go is down. So then you ask yourself why you're doing it."

"Do you love it?"

It was a strange question. He never really thought about it. Rodeo was the family business. He knew there were spare few people for whom that was true. But since he was a kid, his father had been the Commissioner of the Pro Rodeo Association, and it had been a given that they would all grow up and compete. Callie had competed in saddle bronc events for a couple of years; she was taking a break to have a baby, which was great. That had meant a lot to her, breaking that barrier as a woman, and she had paved the way for a whole lot of other women who wanted to do the same thing.

She had a reason for being there.

Kit and Chance were top in their field. He had done bareback broncos for a number of years; he'd ridden bulls. That was all after he and his brothers had done a little bit of tie-down roping in their early years. He didn't know that he loved it so much as that he wore it comfortably like a pair of battered old jeans. And he didn't know what else fit. Ranching. They had a big family ranch.

But it was an interesting thing to grow up in a family where you didn't wonder what you would be when you grew up. There was a legacy that you inherited, and you stepped into that. But then, Cara knew about that. He doubted she owned the bar because she loved it the most. He could see that this hotel thing meant a lot to her but he had to wonder…

He gestured to the room around them.

"Is this actually something that you want, or is this just what Mitch wanted to do?"

"I actually do want it," she said. "I've loved this place since I was a kid. And yeah, some of it is that it makes me feel good to fulfill his dreams. Because he couldn't. And he was there for me. He was there for me when no one else in my family was. My dad was… I still don't know where. My mom was where she is now. Drugged out of her mind in a trailer park somewhere making bad decision after bad decision with men. And… I had Grandpa. I don't think I'm doing it just because I want them to be proud or anything like that. I'm doing it because the things that were important to him became important to me. This town became important."

"Yeah."

"I guess I have to ask you the same question. Are you in the rodeo just because it's what your dad wants you to do?"

"No. To be honest, I don't think my dad cares what we do. In fact, I think he would've been perfectly happy if we had never risked life and limb out on the circuit. He loves it, but he's realistic about the risks. Especially after that kid died a couple of years ago… He was never really the same after that. Never looked at the rodeo the same."

And that was a shame. Because the rodeo had been his dad's escape from his grief. Jace knew that, because he understood it. He moved around, and he moved around a lot. Motion kept you from thinking too deep.

But it felt like he was at a critical point. He didn't want to just keep moving. But staying felt like an invitation to settle into pain.

Of course the alternative to that was processing it, but he'd spent years avoiding that.

Years using Cara as a surrogate.

But watching her now, watching her actually take control of her life and get what she wanted shamed him a bit.

"I'm sorry. I know it was your dream…"

"It wasn't," he said. "The rodeo was easily available to us. And we had to do something. But I think it was more than that. It was easy for us to pivot into it because we knew all about it. It must be different when it's your dream. When you have to chase it. It was more like that for Callie, because Dad sure as hell didn't want her out on the horses. Drove him nuts. Still does, to be honest, but he's accepted that is something he's not gonna win with her. He's accepted that is something she's going to do, and she's a grown woman, so you can't stop her. I mean, she married Jake Daniels just to get access to her money."

He'd never anticipated the money. Didn't care about it. Didn't need it.

That shamed him a bit too.

"I never asked, do you all have trust funds like that?"

"Yeah. But we get it when we turn thirty."

"So you're getting yours soon."

He really hadn't thought much about it. He had whatever he needed. He turned quite a lot of money on the circuit; he got in a fair amount of endorsements. He had it pretty easy, honestly.

"Yeah."

"You don't know what you want to do with it?"

"I guess not."

He didn't like that. But then, thinking about the future wasn't his thing. It was that whole… Well, he guessed it was a lot like what she had accused him of. She hadn't wanted to tell him about her dreams because he had the unfortunate inclination to bring reality down on them. And as for himself… He didn't really dream.

"I don't like to think ahead. I live in the moment. I like to work. It's clarifying. In that sense, I guess I do love to ride in the rodeo. You get a surge of adrenaline not like much else. Not really like anything but sex, to be honest."

And then she blushed. All the way up her neck to the roots of her hair. Then it surprised him, because it wasn't like Cara was a prude. She worked in a bar. She heard rough talk all the time. Hell, she wandered around the place looking like *Coyote Ugly* half the time, which she could do without, and men checked her out all evening. She seemed to get a kick out of it. Because she was in control of that interaction, and could bounce their asses out of the bar if they got unruly.

He hadn't expected her to blush just because he mentioned sex. But then he looked behind her and saw the bed, and the earlier tension returned.

"Anyway," he said, clearing his throat. "I didn't really think about what I would do with it. I didn't really think about what I would do when I was done with the rodeo. And anyway, I could coast on that for a few more years if I wanted to."

"You don't want to, though," she said, reaching out and taking a piece of cheese. She seemed to recover slightly from the earlier incident.

But he had to wonder why it had been an incident at all.

"How do you know that?"

"I know that," she said, "because it's not like you to have doubts, and you do. If you're uncertain, and you're pausing, then there's something else going on."

He didn't like that. Didn't like that shifting sand feeling underneath his feet.

It probably had to do with his brothers getting married. It was just a change.

Made him contemplate what things would look like for him, because they wouldn't look like that.

He also didn't love that she could read him so well. He needed to be able to read her. It was important. He had to protect her. Take care of her. Make sure that she was doing all right. The thing was, he had his whole big family. And since her grandfather's death, Cara had nobody. She'd always had fewer people than him. And it made him really important. It made what he did for her really important.

So yeah, he kind of prided himself on knowing what was going on with her, on keeping track of her. On making sure that everything was all right.

But the fact that she seemed to be able to read him…
He wasn't sure how he felt about that.

"You know, there are some other shops on Main Street
that are being sold. The businesses are still going to be
there, but the buildings are up for sale…"

"Are you suggesting that I invest in real estate?"

"It's an idea."

It was. It was also… Roots. Ties. It wasn't like he was
planning on leaving Little Rock. No, that didn't really
factor into his plans. But he also didn't own land for a
reason.

And what exactly is that reason?

He shoved that thought to the side.

"What movie are we opening with?"

"Oh," she said. "You're going to love this." She settled
onto her sleeping bag, grabbing her tablet and setting it
up on the floor. She rested her elbows on the sleeping
bag, and her chin on her knuckles. "I thought that we
needed some nostalgia."

"Oh no," he said.

"Do you remember when we skipped school and we
drove down to Bend and we went to see our favorite
buddy cop movie?"

"No way."

"Yes way."

"You can quote that movie in its entirety. Do you actually need to watch it again?"

"Yes I do. Because you know that if I were a lion and
you were a tuna…"

"You're ridiculous," he said. But he did find it endear-
ing. He liked that she enjoyed a raunchy comedy, just as
much as he did. Though, this was not his favorite.

"Don't worry," she said. "I also have the terrible dream
movie you love so much."

"Thank you."

"And you know, an array of teen movies. From *Mean Girls* to *Easy A*."

"I don't like those movies."

"I know you don't. I don't care. But we'll probably fall asleep before then, because we are not eighteen—we're old."

"Speak for yourself."

"I'm younger than you," she said.

"Yeah," he said, nudging her with his elbow.

She looked at him and wrinkled her nose, and for some reason, he found his eyes drawn to the freckles there.

They were cute. Just a little sprinkling of them that went from her cheeks over the bridge of her nose. They highlighted her green eyes somehow. Beautiful eyes. Slightly feline. She wasn't wearing makeup tonight, so her lashes were pale. Often, she wore a real dark mascara that made her eyes feel like a punch in the gut. This was more like a slow, spring sunrise. A whole lot of green and gold.

That tension had returned.

"All right. Get the movie going," he said.

"Gladly," she said, pouring a glass of wine and handing it to him, before pouring herself one. He lay back on his sleeping bag and decided to pay attention to the movie, instead of the color of her eyes.

Chapter 4

She was just so aware of him. Of every inch of him. The way that he was lying on the sleeping bag, the way that his arm shifted, the way his whole body shifted when he went to take a drink of his wine.

When he grabbed some cheese off the cheese board.

She was starting to feel light-headed, and she had a feeling she needed to go get some more food, so she wasn't off on her alcohol-to-protein ratio. But she found herself drinking a little bit faster the more her nerves flared up in her gut.

This was ridiculous.

But the problem with choosing movies that they had gone to see together in high school was that it reminded her of being in high school with him. That was when her little crush had started acting up. Oh, it wasn't when she had realized that she wanted to sleep with him—that was a more mature realization. But the butterflies over his arm brushing hers when they sat together in the movie theater… Yeah. That had been pure high school.

And she really wasn't nostalgic for it. And here she was, alone with the man in an empty house—unless there were ghosts, there could be ghosts—as an adult, having those same feelings.

It was almost funny.

It was *almost funny*, that now they were adults, absolutely alone and unsupervised, adjacent to a bed, and she was *still* in no danger of Jace Carson trying to pressure her into sex. No. She was much more likely to try to pressure him into it.

The idea made her feel lit up from the inside out. Entirely too warm. She did her level best to look back at the movie.

The next one was not her favorite. It was too mind-bending and she didn't like it. She liked things that had resolved endings, at least. She would prefer a happy ending. But the ambiguity of it all made her itchy, and she started to get restless.

"I'm going to go downstairs and get another bottle of wine," she said.

"Another bottle of wine?"

"Yes. I think that sounds like a pretty good idea, don't you?"

"Yeah. All right."

She knew it wasn't a great idea. She was already feeling a little bit wobbly and loose, and she was in such a weird precarious place with him it…

Well, she had been friends with the man for thirteen years. It wasn't like she was just suddenly going to break it.

She pondered that when she went to get the package of cupcakes, and the new bottle of wine.

Something crashed to her left and she whipped her head toward the sound and she stopped.

She waited to see if she heard another noise, waited to see if anything else shifted, but all she could hear was her own breathing. Ragged. Too fast.

"For heaven's sake," she muttered to herself.

She was such a mess.

She was being ridiculous because she was tipsy and anticipating ghosts and strung out on Jace. And maybe more wine was the wrong thing, but maybe it was the right thing because she needed to calm down. Maybe if she could loosen up, she'd get her equilibrium back.

She waited a few breaths more and didn't hear anything else, so she took the cake and wine back upstairs.

Jace was sprawled out on the sleeping bag on his back, his arm thrown over his face, his shirt lifted an inch or so, so she could see his flat, toned stomach.

Dear sweet Lord, she needed an intervention. A miracle.

Or maybe just wine.

"I'm back with more," she said, standing over him.

His mouth curved into a smile, his arm still thrown over his face, and she was so fixated on that she never saw his other hand coming.

Suddenly she found herself grabbed at the back of the knee and she shrieked, going down fast. And it was only his muscles that stopped her from crashing to the ground, as he somehow managed to guide her down to the sleeping bag slowly with *one arm*.

"Jace!" she shouted, folding down over the top of him.

He was warm under her.

And hard.

And *oh no*.

She was lying across him, folded at the waist over his

chest. She scrambled hard to get off him but not before her hand made contact with his *very firm* ass.

She rolled the rest of the way off him, then scrabbled back for her wine and cake. "Why are you such a child?"

He was reclining, looking at her like...

She had to look away.

"I'm definitely not a child."

"You're immature. I heard a noise downstairs," she said, desperate to not think about the fact he was so very not a child, but clearly a man. "Maybe it was a ghost."

"Well, it wasn't. Because ghosts aren't real. But that cake looks real and I want some."

She still hadn't quite recovered from the full body Jace contact. "I don't know if you can have any because you're being mean."

"I'll take it from you."

He would too. And if there was one thing she could not handle now it was a wrestling match over cake, so she surrendered it, but she did not do it graciously.

And then she poured herself more wine.

They finished his favorite movie and then went on to hers. And she was definitely more than a little tipsy by the time they decided to put in their final comedy about a bunch of high school seniors' quest to lose their virginity.

They'd seen it a hundred times. She had no idea how they'd ever watched it before without her feeling immeasureably uncomfortable.

"Man, I don't miss high school," he said, tipping back his glass of wine. She watched his throat work, watched his Adam's apple bob up and down, and it made her feel a little bit giddy. She looked away.

"Yeah. Wasn't exactly the greatest time of my life either."

It was a lot of feeling weird and awkward. First with

a flat chest, then with curves. But weird and awkward all the same.

"It's just the ridiculousness of it all. All the kids who think they're kings and queens. Of what? The cafeteria. It's ridiculous... All the hormones. Maybe back then I should've decided what I wanted to do. But I was too busy worrying about things like that. Granted, I was a senior when I lost my virginity."

She blinked. "*No*."

Was he about to confess to her that he was an awkward, college virgin? She didn't know what to think about that.

"No. More like a junior."

In *college*? No. That was when she realized he meant... high school. When they'd been friends.

"Why didn't I know that?" she asked, her tongue feeling loose and lazy. And she was annoyed that she had asked that. But she was annoyed that he had mentioned it.

"Did you want me to tell you that I got a fake ID and went to the next town and hooked up with some woman in a bar?"

"You didn't," she said.

"No. Not kidding. That's what I did. I didn't figure that an inexperienced virgin should inflict their inexperience on another virgin, you know what I mean?"

She frowned and wrinkled her nose. "Yeah. Sure."

"I don't know. It just never seemed like the thing to me. I'm still like that. I don't like to have a fling with women too close to home."

She frowned. "Right."

They should not be having this weird, wine addled conversation because she was already in a strange space, and now she was grumpy with it.

And they were supposed to be watching a comedy.

Granted, one they had watched multiple times before, but still.

"I've never had sex with a virgin, actually," he said.

And that did something weird to her. To her body. Her soul.

And she knew, she knew that she needed to stop herself from saying something. She knew that she needed to get a grip. She knew that none of this whole conversation was about her. Or maybe it was. Maybe it was about their friendship. The fact that they were now, and had always ever been friends. So while maybe he hadn't confessed to his sexual shenanigans when they were in high school, he didn't think anything of telling her now. Which... Hurt, actually. He should be a little bit uncomfortable talking to her about sex. It should make him imagine having sex with her. She had *great* boobs.

And he was a straight man. Why wasn't he into her boobs? It wasn't fair. There were all kinds of random men at the bar who would love to see them. And Jace just seemed immune. And he was sitting there talking about sex. Like it was nothing.

"Well," she said, "I guess you're not half the stud that I thought you were," she said.

"I'm not?"

"Yeah," she said. "I would've thought that you had sex with all kinds of virgins. Corrupter of innocents and whatever."

"No," he said. "One of the few things I haven't done."

"Well," and she could hear it in her head before it came out of her mouth, and there was some reasonable rational part of her that was crouched in the corner shouting: don't say it, Cara. But that rational, reasonable part of her was drowned out by Wine Cara, who had some opinions and wanted to express them. Wine Cara was a bitch, and later, she and Wine Cara were going to have a stern conversation. But she was just on the ride right now. "If you wanted to have sex with a virgin, I can help you with that."

"Excuse me? Are you offering to find me a virgin through your bar contacts?"

He didn't understand.

She could turn back now.

She didn't.

"No," she said, pushing his shoulder. "If you wanted to have sex with a virgin, just have sex with me."

Chapter 5

Jace was frozen. And for a full ten seconds you could've heard a pin drop. Except then suddenly there was a huge crash, and Cara scampered across the distance between them and pressed herself against his chest, her eyes wide. "What the hell was that?"

"I don't know," he said, and he didn't know if he was answering her question about the noise, or if it was about the fact that she had just told him she was a virgin and essentially offered to have sex with him.

His heart was thundering hard, and he told himself it was because of the crash, because it had startled him. And not because Cara was pressed up against him.

Which he told himself was because of the wine. Everything that had just happened was because of the wine. And there was no call getting all worked up about that. No call getting angry. Or reading too much into it or anything like that.

Except, they probably needed to figure out what that noise was.

"Where did it come from?" she asked.

"I don't know," he said, peeling himself away from her. But the heat from her body remained, and he felt somewhat branded by it all.

"It's probably your ghost," he said. "Didn't you want there to be a ghost?"

"I didn't want it *to scare me*," she said.

Then she looked up at him, her expression dazed. "Oh," she said.

"What?"

"I just told you I was a virgin."

"Let's put a pin in that," he said. "By which I mean let's not talk about it again."

He hadn't really meant to say the last part out loud. But he was a little bit tipsy, and even though the noise had done something to sober them up a bit, it wasn't fully complete.

"Fine then. But let's go see what it is."

She got up and started to pull on his shirt. He pushed himself up, and grabbed hold of her arm. "Whoa. Did it ever occur to you that it might actually be an intruder?"

"No," she said, her eyes wide. "I just thought it was a good old-fashioned haunting."

"What if it isn't?" he said. "That's something to keep in mind. That's why I'm staying with you. What if one of those perverts from the bar knew that you were staying here?"

"That's creepy, Jace," she said. "If I thought that the bar patrons were like that that I wouldn't let them in."

"I don't trust anybody. Bottom line. So stay with me, and we'll go see what it is."

"I can't even tell where it's coming from." Suddenly,

there was another crash, and she pressed herself against him, and he became extremely aware of the way her breasts felt against his arm. Firm and full and high. And more than a little bit enticing.

A virgin.

What the hell?

What the hell?

He did not have time to focus on that, because he needed to see what was happening down the hall. Or maybe… He stopped and listened. Maybe down the stairs.

"Did you leave anything open when you went downstairs?"

"No. I didn't open anything."

"Did you hear anything when you went down there?"

"Again," she said, "no. I didn't."

"Come on."

The sound was consistent. And raucous.

"I doubt that's a ghost," she said.

"Oh, because they aren't real?"

"No," she said. "Because it's an easy sound to follow, and anybody who had spent the night here previously could've followed it themselves. I would think that the haunting was a lot more…you know, ambiguous."

"Oh. Ambiguous haunting. As opposed to one of those big, obvious hauntings."

"*Clearly*," she said.

"Come on."

"Do you have like a gun or anything?"

"In a lockbox in my truck, yes. But not in the house."

"But it's where you can get to. If you need to."

"We won't need it. Whatever's going on, I'll finish it hand to hand."

He felt her relax.

"I'll take care of you," he said. "I always take care of you."

And that was when he realized he didn't want her coming toward the noise with him. "I want you to stay here," he said.

And then he turned to face her and felt like he'd been punched in the stomach. She was looking up at him, those pale lashes all spiky, her green eyes searching.

And he couldn't get their previous conversation out of his head.

Except over the top of that he felt a surge of protectiveness.

And without thinking, he reached up and touched her cheek. "Stay here."

Her eyes fluttered closed, and she swayed toward him, just slightly. And everything in him went tight. He took a step back. "I'll be right back."

He went down the stairs and toward the kitchen. The noise was definitely coming from the kitchen. From the pantry.

He heard footsteps behind him and turned sharply. "I told you to wait upstairs," he said.

"I didn't want to," she said.

"I didn't ask what you wanted, Cara. I'm protecting you."

"Well now whatever it is knows we're here," she said. "Because you're being loud."

"You're being loud," he said.

"It's coming from the pantry," she said.

"Yeah. I got that."

He reached out and opened up the pantry door, quickly. And there, inside a flour sack, he saw a big fat ring tail. There was a movement, followed by a cloud of pale white dust, and then a small masked face and two spindly claws appeared over the edge of the bag.

"What the ever-loving hell?"

"It's a raccoon," she said, sounding charmed.

"Those fucking things will eat your face off," he said.

"They're adorable," she said.

"They're menaces," he said. "All right, you little bandit, get out of there."

He was not about to call animal control over one small ring-tailed menace. Hell no. And he didn't think that was just the wine talking. He was going to be able to get it out of there.

"I hope you're happy by the way," he said. "Because I knew there was a very reasonable explanation for why people were hearing noises in the house."

"It's a raccoon," she said. "And a raccoon is not a ghost."

"That is my point."

"No," she said, shaking her head. She wobbled, and he realized that Cara was still a lot more tipsy than he was. "I mean, if it had been a raccoon the whole time, then they would've seen it. But it wasn't a raccoon the whole time. It was a ghost the rest of the time. And it's just a raccoon now."

"Whatever. I would've preferred a ghost, because then we could just have an exorcism or some shit, but it's a raccoon, and now I need to chase it out."

"I want it to be my pet."

"It can't be your pet. Don't be ridiculous." He kept watch on the creature, which was staring at him with beady eyes, and he reached into the corner of the pantry and picked up her broom. "I will use this on you," he said.

"Are you cleaning up the town, Sheriff?" Cara asked.

"You're drunk. Get out of here."

He supposed that he should feel better knowing that she was drunk. Maybe she had been teasing. About the whole virgin thing. That couldn't be true. She worked at a bar. She looked like... Like that.

And she sure as hell had to have been teasing about... Him.

"All right," he said, talking to the raccoon again as he extended the broom. "Get outta here."

It snarled and leaned forward, chewing on the bristles.

"Get out," he said, brushing at its face.

It growled again, but leaped out of the flour sack, shaking itself off like a dog after a bath, and sending white dust everywhere.

It started to come toward the door of the pantry, and he put his arm out over Cara, moving her to the side as the snarling beast loped out of the pantry and through the kitchen.

"And open the door," he said.

"I mean, the question is, how did it get in?"

"That's a good question, but we need to get it out first."

"He's just going to come back."

"Fine. We'll work on raccoon prevention once we've done raccoon eradication."

He went to the side door off the kitchen and propped it open with the doorstop, then took the broom and pushed it against the raccoon's rear.

It growled again, but picked up the pace, scampering out the door and disappearing into the night.

"For God's sake." He lifted up the doorstop and shut the door. "I was not expecting that."

"No. That was ridiculous."

"Really, really ridiculous," he said.

"But cute."

"It was *not* cute."

"I disagree."

"So, you might not have a ghost in the hotel, but you might have raccoons. And, we don't know how they're getting in, which is going to require some kind of a fix. This place is a death trap," he said.

"It is not a death trap. I just wish that I had evidence that it's haunted."

"You're not going to get that, because it is not haunted."

"You don't know that," she said.

"Well, the problem is, I fucking do. Because ghosts don't exist."

He was just glad to be having this argument with her, because at least he was on stable ground.

And it wasn't about… Any of the things that had happened before.

"Let's go back upstairs," he said. "We'll look for raccoon entries in the morning."

"Okay."

They had kept the movie playing, but it didn't matter, since they'd both seen it a whole bunch of times. She drank another glass of wine, and he didn't say anything, because he was actually hoping that they might just get past all that. That she might forget it had happened. And she seemed to have.

When the movie ran out, she fell asleep on the sleeping bag. And he lay back on his own. He was lying on his side, and he could see her, in the moonlight coming through the window. The gentle swells of her breasts rising and falling with each breath.

And he couldn't take his eyes off her.

She was beautiful, and he'd always known that. But…

It was like a cascade of things he had held back for any number of years were suddenly rolling through him.

He had kept any thought of her as being a woman—

a woman who was available to him—entirely subdued for all these years.

And she had undone it all with that tipsy offer. Because suddenly, he couldn't stop making it real. Couldn't stop seeing it as something vivid and specific and possible. Pushing his hands up underneath her shirt and revealing her skin. Had no one ever done that? Would his hands really be the first hands to...

No. He protected her. That was what he did.

He shielded her. From hard emotions, and held her when it was all unavoidable.

And there was no way in the damned world that he could protect her if he was...

He turned over onto his side and faced away from her, desperate to do something to find a way to get his mind out of the damned gutter.

And then she made a little whimpering noise, and he sat up. He couldn't take it. He crossed the room and got up on the bed and lay down on his back. He didn't care how dusty it was.

He needed some space. He just needed some space.

Cara felt dizzy when she woke up. And she couldn't figure out why she woke up, because it was still the middle of the night.

And then suddenly, she saw what looked like a light. A floating orb in the middle of the room. It was low, at eye level with her on the ground. She sat up and looked around, and she saw that Jace wasn't on his sleeping bag. She scrambled up, her heart thundering. And then she noticed him on the bed, sleeping.

She scrambled up on the bed beside him, but he didn't move. He was snoring. "Go away," she said to the floating light. It zigzagged in the room. "Please go away. You're scaring me."

The light seemed to respond. It stopped, and then she swore she saw…that it wasn't an orb or just a light, but it was a butterfly. A bright white butterfly.

And she sat there blinking, completely uncertain of what she had seen. Maybe she just had something in front of her eyes because she was a little bit hungover or whatever from just having drunk too much wine. All she knew was that it creeped her out. She grabbed the ties on the curtains, and let them fall around the bed. She and Jace were completely boxed in there in the canopy.

She curled up in a ball and lay beside him, trying not to breathe too hard.

She just wanted to go back to sleep. And she wanted to hear nothing. So she focused on the sound of her breathing. His breathing. Tried to make it loud so that she wouldn't hear anything unnerving.

Hoped that orbs couldn't come through curtains.

She swallowed hard, trying to get a hold of herself.

And finally, she drifted off into a fitful sleep.

Chapter 6

When Cara woke up, it was dim. She squinted and realized that she was sleeping on a canopy bed. And she could see little shafts of sunlight coming through the cracks in the curtain.

Oh right. She had woken up and thought she'd seen... A ghost last night. An orb. A glowing butterfly? She had read a lot of things written by ghost hunters, and enough to know that orbs usually indicated some kind of paranormal activity. Glowing butterflies, she had no idea.

She immediately questioned that, because the fact that she knew it meant that it was something that had been suggested to her prior to being here. Which meant she could easily have dreamed it, freaked out and...

She turned to look at Jace, who was asleep in bed beside her.

And everything in her stopped. Stopped thinking about ghosts. Stopped thinking about anything.

All she could do was stare at him. He looked a lot

more relaxed sleeping. Way more relaxed than he ever did in person. In person he always looked like he was ready to leap into action. At any moment. To vanquish a raccoon or...

Oh no. There was a raccoon.

Last night had gotten very strange, and it was all a little bit fuzzy, because she had been drunk. She'd had way too much wine because she was nervous. But yes, they heard a noise and it had turned out that it was a raccoon. They'd gone downstairs, Jace had vanquished the raccoon...well, he had scuttled out of the room...

But something had happened before that.

But she was stopped again by the sight of him. His profile.

By everything. Just everything.

She took a deep breath. And the scent of him was almost overwhelming. Then she suddenly felt a little bit creepy, sitting there and staring at him like that. Checking him out. She sat up, pulling her knees up to her chest, and her head gave a decisive, definitive dull thud.

Great. And she had a hangover.

If you wanted to have sex with a virgin, you could have sex with me.

She slapped her hand over her mouth.

No.

She had not said that. She really needed that to be a dream, or just something she had thought, or just...

If she could see it clearly. Play back that whole conversation. Everything that had happened right before the raccoon... The raccoon had interrupted the conversation. She had literally *propositioned* Jace and had told him that she *was a virgin*.

She squeezed her hands even more tightly over her mouth to keep from whimpering out loud.

No. And now she was up here in bed with him, and he was going to think that she was… That she had lost her mind.

I promise I'm not trying to hit on you. It's just that I saw a ghost. And I freaked out.

Yeah. That would go well. Just great.

Her heart was thundering out of control. Was he going to say something? Was he going to call her out for hitting on him? Was he going to ask about her virginity? Oh, she could think of nothing more embarrassing. It was a literal horror. The idea that he knew… No.

She couldn't bear it. She really couldn't bear it.

But maybe he wouldn't remember. He had a little bit of wine himself. And they'd made it through the night in the haunted house. Which was… Pretty haunted. Except maybe that it had been a dream. Because she'd been drunk.

She really didn't know what to think. She didn't know what to hope for.

And suddenly, he made a very masculine noise and stirred in his sleep. And then he turned over and looked at her, and she felt like the whole world lit up.

He was the most beautiful thing she'd ever seen. It hurt to look at him.

You love him.

No. She really didn't need to think that. She tried not to think it. She tried to never, ever think it. Yes, she loved him. As a friend, almost a brother, really. But the feelings…the attraction feelings… Those things she tried to keep separate and in their own box. Desire didn't have to be anything deeper.

But right now, lying next to him in bed, it was hard to keep it separate. They seemed to wrap around her com-

pletely, like invisible vines. Jace. And everything he was
to her, along with how much she wanted to lean in and…

She rolled in the opposite direction. Fast. And went
right off the edge of the mattress, down to the floor.

"Ow!"

She looked around the room, all lit up with daylight
and felt…silly. About the whole ghost thing. About getting into bed with Jace…

"What happened?" She could hear him moving behind the curtain.

"I fell. I…"

"Were you up here?" he asked, and she was thank-
ful he was behind the curtain and she was on the floor.

"Yeah I…something freaked me out last night." She
winced. "So I got in bed and closed the curtains. Sorry."

"No need to apologize."

She heard his feet hit the floor on the other side of the
bed, and she stood up quickly because she didn't need for
him to see her on the floor in an undignified heap when
she was sure she already sounded like an undignified
heap. He didn't need visual confirmation.

She smoothed her hair and tried to lean casually
against the bedpost. He came around the corner of the
bed and she ignored the way her heart throbbed. "Morning," she said.

"You made it. The hotel is yours. Assuming you still
want to buy it after Raccoonageddon."

"Oh, if anything I want it more."

"This is why you need a full-time babysitter, Cara."

"Don't worry. I'm bringing Grandpa's whiskey bottle over."

"Cara… That's not what I mean. Let's go out to the
diner and get some breakfast."

And she was grateful for that. Because she needed to

get back somewhere more familiar with him. On regular old footing. He was acting normal. Unaffected. Standing there in the same jeans and Henley he'd been wearing yesterday, he almost looked like last night hadn't happened. And maybe… Maybe he didn't remember. It wasn't like they'd done anything. It was just that she'd… Told him one of her more embarrassing secrets, and… Really, it wasn't so much like she had propositioned him. She could play it off like it was a joke.

It was just… It had not been a joke. And it hurt her to know that at the very first moment, she had exposed herself like that. Why had she done that to herself? He didn't want her. If he did, there had been ample opportunity for him to let her know along the way. Not that she had really ever let him know. But… There also hadn't been anyone else.

She ignored the ache in her chest that was still there from moments ago. From that terrible, ridiculous thought about love.

She didn't need to go thinking things like that.

And she didn't need to go marinating in all these feelings. They were just Jace and Cara, the same as they'd always been. One weird moment wasn't going to change that.

They packed up their things and went back out to Jace's truck.

"If you want, I can drive us over to the diner, then swing us back by here."

"Sure," she said.

The diner was packed. It was Sunday morning, and a whole lot of people were there for free church bacon and eggs. And a lot of other people were there for a hangover cure. The diner was where every kind of person in Lone Rock met.

"Good morning," said Rosemary, who had been hostess at the diner ever since they had graduated from high school.

"Morning," said Cara.

"Two," said Jace.

Rosemary gave them a sidelong glance.

All right, they had shown up at the diner for breakfast together. But hey, they had spent the night together. It was just it wasn't like that.

It was frustrating. Knowing that everyone in town basically assumed that she and Jace were sleeping together, when they absolutely weren't.

She wanted the diner to be a normalizing moment, and in many ways, she supposed that it was, since these kinds of speculative looks were normal for them. It was just that… She wanted to not think about him that way. And there was a strange kind of intimacy that seemed to linger between them after last night.

They sat down at the booth, and Rosemary handed them the menus. "Coffee?"

"Yes," they both said at the same time.

"I have a bastard of a headache," said Jace.

"You weren't even that drunk," she pointed out.

"It's that sugary girlie wine," he said. "I can drink Jack Daniel's and feel nothing the next day."

"So what you're telling me, is that you're not man enough for girls' night."

"I am not," he said.

"Maybe your toxic masculinity is protecting you."

"I would maintain that," he said.

A few moments later, their coffee arrived.

"Do you need a minute?" Rosemary asked.

"No," said Jace. "Bacon and eggs. Over medium. Hash browns, sourdough toast."

"Same."

Rosemary nodded, then left, and both she and Jace lifted their coffee mugs up and took long drinks.

As soon as that first hit of caffeine touched her soul, she started to feel slightly more human.

"I want to invest in the hotel."

"What?"

"I was thinking. After we talked last night, about the trust fund, and all of that... I want to invest in the hotel."

"You want to invest in the hotel. And when you say that, you mean you actually want to do this, and this isn't you doing some kind of misguided older brother thing?"

She was trying to sort through the tangle of feelings that this offer brought up. There was a certain measure of relief, because having some extra financial support— especially considering that there was clearly a raccoon porthole somewhere—was great. And certainly offered her a little bit of reassurance. But then also, if he remembered that conversation from last night...

Of course, that conversation had only been a couple sips of wine in, and it had come before all the raccoon stuff, way before, meaning she hoped that what had come right before the raccoon stuff, had been swallowed up by both that and the wind.

"So you want to... You want to throw backing behind this?"

"Yeah," he said. "I do need something that I believe in. That I want to invest in. Why not the town?"

"I just can't escape the feeling that actually what you're doing is acting like a mother hen."

"I prefer older brother."

Oh well. He might as well have just taken the butter knife next to his right hand and stabbed her in the heart.

Done a little dance around her body as she bled out for good measure.

"I don't need an older brother," she said, her tone crisp. "Thank you. A friend, who sees me as an equal, sure."

"Me feeling like an older brother doesn't preclude me seeing you as an equal."

But it definitely precluded him seeing her as a woman. Great. Maybe it was even worse than she was thinking. Maybe he did remember what she had said last night, and he was not surprised that she was a virgin, and also didn't take seriously her offer for him to relieve her of it at all, because why would he, because she would've had to be kidding, because obviously they weren't attracted to each other.

She was rescued by the arrival of her breakfast, and she tucked into her eggs fiercely, mixing the yolks up in her hash browns and dipping her toast in the rest.

"You okay?"

"Starving," she said.

"Yeah. All right. Anyway, I figure if you're going to go over to the bank today, maybe I can go with you. And we can maybe have me cosign the paperwork."

"I don't need you to cosign, Jace. And if you're thinking that's a way to help keep me safe or bail me out or whatever…"

"Hey, all right. If you don't want my name on the paperwork, that's fine. I really was just trying to be helpful. I promise that I'm not… Doubting you."

"Whatever your crisis is, it doesn't have anything to do with me."

"Not a crisis," he said. "I've basically lived my life this way on purpose. I don't have a lot of connections. Other than my family, and I love them. And I've got you. But I don't own property, I don't do a job where I am doing any one thing for any length of time. I got all this money that I earned riding bulls, and you tell me what's…meaningful about that? Now I'm going to get a whole bunch of money that I didn't even earn. I don't know. Part of me wants to live that way, but… At this point… It's also starting to seem a little bit pointless. And useless. You want things, and I admire that. You're right. I don't put a lot of stock in dreams. And I'm still not in a place where I want to put any in my own. Or even have any of my own. But I'm happy to invest in yours. Don't see it as anything other than that. Your dreams feel valuable to me. So…"

"Yeah," she said, her heart seizing up. "Okay."

Why was it like this? Why was he like this? It really… It really got her. Right square at the center of her chest. He was doing this for her. And not to be condescending or anything like that, just because he cared.

And she didn't know why in the hell that made him feel like he was sitting further away from her than he had been a moment before. Because it should feel like they were closer.

But there was just something… There was something. Something that was there for her that was missing for him.

And she would never be able to talk to him about it. She would never be able to bridge that gap, because he was all she had. She had made an idiot out of herself last night. But there were a ton of handsome men. A ton of them. She saw them every night at the bar. Little Rock was lousy with hot cowboys. If that was her thing, then there was ample opportunity for her to pursue that. The one thing she would never be able to replicate or re-create was this relationship with him. The one thing she would never be able to have again, with anyone else, was what she had with Jace. This long-standing, completely trusting friendship. Something that was kind of more like family, if she were honest.

And he was the only family she had left, really.

He was important to her. In ways that were so complicated and imperative, there was no untangling it all. "Okay," she said again. "I'll take your help. You can invest, but I'm going to sign the paperwork on my own."

"Fair enough. What I'd like to do is help finance the remodels then."

"All right," she said.

"Then you have yourself a partner."

"A haunted house partner," she said.

"It's not haunted by anything but raccoons."

"Still. That's pretty haunted."

She reached across the table and stuck her hand out. And only when his large, warm, calloused hand wrapped around hers completely, did she recognize the error of her ways. Yeah, maybe that wasn't the smartest thing to have done. But he was her friend; she wasn't going to just not touch him. To not shake his hand.

So she did, firmly. And then brought her hand back over to her side of the table and started shoveling more eggs into her mouth.

"I'm going to make my offer right after breakfast," she said, around her eggs. "Then I'll sign the paperwork, and then… We can make a meeting with the contractor."

"All right. Sounds good."

By the time he got back to the ranch, he almost wasn't thinking about that moment last night, over and over again. Almost.

He thought that he had done a pretty good job playing it cool this morning. But when he'd woken up, it hadn't been the raccoon that he thought of. It had been that moment when she looked at him, all glossy eyed, and told him that she was a virgin.

And that if he wanted to have sex with one...

Holy shit.

He had no idea what he was supposed to do with that.

Because he hadn't been able to get it out of his mind, and he was...

His body stirred.

Hell. And damn.

But he was resolved in his decisions to invest in the hotel. Even more so after last night. She needed him. If he didn't help, she was going to end up neck-deep in debt.

And maybe... Okay, maybe he needed her too.

Maybe he was ready to admit it was time to make something of his own.

But this was the thing. Whatever had happened last night, it was an anomaly. He wasn't going to let that dictate his actions, but it might also be telling him that he needed to stop and make a choice.

He was all thrown off because he was indecisive. So he was indecisive no more.

He was investing in the hotel. He was staying.

He'd realized this morning at breakfast that he couldn't afford to be wishy-washy. Not now. This was the time to make a decision.

He put his truck in Park and got out, stepping toward the barn. There had to be something to do. It was a ranch. There had to be something physical that he could pour himself into.

He was just about to go grab a rake, because God knew he could probably always muck a stall, when his brother Boone appeared from one of the stalls. "Howdy," he said. He looked him over. "You look... Not particularly well rested."

"What's your problem, Boone?"

"I don't have a problem. You seem to."

"No problem. Just thinking about some things."

"Oh yeah?" Boone crossed his arms over his chest and leaned against the stall door. "What kind of things?"

"I decided to invest in Cara's hotel thing."

"Her hotel thing?"

"Yes. You know, she's going to buy the Little Rock hotel. I thought that I would throw some money behind it. What she wants to do is pretty ambitious and... Anyway, I get the trust fund money next week."

"Wow. Well. Good for you. And here I thought you were just going to use it the way that I did."

"Hookers and blow?"

Boone laughed. "I mean, basically."

"I think we both know that isn't true," said Jace.

"Hey. You don't know."

"I think you pretend there's nothing more to you than that, but we all know there is."

"There maybe used to be," he said. "But there's not now." He got a slightly distant look to his eye.

It was impossible to know what Boone thought about anything. And yet, sometimes, Jace thought there was something in his brother that was just plain sad, and it wasn't the same kind of sad the rest of them were—they shared a common grief, so there was a bit of it that was inevitable. But there was something else to Boone, he just couldn't quite say what it was.

"Have you ever thought about investing in property?"

"Sounds dangerously like settling down," said Boone. "And that is also not in the cards for me."

"So you just going to... What? And I'm serious, because I'm trying to figure this out too. You just going to have all this money, and nothing to invest it in. Nothing to make your own."

Boone shrugged. "I have to find something that was worth making my own. Something that didn't belong to someone else, that is."

"Do you want something that does belong to someone else?"

"Story time's over," said Boone. And he knew that he'd hit a nerve.

"What's going on?"

"Nothing. And anyway, none of your business. But there's nothing wrong with just living life. Nothing wrong with... Hell, I mean, we've all accomplished things in the rodeo."

"Yeah. We got a bunch of belt buckles. And a bunch of money. It's just... Sometimes I ask what it's all for."

"What do you mean? It's our family legacy?"

"It's Dad's legacy," Jace said. "It's not mine. I never sat down and decided that it was something I wanted to do. I just did it. And now I guess sometimes I want something that's a little bit more... Mine."

"So that's where this hotel thing comes in?"

"I guess so."

"Well good luck to you. It still sounds an awful lot like an entanglement to me. And honestly, another thing that makes you and Cara basically married. Now you're business partners too? I don't know about that."

"Good thing is I didn't ask you," he said. "Didn't even start to. You're the one who asked. I'm just letting you know."

"Right. Well. I wish you the best of luck with that endeavor. And hopefully whatever else has you tensed up. Because something tells me it's not just that."

And then his brother left, but Jace still felt irritated.

Because damn him, he was right. He was right about the fact that there was something else bothering him.

It was the fact that his body seemed to have developed an irrepressible interest in Cara.

He couldn't claim that it was sudden. It felt sudden. But it was just... He knew that she was beautiful. It was just that he had never let that matter. Because what did beauty matter? There were a lot of beautiful women. But there were very few people in his life that he cared for like he cared for her. And there was no one exactly like her. So he let all that fade to the background, and he never let it become attraction.

But there it was. Just suddenly. He was... He couldn't stop thinking about the way that she'd said that, and the inevitable thoughts that had followed.

How much he wanted...

Hell.

He wanted her.

No. He didn't have to let it go that far. He had a little bit of an interest there, but that was it. That didn't mean that he wanted her. And it didn't have to be anything too deep.

He wouldn't let it be.

In fact, tonight he would go to the bar, meet with her and talk her plans over with her. He wasn't going to let it be weird. He was just going to keep it the same. It was entirely possible Cara didn't even remember saying that to him. She hadn't acknowledged it all day. Not at all. Maybe she had even been kidding. Because he just couldn't imagine...

Except what was becoming easier and easier to imagine was his own hands skimming over her curves.

He could remember when he had pulled her down on top of them last night. How soft she'd been.

It had been a juvenile thing to do, but the feelings that had resulted had been anything but.

And then after that…

You've been tempting it. Teasing it.

He would've said no. That he'd never done that. Not with her. But the way that he had teased her last night, even before she'd said that to him about her virginity… It made him wonder. It made him wonder what he was actually thinking.

He needed to get back on the road, maybe. Maybe that was the issue. He'd been home a long time. And after school, for most of their friendship, they had gotten some decent-sized breaks from one another while he went out on the rodeo. And he usually hooked up when he went out on the rodeo. Quite a bit.

He didn't like the way that thought made him feel. Like it was only having sex with other women that kept him from being attracted to her.

That it was only some weird dry spell now that made him feel different.

He felt like it cheapened what they had between them, and like it cheapened her a bit, and nothing about Cara was cheap. He gritted his teeth and tried to get a grip.

Yeah. Tonight he would make sure that things got back to normal. And pretty soon that little snippet of conversation would fade into the background. It would just become one of the many conversations they'd had, and it wouldn't stand out as being anything more than what had gone on before it.

Just a snippet of things they'd said to each other.

It didn't have to echo in his mind. It didn't have to echo in his body. It really didn't.

So he took one more shovelful of manure and relished the ache in his arms.

He was going to work until he was busted. Then he was going to go have a drink with his best friend. And make some plans for the new business venture.

It wasn't like being married. Because being married wasn't in the cards for him. Not ever.

But this? This felt better. This felt right. This felt like he was getting close to doing the thing that he needed to do. Because something had to change. He wasn't going to turn thirty and just stay the same old way. Boone might be comfortable with that, but Jace wasn't.

And this was the right step forward. He knew it.

So he banished anything that felt wrong and kept on shoveling.

Chapter 7

By the time Jace stumbled into The Thirsty Mule with two of his brothers, he was pretty damned tired. Which was exactly what he wanted. He wanted to be bone-tired by the time he hit his bed tonight. And he definitely didn't want to think. He saw Cara standing behind the bar, glowing. She was lit up like a firecracker. Laughing and talking to two men sitting in front of her who were… Looking down her top.

And suddenly, Jace couldn't look away. Not from down her top, though his eyes definitely drifted there. But just from her. Altogether.

Her blond hair was lit up like a halo, and she looked so damned happy. She had on makeup tonight. Dark mascara and glossy pink lipstick. There was a glow about her cheeks, and he had a feeling she dusted some kind of sparkling powder on there. And yeah… If he wasn't mistaken, she had put a bit of it on her breasts…

"Damn. She is pretty."

That came from Flint.

Jace scowled. "Shut the fuck up."

"Down boy," said Boone.

"Well. If you guys could stop being perverts about my best friend for five minutes, that would really help. You treat her like an object, and I'm sick of it."

"To be clear, when we tease you about her," said Boone, "it has nothing to do with her, and everything to do with you. Right now has a bit to do with her. Because damn."

The problem was, he couldn't even disagree. But it didn't feel like objectifying her. Not really. It felt like something else. Something different. It felt like something singular, like something had reached up and grabbed him by the throat and shaken him hard. And he didn't like it. No, he really didn't. Worst of all, his brothers were there. Worst of all, there was a bar full of people. If there wasn't...

He could see it clearly. Going over to the bar and leaning over, hooking his arm around her waist and...

No. What the hell? She was supposed to be like a sister to him. She was...

There was something unraveling here, and he couldn't quite put a finger on it. And maybe it had to do with all this need to reframe his life. With all these thoughts he had about what he wanted to do with his life and himself. Maybe he was looking for something to hold on to, and there she was.

Hell. She'd always been the thing he'd held on to.

Maybe that was what he was doing now. Just so desperate to find something that he...

He gritted his teeth and went to the empty barstool and sat down. Boone and Flint sat on either side of him.

Cara whipped her head to the side, and the moment that she saw him… There was something on her face, and he couldn't quite read it. But it reminded him of the sun coming up from behind the mountains. It reminded him of some kind of beauty he never considered before. Something that had never been spoken about or written about or even sung about. And he was not a poet by nature. But there was something that stirred inside of his soul that defied words and poetry. Something that made him feel unworthy. Of standing there. Of looking at her.

Of being in this spot.

He looked up behind her, at the Jack Daniel's bottle there that contained Mitch.

And he didn't believe in that sort of thing, but he had to wonder if the old man knew somehow. Maybe he'd just put a hex on him. Left a spell behind here in the bar that would affect any man that ever looked at Cara.

Why was that less insane than thinking he might be here now? He couldn't say.

Except he'd always been pretty clear within himself that… That the end was the end.

But hoping for anything else was just trying to put a Band-Aid on the pain that life brought.

He was resistant to Band-Aids. He preferred to rub a little dirt in it and get on with things.

Yeah. You get on with things so well. You're thirty years old and have no idea what you want.

"Can we get a drink?"

His voice came out harsh, and he felt bad, because he sure as hell didn't need to talk to her that way. Especially not when she just looked at him like that. Her expression fell, and he felt like a dick.

"Yeah." She had recovered quickly, grinning like he was just another bar patron. She often did that. It was part of the show, after all. She didn't break character when she was behind the bar.

She moved over and put her hand on her hip. "Boone? Flint? What can I get for you?"

"Something strong," said Flint.

"I drew the short straw," said Boone. "I'm driving. So I'll just have a beer."

"I know what you like," she said to Jace.

And the words felt like a swipe of her tongue, straight down the center of his chest.

And that was a weird and graphic metaphor that he'd certainly never thought before. Not about her.

"She knows what you like," said Boone.

"I could know what you like too, Boone. If you'd let me."

"Shit," Jace said. "It's bad enough that they pull this kind of stuff to make me mad. Now you're in on it?" he asked.

Cara looked at him blandly, then shrugged. "What's the harm in it?"

"God Almighty," said Jace. "You're all going to be the death of me."

She winked at Boone. *Winked* at him.

"Well," said Boone. "Never mind. I take back everything I said about you practically being married to her. She's obviously single."

"Really, are you just trying to make me mad?"

"Why are you so mad?" Flint asked.

And the problem was, he didn't have an answer. Not a good one. Not a good one at all.

"I want a burger," he said. "If you're done flirting with my brother."

"Yeah, I'm done," Cara said. "For now."

She walked back down the bar, and he couldn't help

but watch the wiggle of her hips, the way her ass looked in those jeans.

It was like the floodgates had opened, and now that he had noticed, he couldn't stop.

If you want to have sex with a virgin...

She couldn't be a virgin. She just couldn't be. And it wasn't because he didn't believe she was capable of making that choice, he just didn't... She exuded sex appeal. She was so comfortable with herself. With her body. The way that she handled the men in the room was... She had them all eating out of the palm of her hand. She just seemed like a woman who was *experienced*. He had accepted that. He didn't really ever think about it. They didn't talk about that sort of thing. That was fine. It wasn't part of their friendship. They were sort of open...

And now that he thought about it, he couldn't remember her ever dating anybody, but the thing was, he was gone sometimes. And anyway, he figured that she probably had her share of hookups working at the bar and...

He looked at all the men sitting around the bar. The thought of any of them putting their hands on her made him so angry he couldn't even see straight.

She leaned forward and started talking to two men down at the other end. They were getting an eyeful down her tank top, and the thing was, he knew that she knew it. And that if she didn't want them to, she wouldn't hold herself in that position. She was a woman in total control of herself. She knew exactly the effect that she had on men, and she was happy to have it.

He just couldn't see...

But maybe that was his own wrongheaded thinking. Maybe it showed what he knew about anything.

It was almost funny. That there was something he

didn't know about Cara Summers. That there was maybe something he didn't understand about women.

And hell, sitting there looking at her like he was, he wondered if there were some things he maybe didn't understand about himself. And that was a whole other Pandora's box of freaky-ass shit he didn't want to open.

His brothers and his burgers arrived a few moments later, along with their drinks, and he did his best to listen to Boone talk about his plans for the next rodeo season.

His plans to get on the road.

Flint had similar plans. And he realized just none of it… Resonated in him. Not anymore.

He shoved down his french fries.

"I think I'm going to stay here," he said.

"Really?" Boone asked. "You're not going back out there?"

"I want everything. I've made tons of money. It's time for me to figure out the next thing. I need something that's… I need something that's mine."

Right when he said that, he looked back behind the bar, and his eyes connected with Cara's and, on God, he had not meant for that to happen. But it had, and it resonated down deep inside of him. Made him feel something he really wished he hadn't.

"I mean, more power to you," said Boone. "But I'm not done with the glory."

"I mean, I could do with a little bit less infamy," Flint mused.

Boone snorted. "It'll pass," he said. "Nobody's going to remember that Tansey Martin wrote a song for you in another year."

"It's not about me," said Flint, practically growling.

"It's not? Because I seem to recall…"

"She didn't love me," said Flint. "If she had, I would've known."

"You think so?" Boone asked.

"Yeah," said Flint. "I think so. It was nothing."

And Jace didn't quite believe that. And maybe it was asinine of him, but he kind of liked the fact that his brother wasn't really as certain about things as he tended to pretend.

Boone and Flint were not as gloriously unattached as they pretended. Commentary from the last couple of days had shown him that.

Of course, that didn't really help much. It only made him wonder if he'd ever been as detached as he pretended. If he'd been lying to himself as well as he ever had to anyone else.

They finished their burgers, and Boone downed another shot, simply because he could.

"Let's go," Flint said. "I'm bored of sitting here sober."

"See you later," said Jace. "I'm going to hang out for a bit."

It was getting crowded in the bar, and he didn't like the idea of leaving. Not with Cara looking like that. Not with all these men here staring at her.

You just want to keep staring at her.

She was his friend. It was more than that. It would always be more than that.

His brothers left, and he kept his position at the bar. Kept it until things started to fade out. Until Cara rang the bell for last call.

Until the very last patron exited the bar, and they were the only two people left inside.

"I'm going to need a ride home," he said.

He wasn't drunk. All the whiskey had left his system a couple hours earlier. He wished he were a little drunk.

"Weird," she said. "I don't seem to recall agreeing to that."

"I figured you probably wouldn't leave me here."

"Well, that's where maybe you don't know everything about me."

It was on the tip of his tongue to say that he knew more about her than he had a week ago. That he knew more about her than he wished he did.

But he was trying to get them back on equal footing.

It was tough. It was damn tough when she was standing there looking like she did. When she was looking like the embodiment of...

He cut that thought off.

He was about to think that his best friend looked like the embodiment of sex.

And that was not what he wanted to be thinking. Not now. Not ever.

"I figured we would talk a little more. About the hotel."

"Oh great," she said, leaning back against the bar. She arched her back slightly, and he couldn't help but notice the way that her breasts thrust upward.

He looked away.

"What are your plans."

"Well. That kind of all depends. On how deep of an investment you're talking about here."

He looked back at her, because even though he was feeling off-kilter at the moment, he would damn sure make eye contact with Cara when he was talking about business. When he was talking about things that mattered. "The thing is, I have more than enough. I've never been one to sit around and be idle. The rodeo might not have been my dream, but if I was going to do something, that I was going to be the best at it."

He cleared his throat. "When you have brothers who are determined to be the best at all the same things... Well, it gets a little bit competitive. And on the youngest. So I came after them. And everything they did, I wanted to have done, done better. Every record they had broken, I wanted to come up behind them and break it too. As you pointed out, I'm not a big visualizer. I'm not a dreamer."

He looked down at his hands. It was high time he did something with those hands. Built something. Made something. And doing it for Cara...that just made sense. "I just put one foot in front of the other. I live in the moment. Because of that... I went. There's no room for nerves to creep in. No room for anxiety. No room for what-ifs. And the point of all that is, I made a lot of money doing that. I'm proud of that money. Because it's mine. The money that I'm getting from the trust fund? It isn't. It's not mine. That comes from my dad. It comes from everything that he built. And the more I think about it, the more I want to invest in something permanent with it. Because I have it, whether I feel like I have a right to it or not. So. The budget's big. Did you want an in-ground pool?"

She laughed. "No. I don't think I need a pool. But... I don't really know what to do with this offer. I don't... We're friends, and I know that you care about me. You always have. But this..."

"It's a business decision. I mean, I expect a cut of it. But at least then I'm working for it. No?"

"For a man who claims he doesn't think ahead... You sure have a plan."

"Look. I just don't..." He looked at her, at the hopeful expression on her face. The glitter in her eyes. "Forget about it," he said.

"Forget about what?"

"Forget I was gonna say anything. It's not anything that we need to talk about."

"I want to talk about it. Tell me. Tell me what's going on."

"All right. You know, when somebody that you love is dying, thinking ahead just means thinking to a future without them. And I never could muster up a belief in miracles. So I just knew that if I imagined what I wanted to be when I grew up… I would be imagining a world without Sophia in it. It's a habit. All right. It's a habit that I never got around to breaking."

It was one reason he was all or nothing. In the moment and never in the future. Black-and-white was easy, and he'd lived a black-and-white life. He'd known there would be a before and an after. Sophia here. Sophia gone. There were no shades of gray in loss.

He found there weren't really any shades of gray in life.

Those glittering eyes went liquid.

"Jace…"

"It's been a long time. I don't live in the past. That's the other thing. You learn to live in the present, and she can't… You can't go back there either."

"Well that's pretty sad. Because even though she's gone, she is your sister. And maybe it would be nice if you could revisit her."

"She's gone."

"I don't believe that the people we love are ever really gone, Jace," she said. She looked back at the bar, up at the bottle that held her grandfather's ashes. "You know I talked to Grandpa every day. He's with me. I believe that."

"Well. Sophia's not with me. She's gone. One day,

she just died. And she was never with me again. That's all I know."

And he didn't know why he had always felt so hardline about that. So rigid. Maybe because if there were miracles to be had in the world, if divine power existed at all, and it had not extended its hand to keep Sophia with him, physically with him, then he didn't see the point of it anyway. And frankly it was a bigger comfort to believe there was just nothing there. That was all.

Maybe some people preferred the comfort of faith. He didn't find it comforting. He didn't find it comforting to think that there was someone who could've lifted a finger to save her, and hadn't.

He didn't find it comforting to think that somebody might be there in spirit when he couldn't actually talk to them.

And he didn't like to think about any of this. Because there was no damned point to it. None whatsoever. It didn't accomplish anything. Didn't fix anything.

He didn't know why she was pushing.

"I'm sorry that I never met her," she said.

He thought back to the boy he'd been when he had met Cara. "Well, you and I never would've met when she was alive. Because we had to live in Portland as long as she was sick. Make sure she was near the hospital."

"I know. I'm just talking about what-ifs."

"I don't get the point of those."

"Not even a little? Like you never ask yourself… What might happen if you set your foot on a different path? This one or that one?" She looked up at him, and her blush pink lips parted. She drew in a breath, and her breasts lifted.

Fuck. Right then, he wanted to ask what if. Wanted

to ask what would happen if he stepped on a different path. But to what end?

Since when do you care about the end?

One foot in front of the other. Just as far as the eye could see. And no farther.

If a man was meant to see beyond the horizon, there wouldn't be a line.

But there was. Firmly drawn. You weren't meant to look ahead too far.

And right now, it was easy to believe that there was nothing outside of this bar. The thing outside of this moment. It was how he felt when he got on the back of a bull.

There was nothing but that. But his thighs pressed against the bull's flanks. The breathing of the animal as he prepared for the chute to open. For the fight to begin. The rush of adrenaline in his own body as he prepared for the fight of his life.

Those were the moments in life he loved, because they narrowed down to fractions of a second. To a single moment.

To everything.

Everything being within reach. Everything being within sight.

There was simply his hand wrapped around the leather strap, the sensation of that pressure pushing the glove more deeply into his palm. The smell of the dust and the animal. The sound of Garth Brooks and the crowd.

This moment was like that. Suddenly, there was nothing. Nothing but her. Nothing but him. Even the edges of the room had gone dark and fuzzy.

The jukebox was playing Luke Bryan. The room smelled like alcohol, fry oil and tobacco. And she looked like heaven. Something bright and glowing against the darkened backdrop.

And there was no moment beyond this one. Nothing beyond the next breath.

And nothing, nothing beyond the last breath.

And so it seemed the easiest thing in the world to take a step toward her. And then another. The easiest thing in the world to square his body right in front of hers, and watch as she pressed herself just slightly against the bar. Away from him, but her eyes told him that she didn't actually want to move farther away.

And then her eyes dropped to his mouth, back up to his eyes. And if he were to ask what they were doing, he wouldn't have an answer. If he were to ask himself why the hell he was about to do this, he wouldn't have an answer.

But he just didn't need an answer. He didn't need a fucking answer. Because that meant that there was something beyond this. And right now he wasn't acknowledging that. Not even a little bit.

It was only this. Only this.

And that was when he planted his hands on the edge of the bar, on either side of her body, and looked at her like he might be able to find some answers at the very bottom of that green gaze.

She lifted one hand and placed it on his chest. Warm fingertips flexing there, shifting the fabric of his shirt over his skin. His heart rate kicked up, like he was about to ride, and the world narrowed even further. Pink cheeks, pink lips, green eyes.

She looked up at him from beneath her lashes and leaned in. He felt her breath against his skin. Then she moved her hand to the back of his neck. Her fingertips were so soft. Impossibly.

Cara shifted, leaned in, stretched up on her toes.

And she kissed him.

Chapter 8

Oh, she was doing it. She was kissing him. Her mouth brushed his, and a streak of heat went through her that she couldn't deny. She pulled away, almost the instant their mouths touched. "I'm sorry," she said. She turned away. "Shit. I'm sorry," she said again.

He grabbed her arm and turned her to face him, his hands curved around her forearms, and gripping the edge of the bar, pinning her there. "You just kissed me."

"I did," she said.

And suddenly, she found herself being hauled toward him, and he wrapped his arm around her waist, pushing her body against his, and when he kissed her, he did not move away.

No. His kiss was deep, hard. Hot.

And it was Jace.

She wanted to pull away and scream with the hysteria of it.

Jace.

It was Jace.

And he was kissing her. His lips were firm and expert, and then he angled his head, and she opened her mouth to him. And his tongue slid against hers. Jace's tongue.

And she was trembling. Immediately wet between her legs. Because her fantasies had primed her for this moment over the course of years, and yet it was so much better than she had ever imagined that it could be.

This kiss was beyond anything that she had ever fathomed a kiss might be. He was everything. And too much all at once. So tall and strong and hot. All-knowing. Like he was demanding a response from her. Like he was willing it from the depths of her soul.

And she couldn't doubt. Because how could she, when she was being kissed by a man who so clearly knew exactly what he was doing. A man who didn't seem to have doubt anywhere in his body, anywhere at all. And she would know, since she was currently plastered against his body.

He pulled her away from him, and looked down at her. "Are you really a virgin?"

"Well. I thought we weren't talking about that."

"You *kissed* me, Cara."

"You also kissed me. So I think we're even."

"Not even a little bit. Were you serious?"

"Was I serious?" She squinted, and tried to look confused.

"You are not fucking confused. You know exactly what I mean. Were you serious?"

"Yeah," she said, realizing that it was all futile now. And if she got weird about it, it was only going to be weirder. If she pretended, after kissing him like that and then returning his kiss like he was oxygen and she was suffocating to death, it was only going to look more extreme. More ridiculous.

So there was just a point where she was going to have to exhibit some honesty. "I was serious. Yes. I haven't ever been with anyone. And you know, it's one of those things… That at this point it's kind of weird and left undone, and if you would like to be the one to help me out with it, then I am okay with it. It just has to be the one… the once. I appreciate the fact that you're already helping me with my hotel. And it might be a little bit much to ask you to pay for renovation and also have sex with me."

Well. She wanted to crawl under the bar. She had just said all those words to Jace, and she wasn't even drunk. She couldn't blame them on anything like that. Couldn't take refuge in the fact that she was maybe being an idiot.

"You're a virgin?"

"Yes."

"And you would like to not be." He said it not so much as a question, but as a clarifying statement.

Though in general, that wasn't true. If she had actually wanted to lose her virginity, if it were even a thing to her, then she would've done it. It was just that she… She was stuck in some kind of weird limbo with Jace.

Weird limbo. Weird way to say: you're in love with him.

Hell. She didn't want to think about being in love with Jace. The very thought made her want to cry. She didn't want to be in love with Jace. It was fucking stupid. She did not want to be in love with Jace.

But as she stood there, looking at him, at that precious, dear, familiar, wonderful face, she knew it was true. And it was why she had never been with anyone else. Because there was just nobody that made her feel even a fraction of what he did. Because being with somebody else would be a mockery of what they had. Because it wouldn't come close to what she actually wanted it to.

"I want you," she whispered.

She wished her voice was stronger. She wished it wasn't so small.

And it was so far from the whole truth that it made her want to laugh. And it was so desperately inadequate that it made her want to cry. And so exposing that she wanted to cover herself. But looking at him, she could see the promise of something. Like the sun rising, flooding the moment with hope. With light.

And what if… What if she could have everything with him?

It was a bright, brilliant moment, but she let herself have it. Even though she didn't think it was realistic. Even though she didn't think it would ever… Ever amount to anything… She let herself dream. If only for a second. She let herself dream, because it felt right. She let herself dream, because sometimes dreams were all you had. And they were beautiful, and magical, and you should hang on to them when you could.

And who knew if she could actually have everything with Jace. She'd never been all that special.

Except to him.

But then, she also knew that he was a difficult bastard. Who didn't have a romantic bone in his body.

He didn't do long term, or even an exclusive kind of short term. Yeah, she also knew that.

"You want me?" His voice was rough and she felt it between her legs.

What was she doing? What was happening right now? He was her friend. Her best friend. Hers. And she was just telling him, and he was looking at her like he might want her too, and she wanted to run. From him and to him.

She cleared her throat. "Is that not apparent?"

He cut her off by pressing his mouth to hers, and a rush of warmth overtook her. He wrapped his arm around her waist and brought her close. And when he kissed her... It was deep. It was real, and it was the most full-on, intense moment of its kind that she imagined anyone had ever experienced. She didn't want to talk. She didn't want to think. She didn't want to do anything but feel. She just wanted to feel. Feel this. Feel him.

She wanted it more than anything.

And she had to laugh, because she sort of wondered if they were being utterly themselves in this moment. If she was trying to manifest forever while he deeply denied any sort of future.

But maybe it didn't matter, because their truth and their beliefs were coming together right in this moment, and it was resulting in a kiss, so... She supposed that was all perfect.

And maybe she would take a page out of his book. Just this once. Because the scrape of his stubble against her cheek was magic, and the slick friction of his tongue against hers was doing wild and reckless things to her insides. Because the feel of his big hands, gripping her waist, smoothing down her hip. Oh, it was her fantasy. Her moment. It was the thing... It was everything.

She started to shake.

And he was Jace, so he noticed.

"You okay?" he asked, brushing his hand over her cheek.

"I'm okay," she said. "I just... I watched you once. Pick up a woman in the bar. The way that you put your hand on her body... I went home and I fantasized about it."

"Fuck," he said. "Don't tell me things like that."

"Why? We're already here."

He huffed a laugh, soft and sexy, and then he smiled. Just a little. "Well. Damned if that isn't true."

And then he kissed her again, and she was drowning.

She pushed her hands up underneath his T-shirt and groaned when she made contact with his hot skin. With his hard-packed muscle.

She started to pull off his shirt.

"Look, as much as I think it would be fun to do this on the bar, I think that we need to bed."

"What?"

"Seriously. You've really never been with anybody?"

"Yes." She moved her hands over his chest. "I've never been with anybody, and I want to be with you, and I'm feeling a little bit desperate."

"And there will be time for hard and fast, I can assure you. I'm all for it. But, we need to do slow and thorough first. Because I take care of you. Bottom line. You're mine, Cara. Mine to protect. And I'm gonna make this good for you. And that means we need to bed. And we need time."

"I'm a virgin," she said. "But I am not an *untouched* virgin. I have a vibrator."

"Praise the Lord, and hallelujah. But, I still want to take my time."

"I just mean… I actually know when I'm about to come. And believe me when I tell you…"

"Save the dirty talk," he said, pressing his thumb against her lips. "We're gonna have me coming a whole lot earlier than either of us want."

It was the fact that he made eye contact with her when he said that that nearly sent her over the edge. The fact that it was Jace.

Her Jace.

The fact that she had looked up and seen him down by

the riverbed when she'd been crying when she was just in middle school, and he looked at her with those same eyes. And now he was looking at her like this, talking to her like that.

It was enough to send her straight over the edge.

Jace. This was *Jace*. And she didn't even have to tell herself that to cement it in her mind, because it could only ever be him.

She had been waiting for this. All this time.

"Well. We can go back to… To the house."

The house that she had inherited from her grandfather wasn't that far out of town.

"Yeah we can."

"It's convenient, since you don't even have your truck here."

"Yeah," he said, his voice ragged. "If I were a different man, I'd be tempted to say that I planned it this way. But you're you, so I definitely shouldn't of done that. And I'm me, so I'm not supposed to… Plan."

"Did you?"

"I'm not going to lie to you. What you said about that got to me. I try to not think of you that way. And when I say try, I mean I decided not to, so I didn't. You must know that you're beautiful."

"I know that men respond to me a certain way. I don't know that I think that is beautiful."

"Well you are. You're basically a damn sunrise. All right? I'm not good at that."

"That's a lie. You pick up women all the time. You must be very good at flattering them."

"I'm good at empty flattery. I'm good at letting those words roll off my lips without even thinking about what they mean. Hey gorgeous. Hey baby. You look beautiful. Like a dress. But it would look better on my bedroom floor."

She blanched. "Please tell me you've never said that."

"I probably have. I probably didn't even pay attention to what it really sounded like. But I guarantee you that neither did she. Because we were both there for one reason, and it didn't matter if we liked each other. It didn't matter. It's the perfect kind of hookup for a man like me. Who doesn't think about tomorrow." His voice pitched lower, and she shivered. "And you know, even though I don't think about my tomorrows, Cara, I know one thing about them. You'll be there. And that matters to me. It matters a hell of a lot."

Her throat went so tight she could hardly speak. "It matters to me too."

"So what I say to you matters. I'm not to give you empty compliments. And maybe that wasn't a great one, but I meant it. I meant it all away from my soul. I promise you that. You're beautiful, and I had to put blinders on to not notice. I did a pretty bad job of it when you first... Filled out."

She laughed, which felt good. "Diplomatic," she said.

"Tonight, I was watching those men look at you... And seeing you the way that they did... Well, it made me want to strangle them, but it also made it impossible to look away from you. But I want to make it very clear it's not like I didn't notice. You don't have the kind of beauty a man doesn't notice."

"Thank you," she said. "But we don't need to talk."

Because it they kept talking, then maybe she would have to share more about what she felt. Maybe she would have to share more about the way that she felt about him. The way that she had always felt about him.

"Take me home and make me feel good." And it wasn't

the smoothest thing, but it was real. It was raw and it was honest. And he seemed to find it undeniable. Because that was when he grabbed her arm and led her out the back door of the bar.

And it was her truck that they needed to take, but she fumbled around looking for the keys, and finally he took pity on her and fished them out of her purse for her and got into the driver's seat.

Her house was a modest one, on one of the streets just a couple of blocks from the bar. All the houses on the street had been built in 1974. All of them the same sort of small and nondescript, or at least they had been originally. Some had been added onto over the years. Made a little bit more fancy a little bit more spacious. But not hers.

It was still the same as when she had lived here with her grandpa. The same green shag carpet. The same daisy pattern countertop in the bathroom.

She loved it because it reminded her of him. Because it reminded her of home.

Jace was a lot like home too, and somehow, right now the combination of the two didn't feel comforting. It simply felt dangerous.

They had spent the night together, shared a bed back at the motel, but this was different. It was different, and so were they.

And she fought against the thought that argued with that. That told her they were just the same. And doing this was risky. As risky as it ever had been. And she needed to be careful. So goddamned careful. And she was taking a risk because she wanted to touch him so badly.

But the fact of the matter was, the horse had bolted. They could turn back now, and things would still be different forever.

Because the acknowledgment of the feelings was the horse in the room. And the sex didn't have to actually happen for it to have been spoken of. And they'd already kissed. So there was no point turning back. Because if it was going to break something, then they'd broken it back at the bar. Maybe they'd broken it back at the hotel.

Maybe they'd broken it at some other point along the path that she couldn't even identify.

Maybe it had shattered for her the moment she had seen him put his hand on that woman's hip and envied her. Maybe that was the point from which she had been too far gone to go back.

And so she really had to be like Jace this moment. And just go forward.

But not look too far ahead.

He got out of the truck and took her keys and unlocked the front door.

She walked in first, and the very familiar room suddenly didn't look so familiar. It looked foreign and a little bit frightening, or maybe that was just her own body right now.

Foreign and a little bit frightening. Not at all what she was used to. Not at all what she expected.

And then he closed the door behind them and locked it, and suddenly it all felt so real.

She was hyperaware of everything. The sound of her breathing. The sound of the forced air coming through the vents as the heater came on. The sound of his footsteps as he walked toward her.

"Jace," she whispered.

"Cara."

It was in affirmation. That he was well aware of who she was. That he saw her. That he wanted her too.

And that was what she really needed to know. More than anything.

"This isn't just the virginity thing, is it? It's not just a novelty for you?"

"I've never found anything about virginity novel. I don't care about it. But I do care about you. I care about what you want. And you waited a long time to do this and… I want it to be good for you. So no. I don't care about that. What I care about is you. That's it. Beginning and end of story. It's you, Cara. You're what matters."

She felt like her heart was being peeled, layer by layer, like all the resistance that she had left was being stripped away. And she really didn't have much. And yet it was brutal. Utterly brutal. She hadn't expected this. That a moment so deeply desired. So anticipated, could be quite so uncomfortable.

But it was like he knew. Right then. Like he knew just what to do. He leaned in and kissed her. And he made it impossible for her to think. And that was just exactly what she needed. A reprieve. And that was what he excelled at. She could see the appeal. Why he lived the way that he did. She could see why it felt great to block out everything but the moment. Absolutely everything.

And so she let his kiss carry her away. Or maybe keep her grounded. To the spot instead of the moments that would follow. The moments where he would see her. Touch her. Tease her in a way that no other man ever had.

Yes. She kept herself in this moment, so she wasn't quite up ahead to those.

His hands were strong and certain as he gripped her waist, rooted her to the spot, to the moment.

Her heart began to throb, her body aching with need.

It was just so good. And it surpassed everything. Every single one of her fantasies. Every single one of those illicit evenings she'd spent thinking about his hands on her body. The reality was so much sweeter. So much better.

And then suddenly, she wanted to see him. Because after all, it was her fantasy. Because after all, she was the virgin.

She pushed her hands up beneath his shirt, and he took the hint, reaching behind his head and gripping the back of his T-shirt, pulling it up over his head in a way that left her mouth ajar.

"How do men do that?"

"What?"

"I dunno. It was just the sexiest thing I've ever seen." At least, it was. It was the sexiest thing she had ever seen until she saw his body. His broad shoulders, his pectoral muscles, with just the right amount of hair sprinkled over them, his lean waist, his corrugated abs.

She licked her lips. She had seen him shirtless any number of times, but this was the first time that it had been okay for her to touch. She could touch him now.

It wasn't inappropriate for her to do that. Because he wanted this. He wanted her.

She reached out and pressed her hand against his chest. It was so hot, and she could feel his heartbeat raging there.

She was actually touching him. His skin. His body.

She hadn't done that, because they were friends. And you didn't do that to your friend. Except she was. And he was still her friend. Every bit as much as he had been before. Before she had touched him. Before everything.

He was still her friend.

She looked at him, searching his face, and suddenly, she couldn't find that assurance there. Because he looked like a stranger just then. There was something about the tension in his expression, the sharpness in his eyes. She had never seen that look on his face before. She wondered how many other women had.

But you have this other part of him. And no one else has that.

It was true. And she knew it. They had a connection, and it was bigger than this. Right then, she needed to expand the moment. To include their past.

It made her heartbeat settle just a little bit.

She continued to move her hands over his muscles, slowly, between his pecs, down to his abs, where she let her fingers drift over the ridges there. She swallowed hard. And she looked back up at him.

"What should I do?"

"Whatever you want."

"Well... I don't know what I want. Could you... Can you take control, please?"

And it was like a blue spark flashed in his eyes. It was like everything shot off like a rocket. An explosion between them.

She had felt safe with Jace, all this time, for all these years, and just now, it was like she was poised on the knife's edge of danger. Like she could see there were vast dimensions to this man that she didn't know, had never known. It was more than just tension in his face. She had opened the door and discovered vast rooms of Jace that she had never realized were there.

And he was the key to her opening the door to those rooms inside of herself too.

She just knew.

But it wasn't only that she was discovering all this about him, she was about to learn a whole lot about herself.

This was terrifying. It really was.

And wonderful too. Amazing. Something more than she had ever imagined possible. Something different.

And her fantasies about Jace hadn't prepared her. Because those were her fantasies. It was her hand on her body. Directing the tempo, directing the speed. Deciding exactly what happened when.

She had just turned the control over to him, and that meant to surrender.

On a level she had never quite dreamed.

"Are you sure?" he asked, his voice rough.

"Yes."

"If there's something I do, and you don't like it, you need to tell me to stop."

"I will." But she couldn't imagine him doing anything she didn't like. That was actually what scared her. That she wasn't sure there were going to be easy limits to this. Because discovering that he wanted her, and further, discovering that she wanted badly to surrender to whatever that meant...

It was like being tossed into the deep endlessness of the sea.

She wasn't sure it had an end.

"I want this," she said. "I want... I want you."

He growled, closed the distance between them and gripped her hands in one of his, effortlessly pinning her wrists behind her back, low, pressed against the dip in her spine right above her rear.

"Good."

The word was hard.

Final. Firm.

She loved it.

And what she loved even more was that taking care of her didn't look like being easy on her.

She didn't want easy. Because nothing had been easy

to get to this point. So why should it be easy now? She just wanted to revel in this. In him.

Jace.

Her best friend with the stranger's eyes.

He kissed her, deep and fierce and hard. And then he trailed the line of kisses down her neck, to her collarbone, on down farther.

Her tank top was low, and when his lips made contact with the plump skin of her breast, she froze. It felt so good. So good. His mouth was hot, and everything in her was blooming with desire.

She had been ready to come from his kiss back at the bar, and this was... This was more extreme. More intense.

He reached down and grabbed the hem of her tank top, pulled it up over her head, leaving her standing there in her black lacy push-up bra.

"Holy hell, Cara. You are really something else."

His eyes were appreciative, hungry, and there was no amount of male appreciation, or compliments, that would ever equal this moment. This moment when Jace Carson looked at her with lust in his eyes.

She had the sudden, ridiculous thought, that this was the highest purpose her breasts had ever had.

And it made her eager for what came next. Not nervous. But before she could unhook her bra, he reached behind her and did it, releasing it and casting it onto the ground. Her nipples went tight underneath his intense scrutiny.

She shivered.

"You are so fucking beautiful," he said, pressing a kiss to her collarbone, down farther, capturing one nipple between his teeth and tugging hard.

"Jace," she said, pushing her fingers through his hair,

holding him to her breast as he sucked her, the sensation going deep between her thighs.

"You like that?"

"Yes," she said. "Basically, whatever you do, assume I like it." Her voice sounded desperate. Panting. She loved every minute of the moment. Of his touch.

He moved his hands up then, cupped her breasts as he took his attention back to her mouth. As he kissed her, deep and thorough while his thumbs skimmed over her breasts.

"Please," she begged.

He unsnapped her jeans, undid the zipper, and she began to kick her shoes off while he pushed her pants and underwear down her legs.

And then she was just naked. In front of him. In front of Jace. And it felt right. It felt good.

The way that he looked at her... Like he wanted to devour her. And she was ready. Ready for it to be more than just a dangerous glint in his eye, a hint, a promise. She was ready for it to be real.

He put his hands around her waist, smoothed them down her hips and back up, skimming the undersides of her breasts, before traversing a path down her body again, and all the while, his eyes were locked onto hers. His gaze intense. She shivered, and she wanted to look away, but she found that she couldn't. All she could do was stand there, trembling beneath his hands.

"So beautiful," he said.

And then he picked her up, like she weighed nothing, held her in his arms as he carried her to her bedroom. Of course he knew exactly where it was. He had been in it any number of times, but not with these dangerous eyes. Not with her naked and him halfway there.

But that he knew where he was spoke again to the familiarity of what they were.

He set her down at the center of the bed and stood back, kicking his boots off, his hands going to his belt.

And she froze. She wanted to see him. Jace. She had never seen him naked. Of course she hadn't. She had never seen a naked man before. She could see the outline of his arousal through the faded denim of his jeans.

He was big. Not that she had any comparison or anything like that. But she could still tell he was big.

She licked her lips as he began to undo the belt buckle. As he began to pull the leather and slide it through the belt loops slowly.

"Yes," she whispered.

"You looking forward to this?" he asked, his voice husky.

"Yes," she confirmed, her own voice sounding scratchy.

"Good. Because it's for you, baby. This is definitely for you."

"Don't call me that," she said.

"Don't call you what?"

"Don't call me 'baby,' please. Call me Cara."

"Cara," he said, his voice coming out a growl.

He pushed his jeans and underwear off and revealed the extent of his arousal.

"Oh my," she said.

"Now that's not like you at all," he said.

He was confident, no nerves at all, and he didn't need them. He was gorgeous. Every inch of him sculpted and lean and glorious.

His manhood was thick and just plain beautiful. She wouldn't have expected she'd think that about male anatomy, but she damn sure did. About Jace.

He moved over to the bed and pushed one knee down

into the mattress, looking at her. Then he put his hands on her knees, smoothed them up her thighs, before forcing her legs apart.

"Jace," she said, the word a protest.

"Don't hide from me," he said, the command so firm she had no choice but to obey. She relaxed her thighs, let her legs fall open.

"That's right," he said. "Show me everything, baby. Show me."

She relaxed even further, and she felt herself getting more and more aroused beneath the sharpness of his gaze. Then he pushed his fingers right between her slick folds, finding her wet with desire for him.

Heat flared in his eyes. "You're so perfect, Cara. So perfect. And I need to taste you now."

She was about to protest, she really was, but then he lowered his head, buried his face between her thighs, and his tongue was so perfect and unerring that she couldn't breathe. Couldn't think.

She looked down, and immediately, her arousal inched its way up higher. Impossibly so. But it was undeniably Jace's head there. Between her legs. Undeniably her best friend licking her, tasting her.

She gasped, the beginnings of her orgasm pulsing from deep within her. And then he pushed a finger inside of her, and she lost it completely. She pulsed around him, arching her hips upward as her release slammed into her.

"You're so hot," he growled, moving up her body and capturing her mouth with a kiss. She could taste her own desire on his lips, and she found herself right back where she had been only moments ago. Turned on and ready to go.

He kissed her as he worked a second finger inside of her, and she moaned, letting her head relax against the pillow. There was so much that she wanted to do. She wanted to pleasure him with her mouth. She wanted to kiss him all over. She wanted… Him. All of him. But she didn't have the words to say that, because she was simply lost. Lost in the moment, lost in him.

He pushed a third finger inside of her and she arched her hips into the stinging discomfort.

"I know you said you had a vibrator. But I still want to make sure you're ready."

"Believe me," she whispered. "I'm ready."

And it was absurd. These impossibly intimate things they were doing. That they could go from being platonic all their whole relationship, to this, in the space of only an hour didn't seem real.

And somehow it seemed right all the same.

Because it had been there. Beneath the surface. Because it wasn't random. Because it hadn't come from nothing. Because it was the truth, was the thing. The truth of how she felt about him.

And she supposed the truth of how he felt about her, even if it was limited to the physical and didn't extend to anything emotional.

Because you couldn't take this. Couldn't manufacture it, and she wasn't even tempted to ask if he was just doing her a favor. Because he was different in this moment. Because it wasn't brotherly Jace who had helped her out of any number of scrapes or taught her how to shoot or anything like that.

She would know if that's what he was doing, because she knew him.

"I hope you have… Condoms," she said.

"Yeah. I do."

The words were strange, the tendons in his neck standing out.

He withdrew from her and went to where he had discarded his jeans, grabbed his wallet and took out a condom packet. He tore it open, then positioned the protection over the head of his arousal, rolling it down slowly, gritting his teeth as he did. It was so erotic to see that. She shivered. And her teeth were still chattering when he came back to the bed, when he steadied her with a kiss, settling between her thighs, and the blunt head of his arousal pressed against the soft, slick entrance of her body, and she held her breath as he filled her.

Yeah, she had penetrated herself with a vibrator before. But that was different. It was hard, and it hadn't been this big.

She could feel him, pulsing inside of her. She could feel how this was different.

And it was… Him.

She looked up at him, and their eyes met. She fought against a strange swell of emotion in her chest. Jace. Jace was inside of her, and she didn't think anything could have prepared her for that. For the enormity of it. For what it meant. And suddenly, it did feel like too much. It felt like too much too fast. Too much for forever. Because one thing she couldn't deny was how deep her feelings ran for him when he pushed himself all the way inside of her and she felt whole. Complete. Felt like she had never wanted anything quite so badly.

Jace.

She didn't know if she said it out loud, screamed it, whispered it, or if it just resonated in her soul. All she knew was that he was there. And she wanted him.

All she knew was that it was too late to turn away. All she knew was that there would be no going back to the way things were before. Because it was too profound. Too real. Too utterly and completely earth-shattering.

And then he began to move, and each thrust of his body within hers pushed her closer and closer to that inevitable peak. She would've thought that it had been too much. Too intense that last time for her to be able to achieve it again, but here she was. His movements became sharp, hard. And that was when it was like being lit on fire. When there was no more control. No more tenderness because he was trying to take her innocence into account. This was hard and rough and primal. It was what she had asked for. She wrapped her legs around his waist, and it made him go deeper. She gasped at the impossibility of it. And how glorious it was.

"Jace…"

"Cara," he ground out, thrusting hard and fast until his control unraveled completely. Until it was like a desperate race to the finish line. She screamed out her pleasure before she even realized her orgasm had crashed over her. And then she was lost. Swept out to sea. Couldn't find a foothold. Couldn't get purchase.

"Jace." She said his name again. It was her battle cry. Her prayer. Her sanctuary and her tempest all at once.

And then his own release took him. He lowered his head, pressing his forehead hard against hers and pumping into her wildly, before going still, and she could feel him pulse deep inside of her. He growled, something feral and uncivilized as his release took hold. And then they lay there together. Sweat slicked and breathing hard.

And she tried to remember the before moment. When they had been the way they'd always been. When they hadn't seen each other naked. When he hadn't been inside of her. And she realized that moment would never be able to stand on its own ever again.

Because they would've always done this.

Because every memory she had of him now would be colored with knowledge.

Of who he was when he made love. What he looked like beneath his clothes. How it felt to have him buried deep within her.

It wasn't just the after that was changed. It was the before.

And she really hadn't taken that into account. But here they were. Inglorious and changed.

Reduced to the very essence of who human beings ever were. Horny, sweaty messes, who had reveled in improbable things only a moment before.

And there was not another person in the world she could have ever done it with. She knew that much. It was clear as could be.

She didn't want him to say anything. Because she didn't want to move from this space into the next one. She didn't think she could handle it. She just needed to sit in the quiet for another second, try to find her breath.

She wasn't sure that was possible. So she just kept on trying until her eyelids got heavy, and the last thing she saw before she drifted off to sleep was him lying beside her.

Chapter 9

He couldn't remember the last time he'd had a cigarette, but thankfully, along with condoms, they were always in his pocket.

Because sometimes, after a night of heavy drinking, only a little nicotine would do. He hadn't been drunk on alcohol tonight, though. It was her.

The night was still and cold, and he sat out there on her back porch, staring off into the darkness. He didn't have his truck, so he couldn't leave. Anyway, leaving after he had just...

After he'd just screwed his best friend's brains out, was maybe not the best way to go. But then, was he screwing her brains out, or had she done it to him? It was hard to say.

It never felt anything like that before. Their connection, combined with the chemistry... It was unreal.

He flicked the switch on the lighter until it started

up, lit the cigarette and took a deep drag off of it, then watched the glowing red end and the smoke curl up into the night.

"What are you doing out there?"

He turned around and saw Cara looking at him through her partially opened window.

"Sorry. Didn't realize the window was open."

"I woke up before I smelled the cigarette smoke."

She shut the window, and a moment later, the glass door slid open, and she stepped outside. "What's this?"

"Nothing. Just… Cigarette break."

"You don't smoke."

"Not usually. But, sometimes."

"Is this when I find out a whole bunch of things about you I didn't know?"

"It wasn't a secret."

"I guess."

She sat in the chair next to him. There was the space of a small, round table between them. She was dressed in an oversize T-shirt and nothing more. Her blond hair was a wreck. And he knew why.

A knot of guilt formed in his chest.

Was it guilt? He didn't think it was. It was something else entirely.

He wanted to call it uncertainty. But the fact of the matter was… It was a resistance of certainty.

He'd taken care of her. It was what he had purposed to do. He had a great time having sex with her. It had been great. They'd both enjoyed it. So there was nothing to feel guilty about. She'd consented enthusiastically, as had he.

It was what he felt like required doing in the aftermath.

"So why don't you tell me why you've never been with anybody before."

"Really?"

"Well. I have licked you between your legs, Cara Summers. So I think that maybe we don't need to have barriers up between us."

"Tell me about the cigarette, first."

"Sometimes I smoke after sex. There. It's that basic. Or when I'm really drunk. Sometimes both of those things are happening at the same time."

"Oh. It's just…"

"It's relaxing," he said. "That's all."

"I see."

And hell, because he had had his face between her legs, he didn't really see the point in holding back the truth of it. "I was never really all that into hard drugs. And let me tell you, there's opportunity for all of that out on the rodeo. I've tried just about everything. But mostly, what I learned was how to smooth out the rough edges incrementally. Little whiskey here and there, an orgasm is a great sleeping pill. A cigarette will finish you off. That's it. When I don't want to think anymore, those are the things that I do. I'm a high-functioning self-medicator."

"Oh. I guess I just… I see you as someone who's amazing and strong and doing really well. I guess sometimes I don't see how much pain you're still in."

"No, didn't you hear what I just said? I'm not in pain, because I know how to keep all that going. An unbroken chain."

"Sure. So it's not really because of me specifically. This is just a thing you do."

"I needed to think."

"Did you… I mean… Was the sex good for you?"

He sat up straight. "You can be in any doubt of that?"

"Yes. I can. Because I'm just a person. A person who is very… Vulnerable, when it comes right down to it. There's a reason that I haven't been with anybody. And that is what you wanted to know. I grew up so isolated in a lot of ways. Everybody here was mean to me. I wasn't cool. I was this poor, very unfashionable girl, who lived with her grandpa. White trash. My mom was a drug addict and everybody knew it. And I never knew who my dad was, and everybody knew that too. I was one of those kids. The ones that nobody wanted to touch. And it was my grandpa, and the bar and the town that ended up grounding me here. And yeah, I like to flirt at the bar. But can you imagine if I actually let any one of those guys sleep with me? Then they would all think that they could. It's all fun and games when it's flirting." She looked away. "And anyway, what I said is true. I saw you touch this woman one time… All I could think about was what that must be like. And I swear to you, Jace, you are my friend, and you always have been. And I feel guilty about this. I do. But I've thought about sleeping with you. A lot."

He took another drag on the cigarette. "Tell me," he said, blowing the smoke out into the air.

"The night before the hotel… The night before I… I told you that I was a virgin… I couldn't sleep. I started thinking about you and… Then it seemed like the easiest thing in the world to touch myself."

He flicked the cigarette down onto the ground and twisted his boot over the top of it. "What are you telling me exactly?"

"I touch myself sometimes and think about you. About you being the one to touch me. About us… In bed together."

"You know, it's a good thing I never knew about that before now. Because you would not have been untouched all this time."

"You don't feel violated by that?"

"Did you really think I would?"

"I don't know. Sometimes I felt really guilty about it. Like it was an invasion of your privacy. But…"

"But, you were too horny to care?"

She laughed, and he could see that her cheeks had been stained dark pink with just a little bit of charming embarrassment. "I guess. Isn't that kind of the human condition?"

"Yeah. Often. I guess tonight is a good example of that. Look, Cara, for me… I decided a long time ago that I wasn't going to look at you that way. I wasn't going to let myself think about you that way because I had to protect you. For all the people that were mean to you, from anything that they might say. Because you're right. There was stuff. About your parents. And I didn't want anybody to think that I was using you like that, and say the kinds of things about you that they said about your mom."

"Oh."

"So that's one reason. The other is just that I wanted to take care of you the way that I would've taken care of Sophia. And so I put you hard in that category. Sister. I wanted to treat you like my sister. But you weren't my sister. That's the thing. And it's funny, because I fancy myself a realist. I don't talk to ash bottles on the shelf in the back of a bar. But I sure as hell have spent my life trying to compensate for her not being here like she could see it. Like she can see what I'm doing. Like it might mean something to her. Shit. I never really realized that about myself. It's a hell of a thing. It really is. I like to tell myself that I'm too… Logical. Realistic. But I'm just living as a tribute for a ghost I claim I don't even believe in. So, what am I supposed to do with that?"

"But not tonight," she said softly, looking down at her hands.

"No. Not tonight. That was about you and me."

And yet again, that feeling rose up inside of his chest. That booming need to do something.

He'd been telling himself that he didn't know what he wanted for the last couple of months, and yet at the end of the day, he was pretty sure he knew what he had to do.

"Will you come back to bed?"

"Yeah," he said. "Just a minute."

"Will you brush your teeth first?"

"Only because you asked nicely," he said.

She stood up, and walked back toward the house and turned and looked at him just one last time before she slipped into the glass door.

And he sat out there for just a few moments longer, until everything inside of him went still. Until all his certainty crystallized.

Then he stood up and went back toward her bedroom. But not before he stopped and brushed his teeth.

He had kissed her goodbye this morning around five o'clock, and she had a feeling that had been on purpose, because they hadn't had a chance to talk.

The kiss hadn't been on her mouth. It had just been on her cheek.

They hadn't had sex again. He pulled her up against him and said something about her being sore, and told her to go to sleep. She didn't know how he got home—if he called one of his brothers or if he'd taken a cab...

She felt a little bit melancholy, and she carried that all through her day. Her offer was accepted on the hotel, and she made an appointment to go and sign papers. It also happened to work out that the contractor she wanted to use was free to meet with her at the property that afternoon. And all of that should've been great and exciting and more than enough of a distraction to stop thinking about Jace.

It was perfectly normal for them to not have communicated on a random Thursday.

It was just that they had never not communicated on a random Thursday the night after they'd had sex.

They'd had sex.

She wasn't a virgin anymore.

Sex sounded so clinical, even in her head.

She would call it making love, but it hadn't been especially sweet either. It had been… Wrenching. A rending.

It had been something else entirely.

And now so was she. And maybe so were they.

She couldn't shake that image of him, sitting with his elbows on his knees in that chair on her back patio, the cigarette between his fingers. His cowboy hat on like he was fixing to leave in the middle of the night.

She had to say something to him. Because he was her friend.

Because she didn't want him to go.

She sighed and pulled her truck up to the front of the hotel. It was almost hers. Just a few signature pages away.

The contractor was already there, his big white truck parked out front. She got out and tried to smile. She'd been trying to smile all day.

"Hey," she said. "Glad you could make it by today."

"Good to see you, Cara."

Mike Colton was a regular at the bar, and they had a pretty good rapport. He was never flirtatious and didn't flirt with any other women in the bar, which was good, considering he was married. So she had a pretty high opinion of him right off the bat. Plus, she knew he did good work.

"Let's take a walk through the place."

She heard the sound of an engine, and turned around. Just as Jace pulled right into the driveway.

"Oh," she said.

Her mind went blank. Jace put the truck in Park and got out, and her tongue was suddenly as dry as a patch of scrub brush. "I didn't… I didn't realize that you were coming," she said.

"Of course. I just figured… You know, it's my investment. I thought I'd come by and look."

Except he hadn't known that she was meeting with the contractor today, because they hadn't talked. So she wondered what had really compelled him to come by here.

Yeah. She really did.

"Good to have you," said Mike. Who, to his credit, did not immediately start deferring to Jace, which made her feel even better about choosing him to be the contractor.

Except suddenly she was resentful. Resentful that she was in the middle of the contractor meeting. Because she wondered why Jace had come to find her. She wondered why he was really here. And she wondered what he was thinking.

She went around to the back, where the lockbox was, and popped it open, taking the key out from the inside. "Here," she said. "I'll show you the inside."

They walked in, and Mike started explaining about the good bones and all kinds of other things that construction types said.

"It's nice," she said. "It just needs some updating."

"Yeah. If you don't mind, I'll take a walk through, and I'll let you know what I think."

"Yeah. Just, you let me know what you think homeowners are always asking you for. I need to make sure that I have all the amenities that I could possibly want for guests."

"I'm betting it's going to focus a lot on the bathrooms," he said. "That can get expensive. But believe me, it's always worth the investment."

"She can afford it," said Jace.

Mike smiled, then started to walk through the room, clipboard in hand, making notes.

She turned to face Jace, the minute they were alone. "How did you know that I would be here?"

"I didn't. I happened to be driving to the bar. I saw your truck parked out front."

"Oh."

"I was looking for you."

"You were?"

"Yeah. I wanted to talk to you. Because…" He stopped talking. He wrapped his arm around her waist and pulled her up against his body, full-length, and then he kissed her. Kissed her the way she wished he would've done this morning. Kissed her the way she wanted so desperately to be kissed.

"Oh," she breathed.

"Cara…"

"Sorry," said Mike, clearing his throat. "I just wanted to show you something concerning."

"It's already concerning," said Jace.

"Is it a hole where raccoons could get in?" Cara asked.

Mike frowned. "No. Am I looking for one of those?"

"Yes," said Jace and Cara at the same time.

Mike's eyebrows shot up. "Look, as long as you're realistic about the place."

"I think we're pretty realistic," she said.

Mike led them back to the pantry area where there was some rotted wood in the back. "I'm just worried I'm going to find more things like this," said Mike.

"Like I said," Jace said. "We really do have the budget. We don't want to cut any corners. This needs to be a luxury escape. Affordable, but the kind of people that want to travel here and stay in a historic place, want it to be charming without being uncomfortable. We don't want them thinking it just feels old and outdated. We definitely don't need soft floorboards."

"Of course not," she said.

Mike looked between the two of them, and she knew that they were now in an uphill battle with gossip. Because he had definitely seen them kiss.

"I'll keep looking around," said Mike.

"Well," she said, when they were alone in the pantry. "He saw that."

"Fine with me," said Jace.

"I mean, the argument could definitely be made that most people will think that we were already sleeping together, but…"

"I wanted to talk to you about that. I'm staying here. I'm not going back to the rodeo. I'm investing in the hotel. It isn't that I don't know what I want, it's that I was resisting what I want. You know I don't like dreams. And you know I like everything locked in place. I like it sure, I like it certain. The hotel's a little bit of a gamble, but I don't mind gambling with money. As for the rest… Nothing in my life is mine. And that's by design. Whatever I don't have, I don't have because I didn't want it. I love my family, but I recognized pretty early that loving people is painful. I've been riding the rodeo because it was there. Because it was something to do. But that's not enough for me anymore. I need something that's mine. I'm going to stay in Lone Rock—that's what I'm trying to tell you."

Her heart started to throb. "And?"

"And I want you. I want you, Cara."

"You… You want me?"

It wasn't really a declaration of love… Did she even want a declaration of love? The very idea was sort of terrifying. She hadn't fully let herself process her feelings for him. And he was… Well, he wasn't a romantic. That much was sure and certain.

"Yes. I want…"

They heard footsteps again. "Hold that thought."

Mike returned. "Sorry," he said. "Just wanted you to look at some things in the bathroom."

"Rain check," he said.

Her heart was thundering so hard, she didn't think she could take a rain check. But they did decide that they would just go ahead and follow Mike while he looked around. "I'll write up a bid," he said an hour later. "One that's based primarily around modernizing the bathrooms, making sure you have new plumbing, good hot water heaters and modern fixtures in the kitchen, which I know won't really have anything to do with the guests, but if you're going to hire anybody to do some cooking… It'll make things easier."

She really didn't care about cooking. Or plumbing. Or anything but what Jace had been about to tell her, but she knew she couldn't completely abandon the point of all of this, not right now. Not when the point of this was business, and not for her to kiss Jace. But she really wanted to kiss Jace.

And find out exactly what he had been about to tell her.

"It all sounds great," she said. "Thanks, Mike."

And she smiled, hoping that he would get the idea that her smile was the period at the end of this sentence. And he did, giving them a half wave and heading out the door.

She looked up at Jace. "I would really like to hear what you were going to tell me."

"Well. You're my best friend. And I want to be part of this venture with you… And you know, I just don't like halfway shit. I think we should get married."

Chapter 10

He'd thought about it. He was confident in it. And he knew that there were a whole lot of people who wouldn't understand how he had gone from friends, to sex once, to wanting to get married, but he wasn't a man who operated in halfway zones. He was a man of absolutes. He hadn't committed to anything, not for all of his life. And if he was going to commit to any one thing, then it was going to be Cara. There was no way he was going to have sex with her, then pretend that it hadn't happened. There was no way that he was going to…

No. There was no way on earth that he was going to be cool with her moving on and being with other people. And that meant that there was only one option available to him. Locking that shit down.

That was it.

He was in on the hotel. He was in on everything. Whatever she wanted, whatever she needed. He wanted to buy land. And he wanted to build a house on it. And he was going to… He was going to do what he had always promised that he would do. He was going to take care of this woman.

That feels perilously close to a dream.

It wasn't a dream. It was action. It was a plan. It was what needed to happen.

"I… I don't understand."

"The way I see it, it's about the only option we have. Do you want me to sleep with someone else?"

"Hell no," she said.

"I don't want you to sleep with anyone else. Do you want to sleep together a couple more times and see where it goes, take the chance that it might burn out?"

"I…"

"No. Because do you think we can possibly go back? Do you think that we can pretend that never happened?"

"No. And it's why it never did before. And it's why it was… Well, I guess it was a bad idea."

"But it wasn't an idea, was it? It was a thing, and it happened. And I think it was undeniable. Neither of us decided to do it. We didn't just think… Well let's see what happens. We didn't think at all. And listen, when it comes to life, one thing I know is that I'm committed to you. I'm committed to you in a way that I never have been to anyone I'm not related to. So one thing I know for sure is that I've always wanted you to be in my life for all my life. I was never planning on having it be any different. So if I'm going to put down roots, those roots are going to tangle up with yours, Cara. That's just a fact."

"I don't know what to say, Jace. I… I really didn't expect for you to be proposing after one time of being together."

"Think about it. How would it have ever ended in another way?"

It couldn't. That was the thing. And yes, they were different. She was sparkly and fantastical, and he was him. But there had never been another person that he had ever known needed to be by his side for the rest of forever.

"The thing is," said Cara. "You usually travel for half the year. And… You're one of my favorite people on earth. Hell, I think you might be my favorite person on earth, but living together and… And we had sex once."

"What do you want from your life? I mean, do you want to work at the bar every night until two thirty in the morning?"

"No. It's why I'm expanding. It's why I'm buying the hotel."

"Did you want to get married? Start a family?"

"Do you?"

It was a good question, because he'd never given much thought to it. It was part and parcel of the whole not thinking ahead thing. "If you want kids, then yeah."

He would give her whatever she wanted. He realized that. Whatever was in his power to give, he was going to. Because she was Cara, and she had been essential to him from the time they were kids. And he never dreamed of a wife and a family, but… He'd have kids. For her.

"But you don't want them."

"No. I think you're misunderstanding. It doesn't matter what I want. Or maybe better put, what I want is tangled up with what you want. With what makes you happy." What he knew, the conclusion he'd come to, after he'd gotten up at the butt crack of dawn and gone out to work himself to death, because it was the only way to get any kind of mental clarity was that he couldn't imagine letting another man take that position in her life. It wouldn't do. There would be no burning out his attraction for her. There would be no forgetting that those things had passed between them.

And that meant making it permanent. Whatever that looked like for her.

He had done his level best to be whatever she needed over all these years, and he would keep on doing it.

"Can I… Take a rain check on that question?"

"You're the one who asked it."

"Yeah. Kind of. I asked what you wanted, and… Never mind." He could see that something was bothering her.

"I want this," he said, something intense tugging at his chest. Undeniable. "Because there's no other way that I can imagine us getting all the things that we want. You and me. Together. And together like we were last night."

"I… You know, half of what bothers me about this is everybody's just going to think they were right all along."

He couldn't help it. He laughed. Because of course of all the things that would bother Cara, what other people thought—not in terms of appearances, but just in terms of her being proved wrong in any kind of way—was high on her list.

"Yeah. We are going to get mercilessly harassed by my brothers."

"I'm not sure anything is worth it," said Cara.

"You know it is," he said. "Come on. Remember last night?"

And she turned pink. From the roots of her blond hair, all the way down to her breasts. At least, the part that he could see.

"Cara. Don't you want that?"

"Yes," she whispered. "I do. But marriage is a big step and I just don't…"

"Remember what I said, about the ride. About the certainty. I don't do halfway. I don't and I won't. The only reason that I felt uncertain these last few months is because I knew I needed to make a decision. It was either go back all the way, or be here all the way. I felt all this time like I didn't have anything that was mine. Like I didn't have anything to claim. While I do now."

"Are you... Claiming me?"

"Yes. I sure as hell am claiming you. As mine. My best friend. My lover. I hope my wife."

"It's just... It's a lot. And it's like a complete one-eighty from where we were just a couple of days ago? I don't..."

"It's not a one-eighty. It was just a step closer to each other. There's not another person that I can think about living in a house with. Building a life with. You know, it really pains me to say that Boone was right. We're in each other's lives, and now we're in business together. We are enmeshed in each other's lives in every single way. It feels right. It feels like time."

And he had never meant anything half so much as he meant this.

"You're really not going to let me even think about this?"

"Do you need to?"

Her eyebrows shot up. "You really are kind of an arrogant son of a bitch."

"Yeah, but you knew that about me. You knew that the whole time."

"I did, but I guess I've never been in a position where it was directed at me."

"Oh it has. It's just that I dial it up in increments, and eventually, you get kind of dead to it."

She laughed. "Apparently not."

He leaned in, and right then, he couldn't take it any-

more. He wanted her. He needed her. He hadn't realized how much until he had showed up at the house and
seen her.

That was the thing—this wasn't going away. And he
was a man who made decisions. A man who went with
the moment.

And the moment had dictated that they kiss. It had
demanded that they go to bed together. And that turn of
events demanded this. And nothing less.

That was the simple truth of it all. And so he kissed
her. On an indrawn breath. Captured it with his lips and
turned it into a sigh of desire.

"Please," he said.

"Oh shit. Now you even said please? That really is a
miracle."

He smiled against her mouth, and he felt her smile
back.

He kissed her, and he was overwhelmed by the reality of it all. That it was her.

And the rightness of it too. Now that he'd made the
decision… It was right. It was just right.

The decisiveness roared through him. And suddenly,
it was like every piece of his life was locked into place,
in perfect alignment. For the first time in maybe ever.

This was right. This was what he was supposed to
be, where he was supposed to be, with who he was supposed to be with.

So he kissed her. Right there in the ghost hotel, right
there, where all this had started. Or maybe it had started
long before. Before she had ever looked up at him with
those starry green eyes and told him that she was still
a virgin.

She wasn't anymore. He'd seen to that. Now she was his.

He picked her up, because he liked to do that, and carried her toward the stairs. She wrapped her arms around his neck and kept on kissing him, and they went down the hall, to that room, where they had shared a bed, because this time, he aimed to share it with her properly.

The curtains were still drawn around it, and he pushed them aside and set her down on the blankets.

"You know," she said. "None of it's actually dusty."

"You know, I wouldn't have cared if it was. Because all I can think about is being inside of you again."

"I might've thought about the dust. But I appreciate that as a ringing endorsement of my sexual prowess."

"You wouldn't have been thinking about dust." He kissed her lips, her cheek, her neck. "I would've made sure of that."

He laid her back on the bed and let the curtain swing shut. It was dim behind the curtains, but he liked the intimacy that it gave. He stripped her shirt slowly from her body, and even in the dim light, he could see her shape just fine.

He unhooked her bra and threw it to the side. And he was in awe. Of the fact that he could do this with her now. That she was his, and he could just look his fill when he wanted to. No more restraint. No more pretending she wasn't the most beautiful woman he'd ever seen.

He moved to her jeans next, stripped her completely of her clothes and admired all of her. Her stomach, the curves, the dips, her belly button. That downy patch of pale curls at the apex of her thighs. Her legs.

All of her.

She had always been the strongest, funniest woman he'd ever known, and on some level, he'd known she was the sexiest, but he'd tried to keep himself from living in that space. And now he'd moved in permanently.

She was everything.

Absolutely everything.

He kissed her neck, her breasts. Kissed her until she was shivering. Teased them both.

And then suddenly, he felt her hand pressed against the center of his chest, pushing him away. She sat up, grabbing hold of the hem of his shirt and pulling it up over his head. It was like she had come alive with need. She explored his body, kissed his chest, went down his abs and started to undo his belt. And he knew where this was going next, and he did not have the fortitude to stop it. She unzipped his jeans and wrapped her hand around his arousal, exposing him. She pushed his pants and underwear down, and with her hand wrapped firmly around the base of him, leaned in and took him into her mouth.

"Shit," he said, grabbing hold of her ponytail and holding tight.

"I've never done this before," she said.

And hell. That just about took him out. Then and there. It was nearly over before it started.

"Damn, woman. You can't just say things like that."

"But I want you. I want this. I want you to know that you're the only one. I want you, with all your marriage proposal, and your certainty to know, that you're the man I fantasized about. You're the man that I wanted. You're the only man I wanted to lick like this." And she made direct eye contact with him while she slid her tongue from the base of his shaft all the way to the tip. "You're the only one I ever wanted to take in deep."

And that was exactly what she did next. And all he could do was hang on. Let her pleasure him. Let her make him his. He wanted her. He wanted this. This was her staking her claim. His had been a marriage proposal, while she was branding him with his own desire. Letting him know that he would never, ever own his own need again. Because it would always be in the palms of Cara Summers's hands.

He let her pleasure him like that until it became too much. Until he got too close to the edge.

"Come on," he said, his voice rough. "I want to be inside you."

"You were inside me," she said, a little grin tugging at the corners of her mouth.

"You know what I mean."

"No, I don't. You're gonna have to tell me."

"I want inside where you're all wet for me. Just for me. You saved that for me too, didn't you?"

And he would never see anything half so beautiful as his best friend blushing over his dirty talk for her.

And if that was his future, and if that was marriage, it made him want to look forward to it just a little bit.

But there was no need to look forward. Because they could just exist in these moments. Every day until the wedding. Because she would say yes. Of course she would. Because how could they ever go back. Which meant it had to be always. They couldn't take a chance on anything else.

He took his wallet out of his back pocket and took a new condom out of there, then kicked his jeans and shoes off the rest of the way, before rolling the protection on quickly. Then he rolled over onto his back, gripped her hips and brought her down over him. "Next lesson. I want you to ride me. So that I can watch you. Give me a show."

He brought her down slowly, positioning her on his aching length. She moaned, grabbing hold of his shoulders as she flexed her hips, taking him in deep. She began to move her hips, gracefully, elegantly. Like dirty poetry. And he had always imagined that his own brand of hedonism and Cara's divinity could never mix, but he was being proven wrong here and now. Because something he would've said was profane, was very definitely not, not here and now. It felt sanctified somehow, and he would never be able to explain that.

And when she reached up and cupped her own breast, squeezed herself, then her nipple, as she continued to flex her hips over him, he just about died, and he'd be hard-pressed to deny the fact that he saw God in that moment.

Her golden hair was wild, and her lips were parted, her eyes closed. As she moved over him, riding them both into a frenzy.

And finally, he lost his patience. He turned her over onto her back, pinning her to the mattress, his thrusts hard and deep. She moaned, arching up against him off the mattress, and her orgasm broke over her, squeezing him tight. "Jace," she said. And when she said his name it was music. When she said his name, it was fuel to the fire.

When she said his name, it was everything.

But it was when she bit her lip and looked up at him, those green eyes staring straight into him, as if she could see all the way down into what he was, that was when he lost it. It was when he looked full in the face of his best friend in all the world, while the wet clasp of her body was tight around his arousal, while her breasts were pressed up against his chest—that was when he lost it.

His orgasm was merciless, grabbing him by the throat and all but tearing it out, the growl that rose up from inside of him a prayer and a curse all in one.

And this seemed right. Sealing their new life together in this place. This place that had triggered it. This place that had been the first step.

He held her close on the bed for a long moment, until their heartbeats calmed down.

"Yes," she said softly. "Yes, Jace, I'll marry you."

"Good," he said, dropping a kiss on the top of her head. Because he could do that now. Because he could kiss her and touch her, and she could do the same to him, because they had erased those barriers between them. And he meant it, that it was good, but he couldn't help but wonder if he'd said the wrong thing, because she didn't look joyously happy, but she buried her face against his shoulder and fell asleep, so he figured it wasn't all bad either.

How could it be?

They were best friends.

Chapter 11

She really wished that she had a different friend, other than Jace. And she had never really wished that before. She was perfectly fine having all of her friendship eggs in one basket. But the problem was, she had her friendship eggs in his basket, and now her relationship eggs, and she just wished that there was somebody that she could talk to. Somebody that would be able to reassure her that she was making the right choice. It was just that... Jace hadn't said anything about being in love with her. And it was because she knew he wasn't.

The thing with Jace was he was hardheaded, and he was stubborn. And he damn sure thought that his way was the best way. But what she couldn't figure out was exactly why he had decided that he wanted this. She could circle around it. But she didn't think she was quite hitting his motivation on the head, and that worried her a little bit. That she couldn't quite parse it. Yes, she understood that he wanted to put down roots.

Yes, she understood that he could only see this going one of two ways.

That they would eventually take other lovers, or they had to commit to each other. And since Jace was kind of a paperwork, lock, stock, and barrel kind of guy, for him, the answer would be marriage, and not just moving in together. She knew him well enough to understand all of that. But she felt like there was something deeper. And the problem with Jace was he would never admit to that. He would never admit to the deeper. He would never even say it to himself. He was the man who swore up and down there was nothing after this life and he was totally fine with it. He was the man who didn't believe in manifesting your dreams or any of that.

And she was the one who still talked to her grandpa like he was right there with her.

A slight smile lifted the corner of her mouth, and she turned and looked up at the Jack Daniel's bottle. "Well. Jace wants me to marry him. I don't know if you already know that. I kind of hope that you haven't been spying on us. All things considered. But I told him yes and I'm worried. I'm kind of in love with him. Or I'm really in love with him. And I don't think that that's part of this for him. And that scares me."

She waited. For something. For a rush of wisdom.

A glowing butterfly.

She didn't get any of it.

"I think that if I told Jace I loved him he would run away. Because it's like… He wants to do all these external things to take control, but it's the stuff that he can't control that he can't deal with. And I get it. It's because of Sophia."

She took a deep breath. She wasn't getting any answers. Not out of the silent whiskey bottle.

There was a knock at the back door of the bar, and she figured it was probably her delivery from the food services company. She went back into the kitchen, and opened the door. There was a stack of crates filled with various things. Frozen beef patties and other assorted things they needed for the kitchen. And then she heard a sound. A hawk. And she looked up, and saw a bird circling. And it filled her with a strange sort of hope. Sort of resolve.

"Is that you, Grandpa?"

And then it was like she could see his face.

I'm dead. I got better things to do than hang around here.

That's what he would say. And it made her laugh.

Well, maybe that was her answer. Her grandpa had better things to do than hang around here, so maybe she needed to get her life in order. Buy the hotel. Marry Jace. She didn't want anything else. She didn't want anyone else. She wasn't losing anything by marrying him. Yes, the emotions would always be tricky with him. But he cared about her. And it wasn't like she had another man who was desperately in love with her waiting in the wings. It was just... It was just knowing that she maybe cared a little bit more than he did. That was the tough thing. But it would be worth it. It would be worth it to be with him.

Her phone buzzed.

She looked down at the text that she had just gotten.

Dinner with my family tonight?

And she knew that her answer would cement this forever.

Yes.

Yes. She was going to marry Jace. And his family was going to say I told you so, and it would be totally worth it.

Chapter 12

It was handy that his sister Callie and her husband, Jake, had been planning on coming to spend a few days anyway. They would be here for the announcement, and that meant that he only had to tell everyone in his family one time what he was going to do. That he was leaving the rodeo, that he was getting married. All of that suited him. It suited him right down to the very ground his boots were standing on.

He had it all mapped out in his mind. Yeah, there might've been some merit to giving his mother at least a warning prior to making the announcement, but he just didn't want to get into it. He only wanted to do it once, and he wanted Cara to be there when he did. Because it would make them behave. Maybe.

He had also spent part of the day looking at land.

He wanted something that was near enough to town that it would be easy for Cara to manage her interests right there on Main Street, but far enough out that they had a good-size plot of land, and opportunity to make it functional.

He was still deciding what exactly he wanted to ranch. Bison, beef or horses. All completely different endeavors.

Roots.

That's what he was doing now. It was the thing he was doing.

What he didn't anticipate, was how Cara would look when she showed up.

He was in his truck, out in front of his parents' palatial country home, all square lines and lots of glass, when Cara rolled up.

He had seen her in a lot of different things. She typically wore blue jeans. She liked her rhinestones, did his girl, and on the evenings that she worked at the bar, she favored a scoop neck, tight tank top all the better to show off her figure. He was used to her in all these things. The casual T-shirt Cara, and sexy nighttime Cara.

But when she got out of the truck and revealed that she was in a soft, floaty sundress, it just about did him in. It had little short sleeves and a rounded neck with a little bow right at the center of her breasts that he desperately wanted to undo immediately. It was short, coming inches above her knees, swinging when she walked. Her blond hair was loose, curling at the ends and blowing in the breeze, and he was suddenly desperate to touch it.

What was this? This shift.

Because somehow, in that moment, it wasn't about being attracted to his friend. It felt bigger somehow. It wasn't just about having permission to find her beautiful—it was about this woman, this relationship, and something deepening.

He had thought of it as adding something on. But

now it seemed like it was just all that they had been, but deeper.

"Look at you," he said.

As he got closer, he could see that she had painted her lips with something glossy and nice, that she had just a little bit of mascara and some gold and green eye shadow that highlighted her eyes.

She was sexy and sweet, exactly how you would want a woman to look that you were bringing home to meet your parents and tell them you were going to marry her.

Of course, she had met his parents before.

So it was more about presenting her as his future wife, rather than his friend.

Except when he reached out and took her hand in his, she was still his friend. And when he leaned in and kissed her lips, she was still his friend. And something expanded in his chest all the same.

They walked up the steps together, hand in hand.

"If we walk in like this they're going to know."

"Yeah. I'm committed to presenting this as if it's a thing they should all be aware of."

She laughed. "Okay. I'm sure Flint and Boone won't give you a hard time in that case."

"As long as you stop flirting with them."

"Probably I won't," she said. "Because it bugs you."

And it was his turn to laugh, because she was so committed to being her, and it was one of the things he liked the very most about her.

That she was cantankerous and stubborn and every inch herself. That she wasn't going to change or become softer or bend just because they were sleeping together. Just because she'd agreed to marry him.

"Yeah, well. I might put my foot down about the men

at the bar," he said. Because he was testing her. Because he couldn't help himself.

"You're going to put your foot down?"

"I said what I said."

A little smile tugged at the corner of her mouth. "Jace Carson, have we met?"

"Yes we have. Intimately. Naked."

She shoved him against his shoulder. "Sometimes I think you're still the same boy from when we were twelve."

"Close enough."

Except he didn't feel like that boy. He wasn't sure what he felt like. Resolved, so there was that.

He opened up the front door into the house so that she didn't knock—and they walked inside. His whole family was sitting in the broad, expansive living room, on the different couches and chairs in front of the floor to ceiling windows that overlooked the brilliant view. They were missing Buck, who could come back but wouldn't. And Sophia, who was simply gone. And it pained him that those were the first things he thought of, seeing them all together. Just that they weren't all together. And probably never would be.

"Hey," he said. He grabbed hold of Cara's hand and led her into the room. He figured this was as good a time as any. "I'm glad everybody's here tonight."

"It's good to see you," said his sister Callie, popping up from her chair and reaching out to pull him into a hug. She was just a little bit pregnant, her belly starting to round out. He wondered if Sophia would've had kids by now, had she lived.

He wondered if he would have.

If his life would've been different.

If he could've believed in miracles of hope and love for longer.

But Cara felt like an anchor behind him, and he would take that instead.

"It's good to see everyone, but there's something that Cara and I want to tell you."

He looked over at his mother, who was looking at him with an expectation and joy he wondered how she still felt. His mother, who had always been so pretty and perfect. His mother, who had been devastated at Sophia's loss, but seemed to figure out how to keep on going once she had Callie. "We're getting married."

The roar that went through the room was massive.

"Pay up," said Chance.

"Fuck you," said Boone, reaching into his back pocket and pulling out his wallet.

"What?" he asked.

"We have had a bet going for a long time about whether or not you guys were really a couple," said Chance. "And I win. You owe me so much money. Brother, I know you don't have that kind of cash in your wallet, and you're gonna have to write me a check. But we're going to have to make sure that check is good."

"I have more money than you do," said Boone. "I have more endorsements. Because my face is prettier."

"Well, you owe money to me now."

"Are you kidding me?" he asked.

"Not at all," said Flint, shaking his head. "I didn't go in as hard as Chance did, but Boone owes me money too. But I figure if he wants to work it off…"

"I'm not doing your chores for you," said Boone angrily. He looked over at Jace. "You know, this should confirm that I'm your favorite brother," said Boone. "Because I believed you. You're a liar."

"What are the particulars of the bet?" Cara asked. She went and sat down on the chair facing his family. He supposed this was the very great perk of Cara knowing his family like she did. "Because, depending on if time lines and the like are part of the bet, you might actually not have won any money from Boone."

"Why?" asked Chance.

"Well, tell me the bet."

"That you been secretly sleeping together the whole time."

"Nope. You lose."

"Shit. Really?"

"Really."

"Well, I collect on the part where I said you would end up together."

"Yep," Cara said. "That you can have."

"When did you start sleeping together?" Chance asked. "Because that is probably something I can work out in terms of how much money I'm owed."

"Chance," said their mother, scolding. "Honestly."

"That's very crass," said Boone. "Why don't you just accept that you lost?"

"I didn't, though," said Chance. "Because they're getting married."

"Congratulations," said Kit. "Really."

"Yes," said his mother, standing up and coming over to them. She went to Cara first and took her hand. Cara stood, and something shifted inside of him as he watched his mother embrace Cara. "You're just perfect for him," she whispered. "Exactly what he needs."

That made something strange reverberate inside of his chest.

"Happy for you," his dad said, getting up from his chair and coming over to clap him on the back. "Damn thrilling to have four of you married. Growing the family like this. It's more than we could've ever hoped for."

"Dinner is ready," said his mother. As if she had cooked it. But then, what his mother was great at was catering. And he appreciated that. "Shall we go into the dining room?"

He walked over to where Cara was and took her hand, lingering in the living room for a moment as the rest of the family filtered in.

"You good?"

She looked up at him and she smiled, and that smile just about broke his heart. "Yes. I love your family. And the idea of actually being part of it is… It's amazing."

I love your family.

That did something to him. Echoed through his soul.

Dinner was a pretty damned beautiful roast duck and sides, and there was something about it that pulled him back to happier times with his family. It wasn't that they hadn't had happier times in the last few years—they had. But there was something that just felt bigger and more right. His sister being here with her husband. His brothers and their wives. Him and Cara. "I'm investing in the hotel. Cara just bought it," he said. "She's going to open it up and revamp it and bring more tourism into town."

"That's fantastic," said his sister-in-law Shelby.

"It'd be nice to get some of your beadwork to sell," said Cara. "And some art, maybe. I think it would be amazing to have work by indigenous artisans, so that people can get an idea of the real Lone Rock."

"Happy to oblige," said Shelby. "I love the idea of local art being featured."

"You can recommend anybody whose work you love locally."

"Now I'm drunk with power."

"Investing in business," said his dad. "That's unlike you."

"Well. I'm changing some things. I'm done with the rodeo."

His dad nodded slowly. "I thought you might be."

"Done with the rodeo and looking to buy land around here. So that Cara and I can build a house and start a family."

"I'm so happy for you," said Callie, beaming. "This is just great."

But for some reason, his family's joy wasn't quite touching him all the way down, and he couldn't for the life of him figure out why. Cara seemed happy, and he wanted more than anything for her to be happy. No question about that. None at all. He was doing all of the things that he had decided to, and he had announced it, he was certain.

He didn't know why uncertainty was following him. Because there really wasn't any reason for uncertainty. They finished up dinner, and Shelby and Cara had gotten involved in discussing logistics for selling art and featuring art throughout the hotel for sale, and he and his brothers took the opportunity to go into his parents' game room and throw some darts.

Usually, Callie would've joined the boys. But not today. Chance threw the first dart and hit the bull's-eye. The problem with this was they were all too good.

"Seriously, though," said Chance, when Kit's dart came from behind and hit his, knocking it out of position. "Congratulations. I'm glad that you finally opened your eyes to what you guys had this whole time."

"Same," said Kit.

Flint and Boone exchanged looks with each other. His

brother-in-law, Jake, raised his glass of whiskey. "Absolutely. Marriage is the best damn thing."

"It is," Chance agreed.

"Spoken like a man who keeps his balls in his wife's purse," said Flint.

"Spoken like a man who has a diss track about him that's currently number one on the country airwaves," Chance shot back.

"It is not a diss track. And it isn't about me."

"It's about you," said Boone.

"You're a turncoat," said Flint.

"The thing is," said Chance, "I think opening yourself up to all this… It's tough. It's tough to let go of all the shit that you've been through and decide that you want to… Hope."

"Don't go too far," said Jace, picking up a dart and flinging it at the dartboard. He missed the bull's-eye. What the hell was that about?

"It's not about hope or anything like that. It's just… It makes sense. I'm not gonna be in the rodeo forever. Not by a long shot. And I needed to decide what to do. I felt uncertain, but it was only because I was avoiding the most obvious thing. Clearly, going all in on being here is the answer. And then… Cara and I… You know, something happened."

"When exactly?" Chance asked.

"Not your business. But a couple of days ago."

"A couple of days ago?" Three of his brothers asked that at once.

"Yes," he said.

"And you just… Decided to marry her when the first time you've actually ever been with her was a couple of days ago?" Kit asked.

"Are you suggesting that I should be uncertain about what I want from her?"

"Not at all," said Kit. "I just thought maybe you guys were engaged in some kind of serious slow burn and you were just now ready to tell us all. I didn't know that it was like best friends, then you finally hooked up, and you're getting married right away. You didn't even have a chance to find out she's pregnant."

"We don't all have unprotected sex, Kit," said Jace. "You got your wife pregnant the first time you hooked up, but I don't think I got Cara pregnant."

"Whatever. It's how I snared Shelby, so I'm not sorry about it. There was no way she was looking for a relationship after losing her husband. The baby is what clarified some things."

"Again. Good for you. But the way I see it, it just kinda clicked into place, and I'm not a guy that does uncertainty. I care about her. So she needs to be in my life. Forever. Also, I can't have her hooking up with anybody else. Not gonna work. Not after that."

"Are you in love with her?" Chance asked.

The word scraped raw up against the inside of him.

"My feelings for her are stronger than my feelings for anyone else."

"No. That doesn't cut it. Are you in love with her? Are you giving her everything?"

"Everything I had to give," he said. "Look. I'm just not… I'm not into that. I'm not into this kind of impossible to define fantasy shit. I like what's tangible. That's why marriage is so fast. I don't just want to see where things go. I know I want her in my life forever. What more do I need to know?"

"I feel pretty damn strongly," said Chance, "that marriage is a lot about hope. And a whole lot about magic that you can't quite see or touch. Hell. Remember, I had to get amnesia to end up with my wife. Don't tell me there wasn't some kind of… Mystical intervention that happened there. It's not about just being practical. It's not about everything that you can see and touch. It's about something more than that."

He rebelled against that. "Not for me. I don't believe in that kind of thing."

"You better start. Otherwise… I think it's going to be tough for you."

"I've made the decision that I'm gonna make, and I've got everything that I want."

"Right now. But what can happen when she wants more from you."

"I don't know what more there could be. She's important to me. Essential enough that I'm willing to tie myself to her forever. I don't want to be with another woman. That became clear the minute that I touched her. I…"

"Why do you think this isn't love?" Kit asked.

"I don't know," he said. "Who cares what you call it. Maybe it is."

But something in him pushed back at that, and hard.

Like walls he had built around his soul were reinforcing themselves. Reminding him why they were there.

"I'm marrying her," he said. "What difference does it make what we call it?"

"I guess no difference,"

"There you go. Just say congratulations and that you're happy for me."

"I am," said Chance. "But the thing is, being with Juniper healed something inside of me. But you can't go into marriage the same and expect for it to work. Expect for it to heal you."

"I'm not looking to be healed," he said.

"Why not?" Kid asked.

"Because," he said. "Sophia is dead, and there's nothing anyone can do about it. She's gone. She'll always be gone. So the wound should never go away."

He looked down at the whiskey glass he was holding and frowned. It had a butterfly painted on the side.

He looked at the other glasses on the table in the room. Each had something different. It wasn't significant.

They didn't talk about him anymore after that. They just finished playing darts.

Chapter 13

Cara felt so surrounded by love and warmth. Her future sisters-in-law fussed over her, and Jace's mother seemed to be just so happy.

And she felt partly like a fraud. She didn't know why. She and Jace were really getting married. They weren't making that up. It was just that… He hadn't said anything about being in love with her. And she couldn't figure out if she was being strange. If she was splitting hairs. Because Jace cared about her. She knew that. She would say it was indisputable even that he loved her. But she just had to wonder if his feelings had actually changed, or if they were just sleeping together.

And then she had to ask herself why it mattered. If it even did.

She had him in her life, the most stable relationship, and they were going to make it legal. So what did it matter what they called it.

Because you love him.

But what did that matter? Why would it be different if he said he loved her, or if he was in love?

She shoved all of her reservations to the side. And when Jace came back from playing darts with his brothers, he took her hand. "Want to drive over to my place?"

And she did. She really did. She wanted to spend the night with him. She wanted to solidify this whole thing. That their relationship had changed. And also that they were still them. Both felt so important right now. Both felt like it might be everything.

"You can follow me over."

She drove in her car behind him, down the bumpy dirt road that led away from the main house and toward the house he lived in on the property. She pulled up to his place, just behind him.

She got out and walked right to him. "Jace…"

She had been about to ask him where they might live when they were first married. If they would live here, if they would live at her place. But he wrapped his arm around her waist and pulled her to him. And pressed a kiss to her mouth. Fervent, hard and glorious. And maybe it wasn't the time to talk. Maybe it was okay for them to just feel for a while. Maybe it was just fine for them to retreat to this, because it felt right. Because it felt real. Because of all the crazy and uncertain things, this felt like a little bit of something. A little bit of certain. His kiss undid her.

And she wanted… She wanted to project everything that she felt right into him. Wished that she could be emitted to his chest. Wished that she could make him understand.

She wanted that more than anything. To show him. He had taken care of her for the first time, and the second time, he had given her confidence. The second time,

he let her ride him, and it had been dirty and glorious
and they'd been them. Even as they'd given each other
pleasure.

But she wanted something else. Something more and
deeper.

She wanted him to know. She wanted to show herself.
The difference between love and being in love.

She wanted to see. If she could make it all for herself.
If what she felt would be enough to sustain them. Would
be enough to keep them together. He lifted her up off the
ground, and she wrapped her arms around his neck, and
she poured everything that she felt, everything that they
were, into that kiss. All the relief that she had felt when
he'd first been kind to her down by the creek all those
years ago. The need she felt to fill that hole left behind
by the sister that he loved so much. The years and years
of friendship. Of telling each other things in confidence.
Of being there for each other.

Her heart, her soul. Her gratitude for how he had been
there when her grandfather had died. For the way that he
had effortlessly folded her into his family. And just the
way she loved him. Her everything. Her heart.

She kissed him like she might die if she didn't, because
she wasn't entirely certain that she wouldn't.

He walked them both back up the porch to his house
and through the front door. But they didn't make it down
the hall. They just barely made it to the couch. He laid
her down on the soft surface, tearing at her clothes. They
didn't talk. Didn't joke. Didn't laugh.

It was like a reckoning.

Everything was stripped away but their need. For each
other. For this.

And already, she was so aroused by him. And already,
she felt like she was lost in him. In this.

She clung to his shoulders and then realized she needed to get those clothes off of him. So she went from clinging to tearing, then her hands went to his belt buckle. Pushing the denim away from his body, as he wrenched her panties down her thighs, her sundress already somewhere on the floor.

His mouth was hungry, his hands demanding, and she loved it.

This man, this man who was desperate for her body—he wasn't a stranger anymore. This was part of them. Part of who they were now. And it was all the more powerful for it.

He put his hand between her thighs and teased her, tested her readiness.

"Now," she said, begging.

He settled himself between her legs and thrust home, establishing a wild rhythm that tested and tormented them both.

It was rough and hard, this coupling. And she loved it. She loved him.

She dug her fingers into the flesh of his shoulders, wrapped her legs around his waist. He said her name. Over and over again. Like a prayer or a curse, she didn't know, but she would take it all. Just as she would take all of him. And that was what he gave.

It was like a storm. The heat generated between them so bright and intense she thought she might be dying of it. And yet at the same time, it wasn't enough. She wondered if it would ever be enough.

She could feel him begin to tremble, shake. Could feel the edge of his control beginning to reach its end.

And when he found his release, it was on a growl and a shout, and she followed after him, squeezing him tight as he poured into her.

And then she kissed his mouth, his face. Said his name over and over again, because it was all she could think to say. Because he felt like the only thing. This moment felt like the only thing.

But then right at the same time, she looked to the future. To a bright, golden future shining with light, and butterflies. And she wanted that. Hoped for it. Reached for it.

And she knew—she knew that it was time. She knew that she had to say it.

"I love you, Jace."

He felt like he was dying. Really, like someone had ripped his lungs out. Like something in him had been broken, irrevocably. Irreparably.

I love you.

Of course she did. She was his best friend. He loved her too. It wasn't anything revolutionary. But it felt revolutionary, with him lying on top of her on the couch, still buried inside of her. Breathing hard. His mind flown from what had just passed between them, because it was more than pleasure. It always had been.

It was more than sex or release. More than orgasms.

It was something bigger. It was something that had changed them fundamentally. He had that feeling, when he'd seen her walking toward him tonight in that summer dress that he just stripped right off, he had that feeling.

He had this strange, crushing feeling all through the whole night. And he knew himself well enough to know it was when he wasn't acting with integrity. When he wasn't being honest about the things that were going on inside of himself. When his actions weren't matching up with what he knew to be important.

Yeah. That was when he felt these things. When he'd

been hesitating to make his move in Lone Rock, to make his move with Cara. Not because he didn't know what to do, but because he hadn't wanted to do it.

And this was another reckoning. Like a gong going off inside of him.

And he didn't know why it felt so different. It was just that it did.

"That was amazing," he said.

And he wanted to cut his own tongue out.

"Yeah. But I said that I love you."

"I know," he said.

She drew away from him, but not all the way. She just sort of wiggled and scooted to the side. "Can you tell me about Sophia? A little bit more."

He nodded slowly. And it wasn't a weird change of subject. Not for him. Not for them.

"She loved butterflies," he said. "Everything had butterflies on it. The canopy on her bed, special hospital gown my parents bought her. Everything." He cleared his throat. "When I saw you that time…with your pink binder thing and it had those butterflies, I… It was like you were supposed to be there."

He heard himself. Heard himself saying all this stuff he wasn't supposed to believe. But he could remember that moment. Like he'd felt led to her. To this other girl who had butterflies.

It hurt to talk about it. It hurt to look back, because there was no good way to look forward. And he didn't like it. But the problem with putting down roots was it demanded a certain level of projecting. And maybe that was all part of the problem. Part of the shift. And maybe it was just that creating the heaviness in his chest.

"Little kids aren't supposed to get cancer," he said, his voice rough. "And a little boy isn't supposed to have to watch his sister die. A mother isn't supposed to have to watch her child die. Just not supposed to happen." And he knew there was no point to this. No point to raging against any of it. There never was. And so he never had. He had just turned everything off. Everything.

But now he felt like raging, for some reason. At what? There was nothing there.

But he wanted to do it all the same.

"She was the brightest, prettiest, most... She was just so fun. And being sick made it so she couldn't be fun. So she couldn't have fun. It wasn't fair. It's not fair. She was just a little girl that loved butterflies. How the hell is it right that she's gone?"

"It isn't. It's one of those big unfair things in the world."

"But how do you believe in miracles, in mysteries? How do you dream and hope and all that shit that you do? How do you do it, Cara? Because I don't get it."

"Because I've accepted that there are things that I'll never know or understand. But I also don't believe that what happens to us here is the end. And so it's a deep tragedy within our understanding, but I just don't think that's where it stops. I can't believe that. Because I look around this world and I see miracles. I see miracles and shafts of sunlight and butterflies. There are always so many butterflies. Around you. Around me. I think she might be with you."

"No. I just... I can't..."

"I get it. It hurts to hope."

"Don't say that. Like you're patronizing me. Like I'm the one who's ridiculous. When you... You're the one that believes in all these things that you can't see."

"But there are so many things that we can't see, Jace. So many things. This, this between us. Don't you see the miracle in that? That you found me? But you found the girl with the pink butterfly Trapper Keeper. That you were there for me, like you were compelled to be. Don't you think there's something magic in that. And here we are, and we were each other's best friends all this time, all this time. And we can be more too. And isn't that a miracle. That not only are you my favorite person to talk to, but when we are together like this… It's so bright and hot and wonderful. What isn't miraculous about that?"

"And why couldn't I have the miracle that I wanted," he said, his words coming out hard. And he could see a brief flash of hurt in her eyes before she dismissed it.

"You know I didn't mean that," he said. "You know I didn't mean I didn't want you."

"I do," she said. "Because I know you. I know you don't want to hurt me. But I think I kind of get that you don't want to love me either."

Her words hit him in the center of his chest. They were quiet. And they weren't angry. They weren't accusing him of anything.

But they cut deep.

And they were true.

"What does that even mean? Between the two of us. What difference would it even make?"

She looked up at him, her eyes sad. "I don't know."

"Well until you know, what's the point of making it an issue?"

"That's fair. Let's go to bed."

"You still want to stay the night?"

"I still want to marry you."

And he would take that. Because he wanted to take care of her. He wanted to be with her. Like they had always been, and like this too. So even though he knew he messed up, he was going to go ahead and accept that.

"All right then. Let's go to bed."

"I just wanted to say… Or I need to make it clear." She said nothing for a moment, and then she looked up at him, her green eyes firm and steely. "I don't need you."

She might as well have shot him directly in the chest. "What?"

"I don't need you. Even when I was a sad, flat-chested middle school girl, I didn't need you. I had been kicking along in my life just fine without you. You were great. You are great. But I would have survived if you weren't in my life."

She stood up then, naked and resolved, and he almost felt like he didn't have the right to look directly at her. "I'm tough. My mom is a drug addict who doesn't want me. Thankfully I don't remember very much from that time of my life. Very, very thankfully. Thankfully, mostly what I remember is my grandfather taking good care of me. I remember you being a good friend. And those things… They matter. But I don't need you. I didn't even need you for the hotel. I had it all worked out by myself, and I could've waited. I could've waited to remodel things and patch the raccoon hole. I could have."

"What exactly is your point?" he asked.

"My point is that I don't need you, Jace Carson. I just want you. So all of these things that you're doing, all of this stuff that you think makes you indispensable, that's not what it is. It's watching stupid movies with you. And it's spending the night in a hotel and fighting about ghosts. And about whether or not raccoons are cute or vicious. It's those little things that feel like the biggest things. The way that we talk about everything and talk about nothing. The fact that I did tell you that I hadn't been with anybody, even though I was drunk. And a little bit hitting on you. But no matter how that had worked out, I knew that I could trust you with that information. Because I've always known that. And that isn't about needing you, in the sense that I'm dependent on you. That is about wanting you around because you are the most trustworthy, wonderful, caring friend that anyone could've ever asked for. And that's not… It's not you needing to be my protector or my caregiver. That's you being you."

And he realized something, as those words came out of her mouth. She was right. She didn't need him. She was hands down the strongest, most incredible woman—person—that he knew. She had been through a lot, and she had a sense of humor and a firebrand personality. She was confident and capable. She had planned all her finances out in order to get the loan for the hotel in the first place, had even taken care of arranging all the logistics for the ghost sleepover.

She didn't need him.

He had told himself that she did for all these years.

But the truth of it was, he needed her.

He had told himself he had to protect her.

But it was himself he was protecting. All along.

And that was what every single movement that had happened since he had offered to spend the night with her at the hotel had been about. He had been looking for purchase, looking for roots, and of course, he had chosen to wrap them around her, because he didn't know what his life would look like without her.

She had become the thing that he leaned on.

He had fashioned her into a surrogate for every single thing that he missed. Everything he wanted and didn't have.

And he was… He couldn't give her what she wanted. He just couldn't do it.

Because he tried to think out that far ahead, and everything just went black. Because the idea of wanting anything, the idea of hoping for anything was something he was afraid to grab hold of.

"You should get dressed," he said, his voice scratchy.

"Why?"

"Because you should go home."

"This is going to be my home after we get married."

She was speaking with such a calm, firm voice, and he felt like an absolute dick for what he was about to say. But then, he felt that way about the entire situation. About everything. About the way that he had lied. To her. To himself. Because he had. He had found a way to convince himself that what he was doing was for her while he... Well he found a way to hold her close so that he could use her as a balm for his wound.

And at first it was all about taking care. Of somebody that he felt was vulnerable. Because he hadn't been able to take care of Sophia, had he? Not in a real way. Not in a meaningful way. She had died. So what had anything he'd done mattered? She had died, and that meant that he'd failed. And she just wasn't there. And there was a void where she should be. And he didn't know what he was, if he wasn't her older brother. Her friend.

And so he had become that for Cara, but that had gotten inconvenient when he'd started to become attracted to her, and for a while he'd been able to suppress it, because he was very, very good at suppressing emotion. Very good.

He had made a whole lifestyle out of it.

And that had worked for years, until she had looked him in the eye and told him that she was a virgin. And offered to let him be the one to change that. Yeah. It had all worked until that moment. And then... It had all gone to bright, burning hell. So he'd recast it. Recast her. Changing and shuffling the narrative into something, anything that allowed him to continue to run from the truth.

Because he really needed that. But she was there, calling him out, the way that she did. Because she was Cara Summers, and he was Jace Carson, and they were honest with each other.

To a point.

They had always lied about these things.

She had never told him that she wanted him, and he had never told her that he sometimes thought his life might fall apart if she wasn't in it.

Yeah, he went and traveled on the rodeo. He was away from her for large chunks of time sometimes, but she was always there. Waiting when he came back home. And it meant something. It mattered.

It was the reason he tried to live through those rides. That was just the truth of it. Knowing that she was there.

He had used her to give himself purpose.

He had used her as a conduit for all the spiritual things that he didn't allow himself to feel. Because she hoped enough for the both of them, was faithful enough for the both of them. Believed enough for the both of them. In the brightness and beauty of life, in a concept of miracles that he couldn't figure out how to hold in his hand, that she cradled in her palm effortlessly. The way she acted like her grandfather was simply a thought and a prayer away. The way she saw beauty in an old hotel, and potential in a half-empty Main Street.

What did he give to her, exactly?

And she said she loved him. And… And he was just broken.

But if he was going to do one thing, one good thing, it would be to stop this. To not continue to let his roots wrap around her, because all he would do is drag her down into the dirt, and she was meant for more than that.

She deserved more than that.

She hadn't chosen to be born to a mother that couldn't love her right. She hadn't chosen to have a father who wanted nothing to do with her. She didn't have to have a husband who was broken.

He'd wanted to keep her, because he was possessive. He wanted to keep her with him, to add security to his own life. And if he really wanted to do something for her, he needed to let her go. He needed to let her be free of him.

She only thought she was in love with him because of the sex. Because she had been a virgin. Because they'd been friends for so long.

"You should go home," he said again.

"Jace, you're scaring me."

"We can't get married, Cara. You want other things. Different things. Things I don't know how to give. And you're right. You're right. You don't need me. You stand on your own two feet just fine. I'm the one that's limping. I'm the one who's leaning on you. It's not right. I can't do it anymore, not now that I know."

"Jace, you idiot. Did it ever occur to you that I was fully aware of that?"

"What?"

"I know you. I know that there are things that are just really really tough."

"Why would you let me lean on you, if you don't need me?"

"I wouldn't fall onto the ground without you. How about that? But I have certainly leaned against you at many points over the years. You have been the single most important relationship in my life. Sorry, Grandpa.

But it's been you, Jace. You taught me what I wanted from a friend. And then you taught me what to want from a lover. Those are huge things. But I've never been blind to the fact that you had cracks in your soul, Jace. Not ever. Because you went out of your way to befriend a sad, crying girl behind the middle school? Especially if he's cool and handsome and has all the friends he wants? You befriend the bird with the broken wing, because your wing is broken too. And neither of you can really fly. But together… We come pretty close."

"It's nice as a metaphor. But what it amounts to is me holding you down."

"I love you. What if I chose to be with you? What if I chose to be with you just because I wanted to be?"

"I'm telling you that I'm not going to be part of it. I'm not going to keep taking from you. Not when I can't give back."

"This is bullshit," she said. "You're just scared. You're scared, and you're too scared to admit that you're scared. I love you. I'm the one that admitted it. I'm the one that took the step. And you can't because…" Her eyes filled with tears, and suddenly she sucked in a sharp breath, like she had a realization in the moment between that last sentence and this coming one. "And you just can't hope, can you? You're afraid. You're afraid to hope that this could become the best that it could be, because you think it's easier to just imagine the worst. Or just imagine nothing. Because you hoped that she would get well, and she didn't."

He growled. "Forget it. Leave it alone."

"But that's it, isn't it? There is nothing that scares you more in this world than hope. Because you've hoped before. And it didn't go your way. It didn't go anyone's way. It devastated you. It devastated you, and you don't know what to do. Because you don't trust that it wouldn't just happen again."

"Don't psychoanalyze me. You don't know what it's like to have gone through what I have. You don't have any idea what it's like. And maybe it's not psychosis to refuse to believe in things that you can't see. Maybe I'm not the one that's crazy."

"Well. Even if I'm wrong, at least I can think of reasons to get out of bed in the morning. At night, when I get under the covers, I think ahead. And that's not a bad thing. I hope. Because what is life without hope? It's what you have. You can't reach out and take the love that is being offered to you, because you can't look ahead. Because you're afraid to want something that you can't…" She reached out and grabbed hold of him, placed her hands in his. "You want what you can hold in your hands. You're holding me. You're holding me. Can't you believe in me?"

No. He couldn't. Because he couldn't see the end of this. He couldn't see a way to fix this. Couldn't see a way to fix himself.

And he could not do that to her. He wouldn't.

"Go home."

And he did something he hadn't done in all the years since they'd met. He pulled away from her. He took a step back.

But she stood firm. She didn't get dressed like he'd ordered her to do. She didn't back away. She didn't even flinch. He could see deep anguish in her face, and he hated that he had put it there. But she didn't back down.

"All right. I will. But when you need somebody to talk to in the middle of the night, because everything is terrible, you call me. Because I'm your best friend. And you might be surprised to find out that I've been supporting you all these years, but I'm not."

"This changes things," he said. "I don't think that we can… I don't think that we can do this anymore."

"So wait a minute, you don't want to marry me, and you don't want to be my friend anymore?"

And that was when she faltered. When strong, beautiful Cara Summers looked like she might shatter. And he really stood there and marinated in his own sense of fear and anguish, because it had been a long time since he had felt anything like this. He thought that he was going to break. And he hadn't thought that there was any fragile thing left inside of him.

"I can't be. Because it would just be me hanging on to you when you need to be let go. It would be me keeping you in a place where you hope that something can be different when it can't be. You can't love me. Not anymore."

"You don't get to tell me what to do."

"I'm right. I'm just… I'm right about this, Cara."

"You're leaving me with nothing," she said, her voice frayed, wretched. "You're leaving me with nobody. You have your whole family, and what are you leaving me with?"

"Cara…"

"No. No. You don't get to do this. You don't get to try to make me feel bad for you. Or make me think that you're doing the right thing, that you're being all brave and self-sacrificing by doing this. You're just being a coward. You're ruining us. You are ruining the life that we could have. Because you're scared. And I will not let you turn it into anything else. I know you too well for that. That's the problem with breaking up with your best friend, Jace. I just see through it. Even if you can't." And then she did pick up her clothes. And she dressed, and she walked out of the house without a backward glance, and he felt like she had taken the entire world with her.

Butterflies and all.

Chapter 14

She should have gone straight back to her house, but she didn't. Instead, she went to the hotel. She went to the hotel, because it just seemed like maybe it would be a little bit more comforting than being by herself. Though, she didn't think that anything could comfort her at this point.

As soon as she walked in, she was comforted by something. Maybe the presence of the raccoon. Maybe the presence of the orb. She didn't know. Or maybe it was just that... She could lie to herself here. She could remember when they had been here last, and they had been full of dreams, and he had stood there and asked her to marry him.

Like they could have a future. A future that looked so different than one she had ever imagined for herself. A future that looked bigger, brighter and better.

She had always been alone. She had always been the

one that people just didn't love enough. And she knew that wasn't fair. Not to herself. She knew it wasn't fair to blame herself for this, not when Jace's fears about love were about him. They weren't about her. But it didn't mean they didn't brush up against all the tender places inside of her. That it didn't feel jagged and wrong. That it didn't make her feel lost and sad and all of fourteen years old again and somehow just not good enough. Just not enough.

Because if she was enough, couldn't she make him... Change?

Couldn't she make him see?

Couldn't she make him let go.

He doesn't want to let go. And if he doesn't want to let go, nothing can make him. Nobody can make him.

She knew that was true. Logically, she knew it was true. But nothing was logical about heartbreak.

She paused at the bottom of the stairs. Jace had broken her heart. She was literally living in her worst nightmare. She had fallen in love with him, and he had rejected her. And he hadn't just broken up with her... He had ended their friendship.

Of all the things she had ever worried about, she had never worried about that one thing. She had thought that it would be torture to be with him, and then have to watch him move on with other women, all the while at his side as his faithful companion.

She had never imagined that he would end the friendship completely.

She stood there. Waiting to fall to pieces. Waiting to fall apart.

And she didn't see any glowing lights, but suddenly, she felt one. At the center of her chest, glowing within her soul. She waited to feel isolated, because Jace had been the only person that she'd ever had in her life long-term. The only one who was still here.

But she didn't feel alone. Because her grandfather was with her. And maybe something else was too. Someone else.

Because whatever he thought, whatever he said, love didn't end when someone died, and neither did they. Everything that they were to you was still there. And all the love that they had ever given you, and that you had ever given in return.

She knew that. It was why she was standing in this hotel. It was why she was here at all.

Her grandfather being gone didn't erase the love that he'd given her.

And Jace ending things didn't undo everything that they been.

She put her hand on her chest, and she felt like she might have a broken heart, but even within that... Even within it... She felt a rush of gratitude.

Because he couldn't undo all these years.

He couldn't take the love that he'd given her already and cut it out of her heart, take it out of her soul. Because it was part of her. Woven into the very fabric of who she was.

This was like a death.

But like death... It wasn't really the end.

Because she loved him. And she had all the years before. She would have all the years after too. And she wished... She wished that it would look different. But it was the same as loving people who were gone, she supposed. She wished that it could look different too. But it couldn't. And yes, it was much more within his control to make this something that was happy instead of sad and painful, but… But it simply was. It simply was what it was.

It was painful. But there was beauty in it too, and he couldn't take the beauty away.

It was part of who she was. And what she had to trust was that it was part of who he was too.

Enough that it would never really go away. Enough that he would never really be able to be rid of her.

Of course, that cut both ways. And she would never be able to get rid of him either.

But she didn't want to.

Even if it hurt, she didn't want to. And that was the difference between the woman she was now, and the girl that he had found crying by the creek. She had needed to be different. She had wanted to escape. Had wanted to fight and run away.

And the woman she was now didn't want to do any of those things. She was ready to stand firm and tall. He had said that he had tried to grow his roots around her, and he had dragged her down. But the reality was, her own roots went deep. She knew who she was. And it would take more than a storm to knock her over.

She knew who she was.

She was a woman who loved a man who wouldn't love her back.

And it hurt.

But she wouldn't falter or dissolve, or hide from the pain in drugs and in other meaningless relationships the way that her mother had done. Or just… Simply not show up the way her father had done.

And she wouldn't let it steal her hope, the way grief and pain had done to Jace.

And it wasn't because she was better. It was simply

because… She had been given enough love in her life, that it sustained her now.

She walked up the stairs to the bedroom that she had shared with Jace. And she wasn't afraid of it. Wasn't afraid of seeing anything potentially spooky. Because there was nothing scary about it. She couldn't see the future. But there was nothing scary about that either.

Because she could believe that there would be something better.

She had to.

She had to.

Well he'd done it. He'd broken everything. He'd broken the world. Utterly and irrevocably. It was like he had reached up and hammered a nail into the sky and let it all shatter. Then it all rained down on him.

And that was more fanciful thinking than he ever allowed himself. Because he never allowed himself to… To hope.

She was right about that.

The other thing he had never allowed himself to truly believe was that he had the potential to be hurt more than he already had been. He thought that he had a clear-eyed view of life. And here he was, standing in the middle of a screwed up situation that he had created, feeling like he would never sort out the wreckage. Feeling like he would never be able to stand up straight again.

What had he done?

He had lost his sister. She had been the single most important person in his life. His best friend. And he had met Cara, and being with her, being near her had done something to finally soothe the ache inside of him. And now… He'd sent her away. He'd chosen to not have her. And he had…

It was him. It was his fault. He ruined it. He couldn't stand to sit here for another minute. He didn't sit. It wasn't the thing that he did. He was decisive.

And look where it got you.

He didn't look ahead because all he could see was blackness. Bleakness. Blank despair.

He walked out of the house, and he started to walk down the trail that went behind the place. The moon was full, so he could see just enough to walk without tripping over anything. The trail wound up the side of the mountain, through a thick copse of trees, where it all went pitch-black.

And this… This seemed right. It seemed fair. It seemed like a look at his life. A look at his future.

But he pressed on through, and when he came to the top of the mountain, he looked up and there were stars. Because, impossibly, the world was still turning, and everything was still up in the sky, and he hadn't shattered it at all. It just felt that way. Because it was him. Because it was his heart.

Dammit all.

And no matter how hard he had tried to make sure that it didn't… That it didn't want anything, not ever again… No matter how hard he tried, she had gotten in there. She was under his skin. She was in him, no matter how hard he had tried.

He sat down, right there on the mountainside, and looked out at the broad expanse of everything.

"She thinks that you're out there, Sophia," he said, feeling like an idiot. But he had nothing. He had nothing to hope for, nothing to lose, nothing to gain. He might as well sit there and talk to the night sky. "But I just can't feel anything. Or I'm afraid to. I wanted to believe that there was nothing left to hope for so that I could never get hurt again, and here I am. I haven't hurt this bad since… Not since you. But I did it to myself. I did it to the person that I care about most in this world." He felt a stabbing sensation in his chest. "I love her. I am in love with her, and I sent her away, because I'm too afraid to claim that. Because I'm too afraid to want it."

He closed his eyes, and he waited for something. For inspiration to strike, a lightning bolt from heaven.

Yeah. Because you could ignore all that and say you didn't believe in it, and then just get a sign the minute that you asked.

It was dark, and so was his soul.

He lowered his head, keeping his eyes closed, and he waited. He waited there all night. Until the sun started to rise up over the view in front of him. And it was the strangest thing. Just as the golden rays of light began to touch the brush on the rocks all around him, the flowers, he saw them. Hundreds of them. Little white butterflies, rising up from every surface. All around.

And he felt…

Love. Like he never imagined before, like he never felt it before. Like everyone who had ever stood in the spot before him was still there, like Sophia wasn't gone.

"You tried to tell me," he said, looking all around. "But I'm a particular kind of dumbass, so you can't just send a few. I guess I needed a whole butterfly storm."

And he could see it, like he was looking straight past that horizon. A life and the world all lit up with this kind of love. And he could see himself with Cara.

His Cara.

And once he could see that… Once he could believe it… In this thing that had felt intangible and impossible only a few hours before, he knew.

That he loved her.

And that life might not come with guarantees or certainty. That the world was a harsh and dangerous place.

But love was what made it worthwhile. Love was what endured.

Love didn't work all by itself. You needed faith to go along with it.

And that's what he'd been missing. The ability to believe, in this thing that was bigger than he was.

In this thing he couldn't control. It had been easier to do when she was beside him. Bright and perfect. But maybe he needed this moment, to try and see the light without taking hers.

Because he needed to bring back what he was taking. Needed to give equal to what he was getting.

And he was ready now.

He could only hope that she would still want him after how badly he had messed up.

But he'd loved her for a very long time. He could see that now. When he looked back and forward, and at the present moment, it all added up to love.

Maybe that was why he so obsessively didn't like to look at his life.

He'd been living a whole life.

But he was done lying. And he was done running.

Unless it was straight to her.

Chapter 15

When she woke up the next morning and heard pounding downstairs, she was afraid that it was a raccoon. Or maybe a ghost.

She got out of bed, and when she moved the curtain, it disturbed a little white butterfly. She paused for a moment and looked at it, watched it flutter around the room, before the knocking became more insistent. And then she ran down the stairs, and she could see him through the window.

Jace.

She flung the door open. "How did you know that I would be here?"

"Well, it's not the first place I've been."

"It's really early," she said.

He took a step inside, and her heart began to throb painfully. "No. It's really late, actually."

"It's sunrise," she said.

"I just mean… I'm late with this. Everything I said last night was me running scared. But you knew that already. And I was… I was wrong. Everything I did to you was wrong. Everything I said to you was wrong. And everything you said to me was true. I was scared. More than scared, I've been paralyzed. When Sophia died, it was like my ability to hope that things would turn out okay was just… Killed along with her. But it's a bad tribute, if nothing else. I'm here. And I'm alive, and I've been acting like a part of me died. Except I had you. And you were that bright spot. And you know what, I didn't have to know very much as long as you were with me. It was only when I was forced to sit in the darkness of what my life looked like without you that I had to try and find the light for myself. That I had to try and see past the horizon line. And I can't see a future without you."

She sucked in a hard breath, and she waited.

"Because I love you," he said.

"Thank God."

"Yeah." She wrapped her arms around his neck and she just hugged him. Held him for a long moment. "I really love you too."

"Still? Even after… After everything?"

"Maybe especially after everything. Because this was a lot of work. I know it was. Because I know you."

"I have to tell you. I wanted a sign. Something. And you know that I was desperate if I was asking for signs. And this morning… There were all these white butterflies, everywhere. And I can't explain it."

She pulled back and looked at him, and she laughed. "I saw one this morning too."

"Cara Summers," he said, his voice rough. "I can't believe that I'm about to say this. But I think that this is meant to be."

Epilogue

They didn't end up rushing down the aisle. They took their time. Because Jace wasn't afraid, and he didn't need all those external things to prove to him that what they had wasn't going to evaporate, and because Cara decided that she wanted to get married at the hotel, so she wanted it finished before the event.

They'd gotten married in the newly landscaped backyard, and had the reception both inside and outside.

The old restaurant and bar in the far wing of the hotel was beautifully renovated, and it was set up with free drinks for all of their guests.

And just behind the bar, on that top shelf, was Grandpa's whiskey bottle.

Late in the evening, when the guests were all leaving, and it was Jace and Cara, sitting in the bar, her in her wedding dress, and him in his tux, she lifted a glass of whiskey up toward the bottle. "To Grandpa," she said.

"To Mitch," Jace agreed. "Thanks, old man. For everything."

She smiled. "You're even talking to him now."

"It just doesn't feel half so strange. Not anymore."

"Why do you think that is? Is it just because of the butterflies?"

He shook his head. "No. It's because of the love. Because that is a miracle, Cara, it really is. And once you believe in one miracle, it's not so hard to start believing in all of them."

She smiled. "I love you, Jace. You're my best friend."

"I love you too. And you know, you're definitely my best friend, but even better… You're my wife."

"I like that, husband."

"I think it's time to go upstairs," he said, tipping his glass back.

"You have a one-track mind."

"Yeah. I do. But you know what… After… After what I really want to do is dream about the future."

"I didn't think you did dreams."

"That was before."

"Before what?"

"Before you made my life the best dream of all."

* * * * *

NEED ME, COWBOY

Prologue

Levi Tucker
Oregon State Penitentiary
2605 State St., Salem, OR 97310

Dear Ms. Grayson,
Due to certain circumstances, my prison sentence is coming to its end sooner than originally scheduled. I've been following your career and I'd like to hire you to design the house I intend to have built.
Sincerely,
Levi Tucker

Dear Mr. Tucker,
How nice that you're soon to be released from prison. I imagine that's a great relief. As you can imagine, my work is in very high demand and I

doubt I'll be able to take on a project with such
short notice.
Regretfully,
Faith Grayson

Dear Ms. Grayson,
Whatever your usual fee is, I can double it.
Sincerely,
Levi Tucker

Dear Mr. Tucker,
To be perfectly frank, I looked you up on Google.
My brothers would take a dim view of me agree-
ing to take this job.
Respectfully,
Faith Grayson

Dear Ms. Grayson,
Search again. You'll find I am in the process of
being exonerated. Also, what your brothers don't
know won't hurt anything. I'll triple your fee.
Sincerely,
Levi Tucker

Dear Mr. Tucker,
If you need to contact me, be sure to use my per-
sonal number, listed at the bottom of this page.
    I trust we'll be in contact upon your release.
Faith

Chapter 1

Levi Tucker wasn't a murderer.

It was a fact that was now officially recognized by the law.

He didn't know what he had expected upon his release from prison. Relief, maybe. He imagined that was what most men might feel. Instead, the moment the doors to the penitentiary had closed behind him, Levi had felt something else.

A terrible, pure anger that burned through his veins with a kind of white-hot clarity that would have stunned him if it hadn't felt so inevitable.

The fact of the matter was, Levi Tucker had always known he wasn't a murderer.

And all the state of Oregon had ever had was a hint of suspicion. Hell, they hadn't even had a body.

Mostly because Alicia wasn't dead.

In many ways, that added insult to injury, because

he still had to divorce the woman who had set out to make it look as though he had killed her. They were still married. Of course, the moment he'd been able to, he'd filed, and he knew everything was in the process of being sorted out.

He doubted she would contest.

But then, how could he really know?

He had thought he'd known the woman. Hell, he'd married her. And while he'd been well aware that everything hadn't been perfect, he had not expected his wife to disappear one hot summer night, leaving behind implications of foul play.

Even if the result hadn't been intentional, she could have resurfaced at any point after she'd disappeared.

When he was being questioned. When he had been arrested.

She hadn't.

Leaving him to assume that his arrest, disgrace and abject humiliation had been her goal.

It made him wonder now if their relationship had been a long tail game all the time.

The girl who'd loved him in spite of his family's reputation in Copper Ridge. The one who'd vowed to stick with him through everything. No matter whether he made his fortune or not. He had, and he'd vowed to Alicia he'd build her a house on top of a hill in Copper Ridge so they could look down on all the people who'd once looked down on them.

But until then he'd enjoyed his time at work, away from the town he'd grown up in. Alicia had gotten more involved in the glamorous side of their new lifestyle, while Levi just wanted things to be simple. His own ranch. His own horses.

Alicia had wanted more.

And apparently, in the end, she had figured she could have it all without him.

Fortunately, it was the money that had ultimately been her undoing. For years prior to her leaving she'd been siphoning it into her own account without him realizing it, but when her funds had run dry she'd gone after the money still in his accounts. And that was when she'd gotten caught.

She'd been living off of his hard-earned money for years.

Five years.

Five hellish years he'd spent locked up as the murderer of a woman. Of his wife.

Not a great situation, all in all.

But he'd survived it. Like he'd survived every damn thing that had come before it.

Money was supposed to protect you.

In the end, he supposed it had, in many ways.

Hell, he might not have been able to walk out of that jail cell and collect his Stetson on his way back to his life if it wasn't for the fact that he had a good team of lawyers who had gotten his case retried as quickly as possible. Something you would've thought would be pretty easy considering his wife had been found alive.

The boy he'd been…

He had no confidence that boy would have been able to get justice.

But the man he was…

The man he was now stood on a vacant plot of land that he owned, near enough to the house he was renting, and waited for the architect to arrive. The one who would design the house he deserved after spending five years behind bars.

There would be no bars in this house. The house that

Alicia had wanted so badly. To show everyone in their hometown that he and Alicia were more, were better, than what they'd been born into.

Only, she wasn't.

Without him, she was nothing. And he would prove that to her.

No, his house would have no bars. Nothing but windows.

Windows with a view of the mountains that overlooked Copper Ridge, Oregon, the town where he had grown up. He'd been bad news back then; his whole family had been.

The kind of guy that fathers warned their daughters about.

A bad seed dropped from a rotten tree.

And he had a feeling that public opinion would not have changed in the years since.

His reputation certainly hadn't helped his case when he'd been tried and convicted five years ago.

Repeating patterns. That had been brought up many times. An abusive father was likely to have raised an abusive son, who had gone on to be a murderer.

That was the natural progression, wasn't it?

The natural progression of men like him.

Alicia had known that. Of course she had. She knew him better than any other person on earth.

Yet he hadn't known her at all.

Well, he had ended up in prison, as she'd most likely intended. But he'd clawed his way out. And now he was going to stand up on the mountain in his fancy-ass house and looked down on everyone who'd thought prison would be the end of him.

The best house in the most prime location in town. That was his aim.

Now all that was left to do was wait for Faith Grayson to arrive. By all accounts she was the premier architect at the moment, the hottest commodity in custom home design.

Her houses were more than simple buildings, they were works of art. And he was bound and determined to own a piece of that art for himself.

He was a man possessed. A man on a mission to make the most of everything he'd lost. To live as well as possible while his wife had to deal with the slow-rolling realization that she would be left with nothing.

As it was, it was impossible to prove that she had committed a crime. She hadn't called the police, after all. An argument could be made that she might *not* have intended for him to be arrested. And there was plausible deniability over the fact that she might not have realized he'd gone to prison.

She claimed she had simply walked away from her life and not looked back. The fact that she had been accessing money was a necessity, so she said. And, proof that she had not actually been attempting to hide.

He didn't believe that. He didn't believe *her*, and she had been left with nothing. No access to his money at all. She had been forced to go crawling back to her parents to get an allowance. And he was glad of that.

They said the best revenge was living well.

Levi Tucker intended to do just that.

Faith Grayson knew that meeting an ex-convict at the top of an isolated mountain could easily be filed directly into the Looney Tunes Bin.

Except, Levi Tucker was only an ex-convict because he had been wrongfully convicted in the first place. At least, that was the official statement from the Oregon State District Attorney's office.

Well, plus it was obvious because his wife wasn't dead.

He had been convicted of the murder of someone who was alive. And while there was a whole lot of speculation centered around the fact that the woman never would have run from him in the first place if he hadn't been dangerous and terrifying, the fact remained that he *wasn't* a killer.

So, there was that.

She knew exactly what two of her brothers, Isaiah and Joshua, would say about this meeting. And it would be colorful. Not at all supportive.

But Faith was fascinated by the man who was willing to pay so much to get one of her designs. And, maybe her ego was a little bit turbocharged by the whole thing. She couldn't deny that.

She was only human, after all.

A human who had been working really, really hard to keep on top of her status as a rising star in the architecture world.

She had designed buildings that had changed skylines, and she'd done homes for the rich and the famous.

Levi Tucker was something *else*. He was infamous.

The self-made millionaire whose whole world had come crashing down when his wife had disappeared more than five years ago. The man who had been tried and convicted of her murder even when there wasn't a body.

Who had spent the past five years in prison, and who was now digging his way back out...

He wanted her. And yeah, it interested her.

She was getting bored.

Which seemed...ungrateful. Her skill for design had made her famous at a ridiculously young age, but, of course, it was her older brothers and their business acumen that had helped her find success so quickly.

Joshua was a public-relations wizard, Isaiah a genius with finance. Faith, for her part, was the one with the imagination.

The one who saw buildings growing out of the ground like trees and worked to find ways to twist them into new shapes, to draw new lines into the man-made landscape to blend it all together with nature.

She had always been an artist, but her fascination with buildings had come from a trip her family had taken when she was a child. They had driven from Copper Ridge into Portland, Oregon, and she had been struck by the beauty that surrounded the city.

But in the part of the city where they'd stayed, everything was blocky and made of concrete. Of course, there were parts of the city that were lovely, with architecture that was ornate and classic, but there were parts where the buildings had been stacked in light gray rectangles, and it had nearly wounded her to see the mountains obscured by such unimaginative, dull shapes.

When she had gotten back to their hotel room, she had begun to draw, trying to find a way to blend function and form with the natural beauty that already existed.

It had become an obsession.

It was tough to be an obsessed person. Someone who lived in their own head, in their dreams and fantasies.

It made it difficult to relate to people.

Fortunately, she had found a good friend, Mia, who had been completely understanding of Faith and her particular idiosyncrasies.

Now Mia was her sister-in-law, because she had married Faith's oldest brother, something Faith really hadn't seen coming.

Devlin was just…so much older. There was more than ten years between he and Faith, and she'd had no idea her friend felt that way about him.

She was happy for both of them, of course.

But their bond sometimes made her feel isolated. The fact that her friend now had this *thing* that Faith herself never had. And that this *thing* was with Faith's brother. Of all people.

Even Joshua and Isaiah had fallen in love and gotten married.

Joshua had wed a woman he had met while trying to get revenge on their father for attempting to force him into marriage, while Isaiah married his personal assistant.

Maybe it was her family that had driven Faith to the top of the mountain today.

Maybe her dissatisfaction with her own personal life was why it felt so interesting and new to do something with Levi Tucker.

Everything she had accomplished, she had done with the permission and help of other people.

If she was going to be a visionary, she wanted—just this once—for it to be on her terms.

To not be seen as a child prodigy—which was ridiculous, because she was twenty-five, not a child at all—but to be seen as someone who was really great at what she did. To leave her age out of it, to leave her older brothers—who often felt more like babysitters—out of it.

She let out a long, slow breath as she rounded the final curve on the mountain driveway, the vacant lot coming into view. But it wasn't the lot, or the scenery surrounding it, that stood out in her vision first and foremost. No, it was the man standing there, his hands shoved into the pockets of his battered jeans, worn cowboy boots on his feet. He had on a black T-shirt, in spite of the morning chill, and a black cowboy hat was pressed firmly onto his head.

Both of his arms were completely filled with ink, the dark lines of the tattoos painting pictures on his skin she couldn't quite see from where she was.

But in a strange way, they reminded her of architecture. The tattoos seemed to enhance the muscle there, to draw focus to the skin beneath the lines, even while they covered it.

She parked the car and sat for a moment, completely struck dumb by the sight of him.

She had researched him, obviously. She knew what he looked like, but she supposed she hadn't had a sense of…the scale of him.

Strange, because she was usually pretty good at picking up on those kinds of things in photographs. She had a mathematical eye, one that blended with her artistic sensibility in a way that felt natural to her.

And yet, she had not been able to accurately form a picture of the man in her mind. And when she got out of the car, she was struck by the way he seemed to fill this vast empty space.

That also didn't make any sense.

He was big. Over six feet and with broad shoulders, but he didn't fill this space. Not literally.

But she could feel his presence like a touch as soon as the cold air wrapped itself around her body upon exiting the car.

And when his ice-blue eyes connected with hers, she drew in a breath. She was certain he filled her lungs, too.

Because that air no longer felt cold. It felt hot. Impossibly so.

Because those blue eyes burned with something.

Rage. Anger.

Not at her—in fact, his expression seemed almost friendly.

But there was something simmering beneath the surface, and it had touched her already.

Wouldn't let go of her.

"Ms. Grayson," he said, his voice rolling over her with that same kind of heat. "Good to meet you."

He stuck out his hand and she hurriedly closed the distance between them, flinching before their skin touched, because she knew it was going to burn.

It did.

"Mr. Tucker," she responded, careful to keep her voice neutral, careful, when she released her hold on him, not to flex her fingers or wipe her palm against the side of her skirt like she wanted to.

"This is the site," he said. "I hope you think it's workable."

"I do," she said, blinking. She needed to look around them. At the view. At the way the house would be situated. This lot was more than usable. It was inspirational. "What do you have in mind? I find it best to begin with customer expectations," she said, quick to turn the topic where it needed to go. Because what she didn't want to do was ponder the man any longer.

The man didn't matter.

The house mattered.

"I want it to be everything prison isn't," he said, his tone hard and decisive.

She couldn't imagine this man, as vast and wild as the deep green trees and ridged blue mountains around them, contained in a cell. Isolated. Cut off.

In darkness.

And suddenly she felt compelled to be the answer to

that darkness. To make sure that the walls she built for him didn't feel like walls at all.

"Windows," she said. That was the easiest and most obvious thing. A sense of openness and freedom. She began to plot the ways in which she could construct a house so that it didn't have doors. So that things were concealed by angles and curves. "No doors?"

"I live alone," he said simply. "There's no reason for doors."

"And you don't plan on living with someone anytime soon?"

"Never," he responded. "It may surprise you to learn that I have cooled on the idea of marriage."

"Windows. Lighting." She turned to the east. "The sun should be up here early, and we can try to capture the light there in the morning when you wake up, and then…" She turned the opposite way. "Make sure that we're set up for you to see the light as it goes down here. Kitchen. Living room. Office?"

Her fingers twitched and she pulled her sketchpad out of her large, leather bag, jotting notes and rough lines as quickly as possible. She felt the skin prickle on her face and she paused, looking up.

He was watching her.

She cleared her throat. "Can I ask you…what was it that inspired you to get in touch with me? Which building of mine?"

"All of them," he said. "I had nothing but time while I was in jail, and while I did what I could to manage some of my assets from behind bars, there was a lot of time to read. An article about your achievements came to my attention and I was fascinated by your work. I won't lie to you—even more than that, I am looking forward to owning a piece of you."

Something about those words hit her square in the solar plexus and radiated outward. She was sweating now. She was not wearing her coat. She should not be sweating.

"Of me?"

"Your brand," he said. "Having a place designed by you is an exceedingly coveted prize, I believe."

She felt her cheeks warm, and she couldn't quite figure out why. She didn't suffer from false modesty. The last few years of her life had been nothing short of extraordinary. She embraced her success and she didn't apologize for it. Didn't duck her head, like she was doing now, or tuck her hair behind her ear and look up bashfully. Which she had just done.

"I suppose so."

"You know it's true," he said.

"Yes," she said, clearing her throat and rallying. "I do."

"Whatever the media might say, whatever law enforcement believes now, my wife tried to destroy my life. And I will not allow her to claim that victory. I'm not a phoenix rising from the ashes. I'm just a very angry man ready to set some shit on fire, and stand there watching it burn. I'm going to show her, and the world, that I can't be destroyed. I'm not slinking into the shadows. I'm going to rebuild it all. Until everything that I have done matters more than what she did to me. I will not allow her name, what she did, to be the thing I am remembered for. I'm sure you can understand that."

She could. Oddly, she really could.

She wasn't angry at anyone, nor did she have any right to be, but she knew what it was like to want to break out and have your own achievements. Wasn't that what she had just been thinking of while coming here?

Of course, he already had so many achievements. She

imagined having all her work blotted out the way that he had. It was unacceptable.

"Look," she said stashing her notebook, "I meant what I said, about my brothers being unhappy with me for taking this job."

"What do your brothers have to do with you taking a job?"

"If you read anything about me then you know that I work with them. You know that we've merged with the construction company that handles a great deal of our building."

"Yes, I know. Though, doesn't the construction arm mostly produce reproductions of your designs, rather than handling your custom projects?"

"It depends," she responded. "I just mean… My brothers run a significant portion of our business."

"But you could go off and run it without them. They can't run it without you."

He had said the words she had thought more than once while listening to Joshua and Isaiah make proclamations about various things. Joshua was charming, and often managed to make his proclamations seem not quite so prescriptive. Isaiah never bothered. About the only person he was soft with at all was his wife, Poppy, who owned his heart—a heart that a great many of them had doubted he had.

"Well, I just meant… We need to keep this project a secret. Until we're at least most of the way through. Jonathan Bear will be the one to handle the building. He's the best. And since you're right here in Copper Ridge, it would make sense to have him do it."

"I know Jonathan Bear," Levi said.

That surprised her. "Do you?"

"I'm a couple years older than him, but we both grew

up on the same side of the tracks here in town. You know, the wrong side."

"Oh," she said. "I didn't realize."

Dimly, she had been aware, on some level, that Levi was from here, but he had left so long ago, and he was so far outside of her own peer group, that she would never have known him.

If he was older than Jonathan Bear, then he was possibly a good thirteen years her senior.

That made her feel small and silly for that instant response she'd had to him earlier.

She was basically a child to him.

But then, she was basically a child to most of the men in her life, so why should this be any different?

And she didn't even know why it was bothering her.

She often designed buildings for old men. And in the beginning, it had been difficult getting them to take her seriously, but the more pieces that had been written about her, the more those men had marveled at the talent she had for her age, and the more she was able to walk into a room with all of those accolades clearly visible behind her as she went.

She was still a little bit bothered that her age was such a big deal, but if it helped…then she would take it. Because she couldn't do anything about the fact that she looked like she might still be in college.

She tried—*tried*—to affect a sophisticated appearance, but half the time she felt like she was playing dress-up in a much fancier woman's clothes.

"Clandestine architecture project?" he asked, the corner of his lips working up into a smile. And until that moment, she realized she had not been fully convinced his mouth could do that.

"Something like that."

"Let me ask you this," he said. "Why do you want to take the job?"

"Well, it's like you said. I—I feel like I'm an important piece of the business. And believe me, I wouldn't be where I am without Isaiah and Joshua. They're brilliant. But I want to be able to make my own choices. Maybe I want to take on this project. Especially now that you've said…everything about needing it to be the opposite of a prison cell. I'm inspired to do it. I love this location. I want to build this house without Isaiah hovering over me."

Levi chuckled, low and gravelly. "So he wouldn't approve of me?"

"Not at all."

"I am innocent," he said. His mouth worked upward again. "Or I should say, I'm not guilty. Whether or not I'm an entirely innocent person is another story. But I didn't do anything to my wife."

"Your ex-wife?"

"Nearly. Everything should be finalized in the next couple of days. She's not contesting anything. Mostly because she doesn't want to end up in prison. I have impressed upon her how unpleasant that experience was. She has no desire to see for herself."

"Oh, of course you're still married to her. Because everybody thought—"

"That she was dead. You don't have to divorce a dead person."

"Let me ask you something," she said, doing her best to meet his gaze, ignoring the quivering sensation she felt in her belly. "Do I have reason to be afraid of you?"

The grin that spread over his face was slow, calculated. "Well, I would say that depends."

Chapter 2

He shouldn't toy with her. It wasn't nice. But then, he wasn't nice. He hadn't been, not even before his stint in prison. But the time there had taken anything soft inside of him and hardened it. Until his insides were a minefield of sharpened obsidian. Black, stone-cold, honed into a razor.

The man he'd been before might not have done anything to provoke the pretty little woman in front of him. But he could barely remember that man. That man had been an idiot. That man had married Alicia, had convinced himself he could have a happy life, when he had never seen any kind of happiness come from marriage, not all through his childhood. So why had he thought he could have more? Could have something else?

"Depends on what?" she asked, looking up at him, those wide brown eyes striking him square in the chest... and lower, when they made contact with his.

She was so very pretty.

So very young, too.

Her pale, heart-shaped face, those soft-looking pink lips and her riot of brown curls—it all appealed to him in an instant, visceral way.

No real mystery, he supposed. He hadn't touched a woman in more than five years.

This one was contraband. She had a use, but it wouldn't be *that* one.

Hell, no.

He was a hard bastard, no mistake. But he wasn't a criminal.

He didn't belong with the rapists and murderers he'd been locked away with for all those years, and sometimes the only thing that had kept him going in those subhuman conditions—where he'd been called every name in the book, subjected to threats that would make most men weep with fear in their beds—was the knowledge that he didn't belong there.

That he wasn't one of them.

Hell, that was about the only thing that had kept him from hunting down Alicia when he'd been released.

He wasn't a murderer. He wasn't a monster.

He wouldn't let Alicia make him one.

"Depends on what scares you," he said.

She firmed those full lips into a thin, ungenerous line, and perhaps that reaction should have turned his thoughts in a different direction.

Instead he thought about what it might take to coax those lips back to softness. To fullness. And just how much riper they might become if he was to kiss them. To take the lower one between his teeth and bite.

He really wasn't fit for company. At least not delicate, female company.

Sadly, it was delicate female company that seemed appealing.

He needed to go to a bar and find a woman more like him. Harder. Closer to his age.

Someone who could stand five years of pent-up sexual energy pounded into her body.

The sweet little architect he had hired was not that woman.

If her brothers had any idea she was meeting with him they would get out their pitchforks. If they had any idea what he was thinking now, they would get out their shotguns.

And he couldn't blame them.

"Spiders. Do you have spiders up your sleeves?"

"No spiders," he said.

"The dark?"

"Well, honey, I can tell you for a fact that I have a little bit of that I carry around with me."

"I guess as long as we stay in the light it should be okay."

He was tempted to toy with her. He didn't know if she was being intentionally flirtatious. But there was something so open, so innocent, about her expression that he doubted it.

"I'm going to go sketch," she said. "Now that I've seen the place, and you've sent over all the meaningful information, I should be able to come up with an initial draft. And then I can send it over to you."

"Sounds good," he said. "Then what?"

"Then we'll arrange another meeting."

"Sounds like a plan," he said, extending his hand.

He shouldn't touch her again.

But he wanted to touch her again.

Pink colored her cheeks. A blush.

Dammit all, the woman had blushed.

Women who blushed were not for men like him.

That he had a sense of that at all was a reminder. A reminder that he wasn't an animal. Wasn't a monster.

Or at least that he still had enough man in him to control himself.

"I'll see you then."

Chapter 3

Faith was not hugely conversant in the whole girls'-night-out thing. Mia, her best friend from school, was not big on going out, and never had been, and usually, that had suited Faith just fine.

Faith had been a scholarship student at a boarding school that would have been entirely out of her family's reach if the school hadn't been interested in her artistic talents. And she'd been so invested in making the most of those talents, and then making the most of her scholarships in college, that she'd never really made time to go out.

And Mia had always been much the same, so there had been no one to encourage the other one to go out.

After school it had been work. Work and more work, and riding the massive wave Faith had somehow managed to catch that had buoyed her career to nearly absurd levels as soon as she'd graduated.

But since coming to Copper Ridge, things had somehow managed to pick up and slow down at the same time. There was something about living in a small town, with its slower pace, clean streets and wide-open spaces all around, that seemed to create more time.

Not having to commute through Seattle traffic helped, and it might actually be the sum total of where she had found all that extra time, if she was honest.

She had also begun to make friends with Hayley Bear, formerly Thompson, now wife of Jonathan. When Faith and her brothers had moved their headquarters to Copper Ridge, closer to their parents, Joshua had decided it would be a good idea to find a local builder to partner with, and that was how they'd met Jonathan, and merged their businesses.

And tonight, Faith and Hayley were out for drinks.

Of course, Hayley didn't really drink, and Faith was a lightweight at best, but that didn't mean they couldn't have fun.

They were also in Hayley's brother's bar.

They couldn't have been supervised any better if they tried. Though, the protectiveness was going to be directed more at Hayley than Faith.

Faith stuck her straw down deep into her rum-and-Coke and fished out a cherry, lifting it up and chewing it thoughtfully as she surveyed the room.

The revelers were out in force, whole groups of cheering friends standing by Ferdinand, the mechanical bull, and watching as people stepped up to the plate—both drunk and sober—to get thrown off his back and onto the mats below.

It looked entirely objectionable to Faith. She couldn't imagine submitting herself to something like that. A ride you couldn't control, couldn't anticipate. Where the only way off was to weather the bucking or get thrown to the mats below.

No, thanks.

"You seem quiet," Hayley pointed out.

"Do I?" Faith mused.

"Yes," Hayley said. "You seem like you have something on your mind."

Faith gnawed the inside of her cheek. "I'm starting a new design project. And it's really important that I get everything right. I mean, I'm going to be collaborating with the guy, so I'm sure he'll have his own input, and all of that, but…" She didn't know how to explain it without giving herself away, then she gave up. "If I told you something…could you keep it a secret?"

Hayley blinked her wide brown eyes. "Yes. Though… I don't keep anything from Jonathan. Ever. He's my husband and…"

"Can Jonathan keep a secret?"

"Jonathan doesn't really do…*friends*. So, I'm not sure who he would tell. I think I might be the only person he talks to."

"He works with my brothers," Faith pointed out.

"To the same degree he works with you."

"Not really. A lot more of the stuff filters through Joshua and Isaiah than it does me. I'm just kind of around. That's our agreement. They handle all of the…business stuff. And I do the drawing. The designing. I'm an expert at buildings and building materials, aesthetics and design. Not so much anything else."

"Point taken. But, yes, if I asked Jonathan not to say something, he wouldn't. He's totally loyal to me." Hayley looked a little bit smug about that.

It was hard to have friends who were so happily…

relationshipped, when Faith knew so little about how that worked.

Though at least Hayley wasn't with Faith's *brother*.

Yes, that made Faith and Mia family, which was nice in its way, but it really limited their ability to talk about boys. They had always promised to share personal things, like first times. While Faith had been happy for her friend, and for her brother, she also had wanted details about as much as she wanted to be stripped naked, had a string tied around her toe and be dragged through the small town's main street by her brother Devlin's Harley.

As in: not at all.

"I took a job that Joshua and Isaiah are going to be really mad about…"

Just then, the door to the bar opened, and Faith's mouth dropped open. Because there he was. Speaking of.

Hayley looked over her shoulder, not bothering to be subtle. "Who's that?" she hissed.

"The devil," Faith said softly.

Hayley blinked. "You had better start at the beginning."

"I was about to," Faith said.

The two of them watched as Levi went up to the counter, leaned over and placed an order with Ace, the bartender and owner of the bar, and Hayley's older brother.

"That's Levi Tucker," Faith said.

Hayley narrowed her eyes. "Why do I know that name?"

"Because he's kind of famous. Like, a famous murderer."

"Oh, my gosh," Hayley said, slapping the table with her open palm, "he's that guy. That guy accused of murdering his wife! But she wasn't really dead."

"Yes," Faith confirmed.

"You're working with him?"

"I'm designing a house for him. But he's not a murderer. Yes, he was in prison for a while, but he didn't actually do anything. His wife disappeared. That's not exactly his fault."

Hayley looked at Faith skeptically. "If I ran away from my husband it would have to be for a pretty extreme reason."

"Well, no one's ever proven that he did anything. And, anyway, I'm just working with him in a professional capacity. I'm not scared of him."

"Should you be?"

Faith took in the long, hard lines of his body, the dark tattoos on his arms, that dark cowboy hat pulled low over his eyes and his sculpted jaw, which she imagined a woman could cut her hand on if she caressed it...

"No," she said quickly. "Why would I need to be scared of him? I'm designing a house for the guy. Nothing else."

He began to scan the room, and she felt the sudden urge to hide from that piercing blue gaze. Her heart was thundering like she had just run a marathon. Like she just might actually be...

Afraid.

No. That was silly. Impossible. There really wasn't anything to be afraid of.

He was just a man. A hard, scarred man with ink all over his skin, but that didn't mean he was bad. Or scary.

Devlin had tattoos over every visible inch of his body from the neck down.

She didn't want to know if they were anywhere else. There were just some things you shouldn't know about your brother.

But yeah, tattoos didn't make a man scary. Or dangerous. She knew that.

So she couldn't figure out why her heart was still racing.

And then he saw them.

She felt a rush of heat move over her body as he raised his hand and gripped the brim of his cowboy hat, tipping his head down slowly in a brief acknowledgment.

She swallowed hard, her throat sticky and dry, then reached for her soda, feeling panicky. She took a long sip, forgetting there was rum in it, the burn making her cough.

"This is concerning," Hayley said softly, her expression overly sharp.

"What is?" Faith asked, jerking her gaze away from Levi.

"You're *not* acting normal."

"I'm not used to subterfuge." Faith sounded defensive. Because she felt a little defensive.

"The look on your face has nothing to do with the fact that he's incredibly attractive?"

"Is he?" Faith asked, her tone disingenuous, but sweet. "I hadn't noticed."

Actually, until Hayley had said that, she hadn't noticed. Well, she had, but she hadn't connected that disquiet in her stomach with finding him…*attractive*.

He was out of her league in every way. Too old for her. Too hard for her.

Levi was the deep end of the pool, and she didn't know how to swim. That much, she knew.

And she wouldn't… He was a client. Even if she was a champion lap swimmer, there was no way.

He was no longer acknowledging her or Hayley, anyway, as his focus turned back to the bar.

"What's going on with you?" Faith asked, very clumsily changing the subject and forcing herself to look at Hayley.

She and Hayley began to chat about other things, and she did her best to forget that Levi Tucker was in the bar at all.

He had obviously forgotten she was there, anyway.

Then, for some reason, some movement caught her attention, and she turned.

Levi was talking to a blonde, his head bent low, a smile on his face that made Faith feel like she'd just heard him say a dirty word. The blonde was looking back at him with the exact same expression. She was wearing a top that exposed her midriff, which was tight and tan, with a little sparkling piercing on her stomach.

She was exactly the kind of woman Faith could never hope to be, or compete with. And she shouldn't want to, anyway.

Obviously, Levi Tucker was at the bar looking for a good time. And Faith wasn't going to be the one to give it to him, so Blondie McBellyRing might as well be the one to do it.

It was no skin off Faith's nose.

Right then, Levi looked up, and his ice-blue gaze collided with hers with the force of an iceberg hitting the *Titanic*.

And damn if she didn't feel like she was sinking.

He put his hand on the blonde's hip, leaning in and saying something to her, patting her gently before moving away...and walking straight in Faith's direction.

Chapter 4

Levi had no idea what in the hell he was doing.

He was chatting up Mindy—who was a sure thing if there ever was one—and close to breaking that dry spell. He'd watched the little blonde ride that mechanical bull like an expert, and he figured she was exactly the kind of woman who could stay on his rough ride for as long as he needed her to.

A few minutes of banter had confirmed that, and he'd been ready to close the deal.

But then he'd caught Faith Grayson staring at them. And now, for no reason he could discern, he was on his way over to Faith.

Because it was weird he hadn't greeted her with more than just a hat tip from across the room, he told himself, as he crossed the roughhewn wood floor and moved closer to her.

And not for any other reason.

"Fancy meeting you here," he said, ignoring the intent look he was getting from Faith's friend.

"Small towns," Faith said, shrugging and looking like she was ready to fold in on herself.

"You're used to them, aren't you? Aren't you originally from Copper Ridge?"

She nodded. "Yes. But until recently, I haven't lived here since I was seventeen."

"I'm going to get a refill," her friend announced suddenly, sliding out of her seat and making her way over to the bar.

Faith was looking after her friend like she wanted to punch the other woman. It made him wonder what he'd missed.

"She leaving you to get picked up on?" he asked, snagging the vacant seat beside her, his shoulder brushing hers.

She went stiff.

"No," Faith said, lowering her head, her cheeks turning an intense shade of pink.

Another reminder.

Another reminder he should go back over and talk to Mindy.

Faith was *young*. She blushed. She went rigid like a nervous jackrabbit when their shoulders touched. He didn't have the patience for that. He didn't want a woman who had to be shown what to do, even if he didn't mind the idea of corrupting her.

That thought immediately brought a kick of arousal straight to his gut.

All right, maybe his body didn't hate the idea of corrupting her. But he was in control of himself, and whatever baser impulses might exist inside of him, he had the final say.

"She vacated awfully quickly."

"That's Jonathan Bear's wife," she said conversationally, as if that was relevant to the conversation.

Well, it might not be relevant. But it was interesting.

His eyebrows shot up, and he looked back over at the pretty brunette, who was now standing at the counter chatting with the bartender. "And that's her brother," Faith continued.

"I didn't pick Jonathan Bear for a family man."

"He wasn't," Faith said. "Until he met Hayley."

Hayley was young. Not as young as Faith, but young. And Jonathan wasn't as old as Levi was.

That wasn't relevant, either.

"I haven't been to the bar since it changed ownership. Last I was here was…twenty years ago."

"How old are you?"

"Thirty-eight. I had a fake ID."

She laughed. "I didn't expect that."

"What? That I'm thirty-eight or that I had a fake ID?"

"Either."

Her pink tongue darted out and swept across her lips, leaving them wet and inviting. Then she looked down again, taking a sip of whatever it was in her glass. He wondered if she had any idea what she was doing. Just how inviting she'd made her mouth look.

Just how starving he was.

How willing he would be to devour her.

He looked back at Mindy, who was watching him with open curiosity. She didn't seem angry or jealous, just watching to see how her night was going to go, he imagined.

And that was exactly the kind of woman he should be talking to.

He was still rooted to the spot, though. And he didn't make a move back toward her.

"Are you going to be too hungover after tonight to come over to my place and discuss your plans?"

She looked behind him, directly at Mindy. "I figure I should ask you the same question."

"I'm betting I have a lot more hard-drinking years behind me than you do."

"I'm twenty-five," she said. Like that meant something.

"Oh, nothing to worry about, then."

"Four whole years of drinking," she said.

"Did you actually wait to drink until you were twenty-one?"

She blinked. "Yes."

"You know most people don't."

"That can't be true."

He didn't bother to hold in his laugh. "It is."

"I'm sure the…" She frowned. "I was about to say that I'm sure my brothers did. But… I bet they didn't."

She looked comically shocked by that. Who was this girl? This girl who had been lauded as a genius in a hundred articles, and designed the most amazing homes and buildings he'd ever seen. And seemed to know nothing about people.

"You know the deal about the Easter Bunny, too, right?" he asked.

She twisted her lips to the side. "That he has a very fluffy tail?"

He chuckled. "Yeah. That one."

He didn't know why it was difficult to pull himself away. It shouldn't be.

Dammit all, it shouldn't be.

"How about we meet up after lunch?" he asked, pushing the subject back to the house.

"That sounds good to me," she said, her tone a little bit breathless.

"You have the address where I'm staying?"

"Text it to me."

"I will."

He stood and walked away from her then, headed back toward the woman who would have been his conquest. He had another drink with Mindy, continuing to talk to her while she patted his arm, her movements flirtatious, her body language making it clear she was more than ready to have a good time. And for some reason, his body, which had been game a few moments earlier, wasn't all that interested anymore. He looked back over to where Faith and her friend had been sitting, and saw that the table was empty now.

He didn't know when she had left, and she hadn't bothered to say goodbye to him.

"You know what?" he said to Mindy. "I actually have work tomorrow."

She frowned. "Then why did you come out?"

"That's a good damn question." He tipped back his drink the rest of the way, committed now to getting a cab, because he was getting close to tipsy. "I'll make it up to you some other time."

She shrugged. "Well, I'm not going home. Tonight might not be a loss for me. Enjoy your right hand, honey."

If only she knew that his right hand was even a luxury. In shared living quarters with all the stuff that went down in prison, he'd never had the spare moment or the desire.

There was shame, and then there was the humiliation of finding a quiet corner in the dirty cell you shared with one or two other men.

No thank you.

He would rather cut off his right than use it to add to all that BS.

It was better to just close off that part of himself. And he'd done it. Pretty damn effectively. He'd also managed to keep himself safe from all manner of prison violence that went on by building himself a rather ruthless reputation.

He had become a man who felt nothing. Certainly not pleasure or desire. A man who had learned to lash out before anyone could come at him.

The truly astonishing thing was how easy that had been.

How easy it had been to find that piece of his father that had probably lived inside of him all along.

"Maybe I will," he responded.

"So, are you really working early?" Mindy asked. "Or are you intent on joining that little brunette you were talking to earlier?"

Fire ignited in his gut.

"It'll be whatever I decide," he said, tipping his hat. "Have a good evening."

He walked out of the bar with his own words ringing in his head.

It would be what he would decide.

No one else had control over his life. Not now. Not ever.

Not anymore.

Chapter 5

The next morning, Faith's body was still teeming with weird emotions. It was difficult to untangle everything she was feeling. From what had begun when Hayley had called him attractive, to what she'd felt when she'd watched him continue to chat with the blonde, to when she had ultimately excused herself because she couldn't keep looking at their flirtation.

She realized—when she had been lying in her bed—that the reason she had to cut her girls' night short was that she couldn't stand knowing whether or not Levi left the bar with the pretty blonde.

She was sure he had. Why wouldn't he? He was a healthy, adult man. The kind who had apparently had a fake ID, so very likely a bad-boy type. Meaning that an impromptu one-night stand probably wouldn't bother him at all.

Heck, it had probably been why he was at the bar.

Her stomach felt like acid by the time she walked into the GrayBear Construction building.

The acidic feeling didn't improve when she saw that Joshua was already sitting there drinking a cup of coffee in the waiting room.

"What are you doing here?" she asked, then kicked the door shut with her foot and made her way over to the coffeemaker.

"Good morning."

"Shouldn't you be home having breakfast with your wife and kids?"

"I would be, but Danielle has an OB appointment later this morning." Joshua's wife was pregnant, and he was ridiculously happy about it. And Faith was happy for him. Two of her sisters-in-law were currently pregnant. Danielle very newly so, and Poppy due soon. Mia and Devlin seemed content to just enjoy each other for now.

Her brothers were happy. Faith was happy for them.

It was weird to be the last one so resolutely single, though. Even with her dating life so inactive, she had never imagined she would be the last single sibling in her family.

"I need to be at the appointment," he said. "She's getting an ultrasound."

"I see. So you came here to get work done early?"

"I've been here since six."

"I guess I can't scowl at you for that."

"Why are you scowling at all?"

She didn't say anything, and instead, she checked her buzzing text. It was from Levi. Just his address. Nothing more. It was awfully early. If he had a late night, would he be up texting her?

Maybe he's just still up.

She wanted to snarl at that little inner voice.

"You busy today?" Joshua asked casually.

"Not really. I have some schematics to go over. Some designs to do. Emails to send." She waved a hand. "A meeting later."

He frowned. "I don't have you down for a meeting."

Great. She should have known her PR brother would want to know what meeting she would be going out for.

"It's not like a work meeting. It's like, for…a school talk." She stumbled over the lie, and immediately felt guilty.

"No school contacted me. Everything is supposed to go through me."

"I can handle community work in the town of Copper Ridge, Joshua. It's not like this is Seattle. And there's not going to be press anywhere asking me stupid questions or trying to trip me up. It's just Copper Ridge."

"Still."

The door opened and Isaiah came in, followed by his wife, Poppy, who was looking radiant in a tight, knee-length dress that showed off the full curve of her rounded stomach. They were holding hands, with their fingers laced together, and the contrast in their skin tones was beautiful—it always ignited a sense of artistic pleasure in Faith whenever she saw them. Well, and in general, seeing Isaiah happy made her feel that way. He was a difficult guy. Hard to understand, and seemingly emotionless sometimes.

But when he looked at Poppy… There was no doubt he was in love.

And no doubt that his wife was in love right back.

"Good morning," Isaiah said.

"Did you know Faith had a meeting with one of the schools today to give some kind of community-service talk?" Joshua launched right in. The dickhead.

"No," Isaiah said looking at her. "You really need to clear these things with us."

"Why?"

"That's not on my schedule," Poppy said, pulling out her phone and poking around the screen.

"Don't start acting like my brothers," Faith said to her sister-in-law.

"It's my job to keep track of things," Poppy insisted.

"This is off the books," Faith said. "I'm allowed to have something that's just me. I'm an adult."

"You're young," Joshua said. "You're incredibly successful. Everyone wants a piece of that, and you can't afford to give out endless pieces of yourself."

She huffed and took a drink of her coffee. "I can manage, Joshua. I don't need you being controlling like this."

"The company functions in a specific way—"

"But my life doesn't. I don't need to give you an accounting of everything I do with my time. And not everything is work-related."

She spun on her heel and walked down the hall and, for some reason, was immediately hit with a flashback from last night. Levi didn't talk to her like she was a child. Levi almost…flirted with her. That was what last night had been like. Like flirting.

The idea gave her a little thrill.

But there was no way Levi had been flirting with… her. He had been flirting with that pretty blonde.

Faith made sure the door to her office was shut, then she opened up her office drawer, pulling out the mirror she kept in there, that she didn't often use. Just quick checks before meetings. And not to make sure she looked attractive—to make sure she didn't look twelve.

She tilted her chin upward, then to the side, examining her reflection. It was almost absurd to think of him wanting to flirt with her. It wasn't that she was unattractive, it was just that she was…plain.

She had never really cared. Not really.

She could look a little less plain when she threw on some makeup, but then, when she did that, her goal was to look capable and confident, and old enough to be entrusted with the design of someone's house. Not to be pretty.

She twisted her lips to the side, then moved them back, making a kiss face before relaxing again. Then she sighed and put the mirror back in her drawer. It wasn't that she cared. She was a professional. And she wasn't going to… act on any weird feelings she had.

Even if they were plausible.

It was just… When she had talked to Levi last night she had left feeling like a woman. And then she had come into work this morning and her brothers had immediately reset her back to the role of little girl.

She thought about that so effectively that before she knew it, it was time for her to leave to go to Levi's place.

She pulled another bag out of her desk drawer—her makeup bag—and made the snap decision to go for an entirely different look, accomplished with much internet searching for daytime glamour and an easy tutorial. Then she fluffed her hair, shaking it out and making sure the curls looked a little bit tousled.

She threw the bag back into her desk and stood, swaggering out of her office, where she was met by Isaiah, who jerked backward and made a surprised sound.

"What?" she asked.

"You look different."

She waved a hand. "I thought I would try something new."

"You're going to give a talk at one of the…schools?"

"Yes," she said.

"Which school?" he pressed.

She made an exasperated sound. "Why do you need to know?" He said nothing, staring at her with his jaw firmed up. "You need to know because you need it to be in Poppy's planner, because if it's not in Poppy's planner it will feel incomplete to you, is that it?"

She'd long since given up trying to understand her brother's particular quirks. He had them. There was no sense fighting against them. She was his sister, so sometimes she poked at them, rather than doing anything to help him out. That was the way the world worked, after all.

But she'd realized as she'd gotten older that he wasn't being inflexible to be obnoxious. It was something he genuinely couldn't help.

"Yes," he responded, his tone flat.

If he was surprised that she had guessed what the issue was, he didn't show it. But then, Isaiah wouldn't.

"Copper Ridge Elementary," she said, the lie slipping easily past her lips, and she wondered who she was.

A *woman*. That's who she was.

A woman who had made an executive decision about her own career and she did not need her brothers meddling in it.

And her makeup wasn't significant to anything except that she had been sitting there feeling bad about herself and there was no reason to do that when she had perfectly good eyeliner sitting in her desk drawer.

"Thank you," he said.

"Are we done? Can you add it to the calendar and pacify yourself and leave me alone?"

"Is everything okay?" he asked, the question uncharacteristically thoughtful.

"I'm fine, Isaiah. I promise. I'm just… Joshua is right. I've been working a lot. And I don't feel like the solution is to do less. I think it might be…time that I took some initiative, make sure I'm filling my time with things that are important to me."

Of course, she was lying about it being schoolchildren, which made her feel slightly guilty. But not guilty enough to tell the truth.

Isaiah left her office then, to update the planner, Faith assumed. And Faith left shortly after.

She put the address to Levi's house in her car's navigation system and followed the instructions, which led her on much the same route she had taken to get up the mountain to meet him the first time, at the building site. It appeared that his rental property was on the other side of that mountain, on a driveway that led up the opposite side that wound through evergreen trees and took her to a beautiful, rustic-looking structure.

It was an old-fashioned, narrow A-frame with windows that overlooked the valley below. She appreciated it, even if it wasn't something she would ever have put together.

She had a fondness for classic, cozy spaces.

Though her designs always tended toward the open and the modern, she had grown up in a tiny, yellow farmhouse that she loved still. She loved that her parents still lived there in spite of the financial successes of their children.

Of course, Levi's house was several notches above the little farmhouse. This was quite a nice place, even if it was worlds apart from a custom home.

She had been so focused on following the little rabbit trails of thought on her way over that she hadn't noticed the tension she was carrying in her stomach. But as soon as she parked and turned off the engine, she seemed to be entirely made of that tension.

She could hardly breathe around it.

She had seen him outside, out in the open. And she had talked to him in a bar. But she had never been alone indoors with him before.

Not that it mattered. At all.

She clenched her teeth and got out of the car, gathering her bag that contained her sketchbook and all her other supplies. With the beat of each footstep on the gravel drive, she repeated those words in her head.

Not that it mattered.

Not that it mattered.

She might be having some weird thoughts about him, but he certainly wasn't having them about her.

She could only hope that the blonde had vacated before Faith's arrival.

Why did the thought of seeing her here make Faith feel sick? She couldn't answer that question.

She didn't even *know* the guy. And she had never been jealous of anyone or anything in her life. Okay, maybe vague twinges of jealousy that her brothers had found people to love. Or that Hayley had a husband who loved her. That Mia had found someone. And the fact that Mia's someone was Faith's brother made the whole thing a bit inaccessible to her.

But those feelings were more like…envy. This was different. This felt like a nasty little monster on her back that had no right to be there.

She steeled herself, and knocked on the door. And waited.

When the door swung open, it seemed to grab hold of her stomach and pull it along. An intense, sweeping sensation rode through her.

There he was.

Today, he'd traded in the black T-shirt and hat from the last couple of days for white ones.

The whole look was…beautiful and nearly absurd. Because he was *not* a white knight, far from it. And she wasn't innocent enough to think that he was.

But there was something about the way the light color caught hold of those blue eyes and reflected the color even brighter that seemed to steal every thought from her head. Every thought but one.

Beautiful.

She was plain. And this man was *beautiful*.

Oh, not pretty. Scars marred his face and a hard line went through his chin, keeping him from being symmetrical. Another one slashed his top lip. And even then, the angles on his face were far too sharp to be anything so insipid as pretty.

Beautiful.

"Come on in," he said, stepping away from the door.

She didn't know why, but she had expected a little more conversation on the porch. Maybe to give her some time to catch her breath. Sadly, he didn't give it to her. So she found herself following his instructions and walking into the dimly lit entry.

"It's not that great," he said of his surroundings, lifting a shoulder.

"It's cozy," she said.

"Yeah, I'm kind of over cozy. But the view is good."

"I can't say that I blame you," she said, following his lead and making her way into the living area, which was open. The point from the house's A-frame gave height to the ceiling, and the vast windows lit the entire space. The furniture was placed at the center of the room, with a hefty amount of space all around. "That must've been really difficult."

"Are you going to try to absorb details about my taste by asking about my personal life? Because I have to tell you, my aesthetic runs counter to where I've spent the last five years."

"I understand that. And no, it wasn't a leading question. I was just...commenting."

"They started the investigation into my wife's disappearance when you were about eighteen," he said. "And while you were in school I was on house arrest, on trial. Then I spent time behind bars. In that time, you started your business and... Here you are."

"A lot can happen in five years."

"It sure can. Or a hell of a lot of nothing can happen. That's the worst part. Life in a jail cell is monotonous. Things don't change. An exciting day is probably not a good thing. Because it usually means you got stabbed."

"Did you ever get—" her stomach tightened "—stabbed?"

He chuckled, then lifted up his white T-shirt, exposing a broad expanse of tan skin. Her brain processed things in snatches. Another tattoo. A bird, stretched across his side, and then the shifting and bunching of well-defined muscles. Followed by her registering that there was a sprinkling of golden hair across that skin. And then, her eye fell to the raised, ugly scar that was just above the tattooed bird's wing.

"Once," he said.

He pushed his shirt back down, and Faith shifted uncomfortably, trying to settle the feeling that the bird had peeled itself right off his skin and somehow ended up in her stomach, fluttering and struggling for freedom.

She looked away. "What happened?"

She put her hand on her own stomach, trying to calm her response. She didn't know if that intense, unsettled feeling was coming from her horror over what had happened to him, or over the show of skin that had just occurred.

If it was the skin, she was going to be very disappointed in herself and in her hormones. Because the man had just told her he'd been stabbed. Responding to his body was awfully base. Not to mention insensitive.

"I made the man who did it regret that he'd ever seen me." Suddenly, there was nothing in those ice-blue eyes but cold. And she didn't doubt what he said. Not at all.

"I see."

"You probably don't. And it's for the best. No, I didn't kill him. If I had killed him, I would still be in prison." He sat down in a chair that faced the windows. He rested his arms on the sides, the muscles there flexing as he moved his fingers, clenching them into fists. "But a brawl like that going badly for a couple of inmates? That's easy enough to ignore. I got a few stitches because of a blade. He got a few more because of my fists. People learned quickly not to mess with me."

"Apparently," she said, sitting down on the couch across from him, grateful for the large, oak coffee table between them. "Is any of this furniture yours?"

"No," he responded.

"Good," she replied. "Not that there's anything wrong with it, per se. But—" she knocked on the table "—if you were married to a particular piece it might make it more difficult, design-wise. I prefer to have total freedom."

"I find that in life I prefer to have total freedom," he said, the corner of his mouth quirking upward.

A rash of heat started at Faith's scalp and prickled

downward. "Of course. I didn't mean... You know that I didn't..."

"Calm down," he said. "I'm not that easily offended. Unless you stab me."

"Right," she responded. She fished around in her bag until she came up with her notepad. "We should talk more about what you have in mind. Let's start with the specifics. How big do you want the house to be?"

"Big," he replied. "It's a massive lot. The property is about fifty acres, and that cleared-out space seems like there's a lot of scope there."

"Ten thousand square feet?"

"Sure," he responded.

She put her pen over the pad. "How many bedrooms?"

"I should only need one."

"If you don't want more than one, that's okay. But... guests?"

"The only people who are going to be coming to my house are going to be staying in my bed. And even then, not for the whole night."

She cleared her throat. "Right." She tapped her pen against the side of her notebook. "You know, you're probably going to want more bedrooms."

"In case of what? Orgies? Even then, we'd need one big room."

"All right," she said. "If you want an unprecedented one-bedroom, ten-thousand-square-foot house, it's up to you." She fought against the blush flooding her cheeks, because this entire conversation was getting a little earthy for her. And it was making her picture things. Imagining him touching women, and specifically the blonde from last night, and she just didn't need that in her head.

"I wasn't aware I had ordered judgment with my custom home. I thought I ordered an entirely custom home to be done to my specifications."

She popped up her head. Now, this she was used to. Arrogant men who hired her, and then didn't listen.

"You did hire me to design a custom home, but presumably, you wanted my design to influence it. That means I'm going to be giving input. And if I think you're making a decision that's strange or stupid I'm going to tell you. I didn't get where I am by transcribing plans that come from the heads of people who have absolutely no training. If there's one thing I understand, it's buildings. It's design. Homes. I want to take the feeling inside of you and turn it into something concrete. Something real. And I will give you one bedroom if that's what you really want. But if you want a computer program to design your house, then you can have no feedback. I am not a computer program. I'm an…artist."

Okay, that was pushing it a lot further than she usually liked to go. But he was annoying her.

And making her feel hot.

It was unforgivable.

"A mouthy one," he commented.

She sniffed. "I know my value. And I know what I do well."

"I appreciate that quality in…anyone."

"Then appreciate it when I push back. I'm not doing it just for fun."

"If it will make you feel better you can put a few bedrooms in."

"There will definitely be room," she said. "Anyway, think of your resale value."

"Not my concern," he said.

"You never know. You might care about it someday." She cleared her throat. "Now, bathrooms?"

"Put down the appropriate number you think there should be. Obviously, you want me to have multiple bedrooms, I would assume there is an appropriate bathroom number that coincides with that."

"Well, you're going to want a lot. For the orgies." She bit her tongue after she said the words.

"Yeah, true. The last thing you want is for everyone to need a bathroom break at once and for there not to be enough."

She took a deep breath, and let it out slowly. The fact of the matter was, this conversation was serving a bigger purpose. She was forming a lot of ideas about him. Not actually about orgies, but about the fact that he was irreverent. That there was humor lurking inside him, in spite of the darkness. Or maybe in part because of it. That he was tough. Resilient.

That things glanced off him. Like hardship, and knife blades.

A small idea began to form, then expanded into the sorts of things she had been thinking when they had first met. How she could use curves, angles and lines to keep from needing doors, but to also give a sense of privacy, without things feeling closed off.

"Can you stand up?" she asked.

She knew it was kind of an odd question, but she wanted to see where his line of sight fell. Wanted to get an idea of how he would fill the space. He wasn't a family man. His space was going to be all about him. And he had made it very clear that was what he wanted.

She needed to get a sense of him.

"Sure," he responded, pushing himself up onto his feet, arching an eyebrow.

She walked around him, made her way to the window, followed where she thought his line of sight might land. Then she turned to face him, obscuring his view.

"What are you doing?"

"I'm just trying to get a sense for how a room will work for you. For where your eye is going to fall when you look out the window."

"I can send you measurements."

She made a scoffing sound. "You're six-foot-three."

"I am," he said. "How did you guess?"

"I can visualize measurements pretty damn accurately. I'm always sizing up objects, lots, locations. That's what I do."

"It's still impressive."

"Well, I did have to see you stand before I could fully trust that I was right about your height."

"And how tall are you?"

She stretched up. "Five-two."

A smile curved his lips. "You wouldn't even be able to reach things in my house."

"It's no matter. I can reach things in mine."

"How would you design a house for two people with heights as different as ours?"

She huffed out a laugh, her stomach doing an uncomfortable twist. "Well, obviously when it comes to space, preference has to be given to the taller person so they don't feel like things are closing in on them."

He nodded, his expression mock-serious. "Definitely."

"Mostly, with a family," she said, "which I design for quite a bit, I try to keep things mostly standard in height, with little modifications here and there that feel personal and special and useful to everyone."

"Very nice. Good deflection."

"I wasn't deflecting."

He crossed his arms, his gaze far too assessing. "You seemed uncomfortable."

"I'm not."

"You would want space for a big bed."

"I would?" Her brain blanked. Hollowed out completely.

"If you were designing a room for a man my size. Even if the woman was small."

She swallowed, her throat suddenly dry. "I suppose so."

"But then, I figure there's never a drawback to a big bed."

"I have a referral I can give you for custom furniture," she said, ignoring the way her heart was thundering at the base of her throat, imagining all the things that could be done in a very large bed.

In gauzy terms. Seeing as she had no actual, real-world experience with that.

"I may take you up on that offer," he said, his words like a slow drip of honey.

"Well, good. That's just…great. It's a custom…sex palace." She pretended to write something down, all while trying to hide the fact her face was burning.

"No matter what it sounds like," he said, "I'm not actually asking you for a glorified brothel. Though, I'm not opposed to that being a use. But I want this house to be for me. And I want it to be without limits. I'm tired of being limited."

Her heart twisted. "Right. I—I understand."

She sucked in a sharp breath, and went to move past him, but he spoke again, and his voice made her stop, directly in front of him. "I shared a cell with, at minimum, one other person for the last five years. Everything was standard. Everything. And then sized down. Dirty.

Uncomfortable. A punishment. I spent five years being punished for something I didn't do."

She tilted up her face, and realized that she was absurdly close to him. That she was a breath away from his lips. "Now you need your reward."

"That I do."

His voice went low, husky. She felt…unsteady on her feet. Like she wanted to lean in and press her lips to his.

She should move. She was the one who had placed herself right there in front of him. She was the one who had miscalculated. But she wasn't moving. She was still standing there. She couldn't seem to make herself shift. She licked her lips, and she saw his gaze follow the motion. His eyes were hot again.

And so was she. All over.

She was suddenly overcome by the urge to reach out her hand and touch that scar that marred his chin. The other one that slashed through his lip.

To push her hand beneath his shirt and touch that scar he had shown her earlier.

That thought was enough to bring her back to earth. To bring her back to her senses.

She took a step back, a metallic tang filling her mouth. Humiliation. Fear.

"You know," he said slowly. "They lock men like me up. That's a pretty good indication you should probably keep your distance."

"You didn't do anything," she said.

"That doesn't mean I'm not capable of doing some very bad things." His eyes were hot, so hot they burned. And she should move away from him, but she wasn't.

Heaven help her, she wasn't.

She tried to swallow, but her mouth was so dry her

tongue was frozen in place. "Is that a warning? Or a threat?"

"Definitely a warning. For now." He turned away from her and faced the window. "If you listen to it, it'll never have to be a threat."

"Why?"

What she felt right now was a strange kind of emotion. It wasn't anger; it wasn't even fear. It was just a strange kind of resolve. Her brothers already treated her like a child who didn't know her own mind—she wasn't about to let this man do the same thing. Let him issue warnings as if she didn't understand exactly who she was and what she wanted.

She might not know who he was. But she damn well knew who she was.

And she hadn't even done anything. Maybe she wouldn't. Maybe she never would.

But maybe she wanted to, and if she did, the consequences would be on her. It wouldn't be for anyone else to decide.

Least of all this man. This stranger.

"Little girl," he said, his voice dripping with disdain. "If you have to ask why, then you definitely need to take a step back."

Little girl.

No. She wouldn't have this man talk down to her. She had it all over her life, from well-meaning people who loved her. People whose opinions she valued. She wasn't going to let him tell her who she was or what she wanted. To tell her what she could handle.

She didn't step back. She stepped forward.

"I have a feeling you think you're a singular specimen, Levi Tucker. You, with your stab wound and your rough edges." Her heart was thundering, her hands shaking, but she wasn't going to step away. She wasn't going to do what he wanted or expected. "You're not. You're just like every other man I've ever come into contact with. You think you know more than me simply because you're older, or maybe because you have a—a *penis*."

She despised herself for her stutter, but as tough as she was trying to be, she couldn't utter that word a foot away from a man. Not effortlessly. She sucked in a sharp breath. "I'm not exactly sure what gives men such an unearned sense of power. But whatever the reason, you think it's acceptable to talk down to me. Without acknowledging the fact that I have navigated some incredibly difficult waters. They would be difficult for *anyone*, much less someone my age. I'm a lot harder and more filled with resolve than most people will ever be. I don't do warnings or threats. *You* might do well to remember that."

He reached out, the move lightning-fast, and grabbed hold of her wrist. His grip was strong, his hands rough. "And I don't take lectures from prim little misses in pencil skirts. Maybe you'd do well to remember that."

Lightning crackled between them, at the source of his touch, but all around them, too. She was so angry at him. And judging by the fire in his eyes, he was mad at her, too.

She arched forward, and he held her fast, his eyes never leaving hers.

"Do they offer a lot?" she asked. "Prim little misses, I mean. To lecture you?"

"I can't say any of them have ever been able to bring themselves to get this close to me."

She reached out, flexing her fingers, then curled them into a fist, before resting her fingers flat onto his chest. She could feel his heartbeat raging beneath her hand.

She could feel the rhythm echoed in her own labored breathing.

This was insane. She'd never…*ever* touched a man like this before. She'd never wanted to. And she didn't know what kind of crazy had taken over her body, or her mind right then.

She only knew that she wanted to keep touching him. That she liked the way it felt to have him holding tightly to her wrist.

That she relished the feeling of his heartbeat against her skin.

He smelled good. Like the pine trees and the mountain air, and she wondered if he'd been outside before she'd come over.

A man who couldn't be contained by walls. Not now.

And her literal job was to create a beautiful new cage for him.

She suddenly felt the urge to strip him of everything. All his confines. All his clothes. To make him free.

To be free with him.

The urge was strong—so strong—she was almost shocked to find she hadn't begun to pull at his T-shirt.

But what would she even do if she…succeeded?

He released his hold then, but she could still feel his touch lingering long after he'd taken away his hand. She felt dazed, thrown.

Stunned to discover the world hadn't collapsed around them in those moments that had seemed like hours, but had actually been a breath.

"You should go."

She should. She really, really should.

But she didn't want him to know he'd scared her.

It's not even him that scares you. You're scaring yourself.

"I'm going to go sketch," she said, swallowing hard. "This has been very enlightening."

"If your plan is to go off and design me a prison cell now…"

"No," she said. "I'm a professional. But trust me, I've learned quite a bit about you. And my first question to you wasn't leading, not necessarily. But everything that we've discussed here? It will definitely end up being fodder for the design. You're truly going to be in a prison of your own making by the time I'm through, Levi. So you best be sure you like what you're using to build it."

She didn't know where she got the strength, or the wit for all of that. And by the time she turned on her heel and walked out of the A-frame, heading back to her car, she was breathing so hard she thought she might collapse.

But she didn't.

No, instead she got in her car and drove away, that same rock-solid sense of resolve settling in her stomach now as had been there only a moment before.

Attraction.

Was that what had just happened back there? Attraction to a man who seemed hell-bent on warning her off.

Why would he want to warn her off?

If he really did see her as a little girl, if he really did see her as someone uninteresting or plain, he wouldn't need to warn her away.

What he'd said about threats…

By the time she pulled back into GrayBear Construction, she wasn't hyperventilating anymore, but she was certain of one thing.

Levi Tucker was attracted to her, too.

She was not certain exactly what she was supposed to do with that knowledge.

She felt vaguely helpless knowing she couldn't ask anyone, either.

Her brothers would go on a warpath. Hayley would caution her. Mia would…well, Mia would tell Devlin, because Devlin was her husband and she wouldn't want to keep secrets from him.

Faith's network was severely compromised. For one moment that made her feel helpless. Then in the next…

It was her decision, she realized.

Whatever she did with this… It was her decision.

She wasn't a child. And she wasn't going to count on the network of people she was used to having around her to make the choice for her.

And she wasn't going to worry about what they might think.

Whatever she decided…

It would be her choice.

And whatever happened as a result… She would deal with the consequences.

The resolve inside of her only strengthened.

Chapter 6

He was back at the bar. Because there was nothing else to do. As of today, he was officially a divorced man, and he'd been without sex for five years.

And earlier today he had been about a breath away from taking little Miss Prim and Proper down to the ground and screwing them both senseless.

And he had already resolved that he wouldn't do that. He wouldn't *be* that.

His post-divorce celebration would not be with Faith Grayson. With her wide eyes and easy blush. And uncommon boldness.

He couldn't work out why she wasn't afraid of him. He had thought... A little, soft thing like her... The evidence of a knife fight and talk of prison, jokes about orgies... It all should have had a cowering effect on her.

It hadn't.

No, by the end of the interaction she'd only grown

bolder. And he couldn't for the life of him figure out how that worked.

She was fascinated by him. That much was clear. She might even think she wanted to have a little fun with some kind of bad-boy fantasy, but the little fool had no idea.

He was nobody's fantasy.

He was a potential nightmare, but that was it.

He flashed back to the way it had felt to wrap his hand around her wrist. Her skin soft beneath his. To the way she'd looked up at him, her breath growing choppy and fast.

Those fingertips on his chest.

Shit, he needed to get laid.

He ordered up a shot of whiskey and pounded it down hard, scanning the room, looking for a woman who might wipe the image of Faith Grayson from his mind.

Maybe Mindy would be back. Maybe they could pick up where they left off.

But as he looked around, his eye landed on a petite brunette standing in line for the mechanical bull. She was wearing a tight pair of blue jeans, and a fitted T-shirt, and when she turned, he felt like he'd been punched in the stomach.

Faith Grayson.

With that same mulish expression on her face she'd had when she'd left his house earlier.

The rider in front of her got thrown, and Faith rubbed her hands together, glaring at the mechanical beast with intensity. Then she marched up to it, and took her position.

She thrust her hips forward, wrapping one hand around the handle and holding the other up high over her head. She looked more like a ballerina than a bull rider. But her expression…

That was all fire.

He should look away. He sure as hell shouldn't watch as the mechanical bull began its forward motion, shouldn't watch the way Faith's eyes widened, and then the way her face turned determined as she gripped more tightly with one hand, and tensed her thighs around the beast, moving her hips in rhythm with it.

It didn't last long.

On the creature's second roll forward, Faith was unseated, her lips parting in an expression of shock as she flew forward and onto the mats below.

And before he could stop himself, he was on his feet, making his way across the space. She was on her back, her chin-length curls spread around her head like a halo on a church window. But her expression was anything but angelic.

"Are you okay?" he asked.

She looked up at him, and all the shock drained from her face, replaced instead by a spark of feral-looking rage. "What are you doing here?"

"What are you doing getting on the back of that thing?" He moved closer, ignoring the crowd of people looking on. "You clearly have no business doing it."

"It's not your business...what I have business doing or not doing. Stop trying to tell me what to do."

He put out his hand, offering to take hold of hers and help her up, but she ignored him, pushing herself into a sitting position and scrabbling to her feet.

"I'm fine," she said.

"I know you're fine," he returned. "It's not like I thought the thing was going to jump off its post and trample you to death. But it's also clear you're being an idiot."

"Well, look at the whole line of idiots," she said, indicating the queue of people. "I figured I would join in."

"Why exactly?"

"Because," she said. "Because I'm tired of everyone treating me like a kid. Because I'm tired of everyone telling me what to do. Do you know, that it was almost impossible for me to sneak away to our meeting today because my brothers need to know what I'm doing every second of every day. It's like they think I'm still fifteen years old."

He shrugged. "As I understand it, that's older brothers, to a degree."

"Are you an older brother?"

"No," he said. "Only child. But still, seems a pretty logical conclusion."

"Well, whatever. I went to boarding school from the time I was really young. Because there were more opportunities for me there then here. I lived away from my family, and somehow... Everyone is more protective of me. Like I didn't have to go make my own way when I was a kid." She shook her head. "I mean, granted, it was an all-girls boarding school, and it was a pretty cloistered environment. But still."

"Let me buy you a drink," he said, not quite sure why the offer slipped out.

You know.

He ignored that.

"I don't need you to buy me a drink," she said fiercely, storming past him and making her way to the bar. "I can buy my own drink."

"I'm sure you can. But I offered to do it. You should let me."

"Yeah, you have a lot of opinions about what I should and shouldn't do in a given moment, don't you?"

Still, when he ordered her a rum-and-Coke, she didn't argue. She took hold of it and leaned against the bar, angling toward him. His eyes dropped down to her breasts, a hard kick of lust making it difficult for him to breathe.

"What are you doing here?" He forced his gaze away from her breasts, to her face.

She narrowed her eyes. "I'm here to ride a mechanical bull and make a statement about my agency by doing so. Not to anyone but myself, mind you. It might be silly, but it is my goal. What's yours?"

"I'm here to get laid," he said, holding her eyes and not blinking. That should do the trick. That should scare her away.

Unless…

She tilted her head to the side. "Is that what you were here for last night?"

"Yes, ma'am," he responded.

Her lips twitched, and she lifted up her glass, averting her gaze. "How was she?" She took a sip of the rum-and-Coke.

"As it happens," he said, "I didn't go home with her."

She spluttered, then set down the glass on the bar and looked at him. She didn't bother to disguise her interest. Her curiosity. "Why?"

"Because I decided at the end of it all I wasn't really that interested. No one was more surprised by that than I was."

"She was beautiful," Faith said. "Why weren't you… into her?"

He firmed his jaw, looking Faith up and down. "That is the million-dollar question, honey."

That same thing that had stretched between them back at the house began to build again. It was like a physical force, and no matter that he told himself she was all wrong, his body seemed to disagree.

You dumbass. You want something harder than she

*can give. Something dirtier. You don't want to worry
about your partner. You want a partner who can handle herself.*

But then he looked back at Faith again, her cheeks
rosy from alcohol and the exertion of riding the bull, and
maybe from him.

He wanted her.

And there wasn't a damn thing he could do to change
that.

"I have a theory," Faith said.

"About?"

"About why you didn't want her." She sucked her straw
between her lips and took a long sip, then looked up
at him, as if fortified by her liquid courage. "Is it because...?" She tilted her chin upward, her expression defiant. "Are you attracted to me, Levi?"

He gritted his teeth, the blood in his body rushing
south, answering the question as soon as she asked it.
"You couldn't handle me, baby girl."

"That's not what I asked you."

"But it's an important thing for you to know."

She shrugged her shoulders. "That's what you think.
Again, putting you on the long list of men who think
they know what I should and shouldn't do, or want, or
think about."

He leaned in and watched as the color in her cheeks
deepened. As that crushed-rose color bloomed more fully.
She was playing the part of seductress—at least, in her
funny little way—but she wasn't as confident as she was
hoping to appear. That much he could tell.

"Do you have any idea what I would do to you?" he
asked.

She wrinkled her nose. "I would assume...the normal
sort of thing."

He chuckled. "Sweetheart, I was locked up for five years. I'm not sure I remember what the normal sort of thing is anymore. At this point, all I have to go on is animal instinct. And I'm not totally sure you should feel comfortable with that."

She shifted, and he noticed her squeezing her thighs together. The sight sent a current of lust straight through his body. Dammit. He was beginning to think he had underestimated her.

"That still isn't what I asked you," she said softly. She looked up at him, her expression coy as she gazed through her thick lashes. "Do you want me?"

"I'd take you," he said through gritted teeth. "Hard. And believe me, you'd like it. But I don't want *you*, sweetheart. I just want. It's been a hell of a long time for me, Faith. I'm all about the sex, not the woman. I'm not sure that's the kind of man you should be with."

She squared her shoulders and looked at him full on, but the color in her cheeks didn't dissipate. "What kind of man do you think I should be with?"

He could see it. Like a flash of lightning across the darkness in his soul. A man who would get down on one knee and ask Faith to be his. Have babies with her. Live with her, in a house with a lot of bedrooms for all those babies.

A man she could take to family dinners. Hold hands with.

A man who could care.

That was what she deserved.

"One who will be nice to you," he said, moving closer. "One you can take home to your family." He cupped her cheek, swept his thumb over her lower lip and felt her tremble beneath his touch. "A man who will make love to you." She tilted her face upward, pressing that tempting mouth more firmly against his thumb. "All I can do is screw you, sweetheart."

She looked down, then back up. And for once, she didn't have a comeback.

"You deserve a man who will marry you," he continued.

That mobilized her. "Get married? And then what? Have children? I'm twenty-five years old and my career is just starting to take off. Why would I do anything to interrupt that? Why would you think that's what I'm looking for right now? I have at least ten years before worrying about any of that. A few affairs in the meantime…"

He snorted. "Affairs. That sounds a hell of a lot more sophisticated and fancy than what I've got in mind, princess."

"What have I ever done to make you think I'm a princess? To make you think I need you to offer more than what I'm standing here showing interest in? You don't have access to my secret heart, Levi."

"If you had any sense in your head, you would walk out of this bar and forget we had this conversation. Hell, if you had any sense at all you would forget today happened. Just do the job I hired you to do and walk away. My wife let me go to jail for her murder while she was alive. And whatever the authorities think, whatever she says…"

He bit down hard, grinding his teeth together. "She was going to let me rot there, in a jail cell. While letting me think she was dead. Do you know… I grieved her, Faith. I didn't know she was in hiding. I didn't know she had left me on her own feet. All I knew was that she was gone, and that I hadn't killed her. But I believed some other bastard had. My motivation while I was in prison was to avenge my wife, and in the end? She's the one who did this to me." He laughed hard, the sound void of humor. "Love is a lie. Marriage is a joke. And I'm not going to change my mind about that."

"Marriage is an impediment to what I want," Faith said. "And I'm not going to change my mind about that. You're acting like you know what I want. What I should want. But you don't."

"What do you want, sweetheart? Because all I've got to give you is a few good orgasms."

She drew in a sharp breath, blinking a couple of times. Then she looked around the bar, braced herself on the counter and drew up on her toes as high as she could go, pressing a kiss to the lower corner of his mouth. When she pulled away, her eyes were defiant.

If she was playing chicken with him, if she was trying to prove something, she was going to regret it. Because he was not a man who could be played with.

Not without consequences.

He wrapped his arm around her waist, crossed her to his chest and hauled her up an extra two inches so their mouths could meet more firmly.

And that's when he realized he had made a mistake.

He had been of a mind that he would scare her off, but what he hadn't anticipated was the way his own control would be so tenuous.

He had none. None at all.

Because he hadn't been this close to a woman in more than five years. And he'd imagined his wife a victim. Kidnapped or killed. And when he'd thought of her his stomach had turned. And not knowing what had happened to Alicia…

It hadn't felt right to think of anyone else.

So for most of those five years in prison he hadn't even had a good go-to fantasy. It had been so long since he'd been with a woman who hadn't betrayed him, and it was hard for him to remember a woman other than his wife.

But now... Now there was Faith.

And she burned brighter, hotter, than the anger in his veins. He forgot why he had been avoiding this. Forgot everything but the way she tasted.

It was crazy.

Of all the women he could have touched, he shouldn't touch her. She worked for him. He had hired her to design his house and he supposed that made this the worst idea of all.

But she was kissing him back as though it didn't matter.

Maybe he was wrong about her. Maybe she made a habit of toying with her rich and powerful clients. Maybe that was part of why she'd gotten to where she was.

No skin off his nose if it was true. And it suited him in many ways, because that meant she knew the rules of the game.

Because you need justification for the fact that you're doing exactly what you swore to yourself you wouldn't?

Maybe his reaction had nothing to do with his ex-wife making him into a monster. Maybe it had everything to do with Faith making him a beast.

Uncontrolled and ravenous for everything he could get.

He cupped her chin, forcing her lips apart, and thrust his tongue deep. And she responded. She responded beautifully. Hot and slick and enthusiastic.

"You better give an answer and stick to it," he said when they pulled away, his eyes intent on hers. "Say yes or no now. Because once we leave this bar—"

"Yes," she said quickly, a strange, frantic energy radiating from her. "Yes. Let's do it."

"This isn't a business deal, honey."

"That's why I didn't shake your hand." She sounded breathless, and a little bit dazed, and damn it all if it wasn't a thousand times more intoxicating than Mindy's careful seduction from last night.

"Then let's go." Now he was in a damn hurry. To get out of here before she changed her mind. Before he lost control completely and took her against a wall.

"What about my car?" she asked.

"I'll get you back to it."

"Okay," she said.

He put down a twenty on the bar, and ignored the way the bartender stared at him, hard and unfriendly-like, as though the man had an opinion about what was going on.

"Tell the man you're with me," he said.

Faith's eyes widened, and then she looked between him and the bartender. "I'm with him," she said softly.

The bartender's expression relaxed a fraction. But only a fraction.

Then Levi took her hand and led her out into the night. The security lights in the lot were harsh, bright blue, and she still looked beautiful beneath them. That was as close to poetry as he was going to get. Because everything else was all fire. Fire and need, and the sense that if he didn't get inside her in the next few minutes, he was going to explode.

"Levi..."

He grabbed her and pulled her to him, kissing her again, dark and fierce and hard. "Last chance," he said, because he wasn't a gentleman, but he wasn't a monster, either.

"Yes."

Chapter 7

Faith felt giddy. Drunk on her own bravery. Her head was swimming, arousal firing through her veins. She had never felt like this before. Ever. She had gone on a couple of dates, all of which had ended with sad, sloppy kisses at the door and no desire at all on her part for it to go any further.

She had begun to think the only thing she was really interested in was her career. That men were irrelevant, and if men were, then sex was, too. She had just figured that was how she was. That maybe, when the time came, and she was ready to settle down, or ready to pull back on her career, she would find her priorities would naturally restructure and sex would suddenly factor in. But she hadn't worried about it.

And now… It wasn't a matter of making herself interested. No. It was a matter of life and death. At least it felt like it might be.

He took her hand to his heart, and helped her into his truck. She didn't say a word as he started the engine and they pulled out of the parking lot.

Her heart was thundering, and she was seriously questioning her sanity. To go from her first make-out session to sex in only a few minutes might not be the best idea, but it might also be…the only way. She was half out of her mind with desire, just from feeling his lips on hers. Even so, she honestly couldn't imagine wanting more than sex.

This man, her secret.

It had been almost funny when he had said something about taking a man home to meet her family. There would be no way she could ever take him home to meet her parents.

His frame would be so large and ridiculous in that tiny farmhouse. The ice in his veins, the scars on his soul, so much more pronounced in that warm, sweet kitchen of her mother's.

No, Faith didn't want to take him home. She wanted him to take her to bed.

And maybe it was crazy. But she had never intended to save herself for anything in particular. Anything but desire, really.

And this was the first time she had ever felt it.

What better way to get introduced to sex, really? An older man who knew exactly what he was doing. Because God knew she didn't.

And for once, she wasn't going to think. She wasn't going to worry about the future, wasn't going to worry about anyone else's opinion, because no one was ever going to know.

Levi Tucker was already her dirty secret in her professional life. Why couldn't he be her personal one, too?

Suddenly, he jerked the car off the highway, taking it

down a narrow, dirt road and into the woods. "This isn't the way to your house."

"Can't wait," he growled.

"What's this?" she asked, her heart pounding in her chest.

"A place I know about from way back. Back when I used to get in trouble around these parts."

Get in trouble.

That's what she was about to do. Get in trouble with him.

She felt…absolutely elated. She had gone out to the bar tonight to do *something*. To shake things up. She had seen riding the bull as a kind of kickoff tour for her mini Independence Day.

Oh, it wasn't one she was going to flaunt in front of her brothers or anything like that. It was just acknowledging that sense of resolve from earlier. She was going to have something that was just hers. Choices that were hers.

It had all started with taking this job, she realized. So, it was fitting that the rest of it would involve Levi, too.

"Okay," she said.

"Still good?"

She gritted her teeth, and then made a decision, feeling much bolder than she should have. She moved her hand over and pressed it against his thigh. He was hard, hot. Then she slid her hand farther up, between his legs, capturing his length through denim. He was big. Oh, Lord, he was big. She hadn't realized… Well, that just went to show how ignorant she was. Maybe he was average, she didn't know. But it was a hell of a lot bigger than she had imagined it might be.

It was going to be inside her.

Her internal muscles clenched, and she realized that rather than fear, she was overcome completely by excitement. Maybe that was the perk of waiting twenty-five years to lose your virginity. She was past ready.

He growled, jerking his car off the road and to a turn-out spot next to the trees. Then he unbuckled his seat belt and moved over to the center of the bench seat, undoing her belt and hauling her into his lap. He kissed her, deep and hard, matching what had happened back at the bar.

Her head was spinning, her whole body on fire.

He stripped off her T-shirt, quickly and ruthlessly, his fingers deft on her bra. She didn't even have time to worry about it. Didn't have time to think. Her breasts were bare, and he was cupping them, sliding calloused thumbs over her nipples, teasing her, enticing her.

She felt like she was flying.

She wanted him to take her wherever this was going. She wanted him to take control. She was used to being the one in control. The one who knew what she was doing. She was a natural in her field, and that meant she always walked in knowing what she was doing. Being the novice was a strange, amazing feeling, and she had the sense that if she'd been with a man any less master-ful, it might feel diminishing.

Instead it just felt like—like a weight on her shoulders suddenly lifted. Because he was bearing responsibility for all these feelings of pleasure in her body. He was stoking the need, and soothing it just as quickly. But all the while, a deep, endless ache was building between her legs and she wanted… She needed… She didn't know.

But she knew that he knew. Oh, yes, he did.

He kissed her neck, cupping her head as he moved lower, as he captured one nipple between his lips and sucked her in deep. It was so erotic, so filthy, and she couldn't do anything but arch into his touch as he moved his attention to her other breast. He was fulfilling fantasies she hadn't even known she'd had.

She had just never…thought about doing such a thing. And here he was, not only making it seem appealing, but it was also as if she might die if she didn't have it.

He pulled his own shirt over his head, tugging her heart against his chest, his muscles, the hair there, adding delicious friction against her nipples, and she squirmed. He wrapped his arm tightly around her waist, cupped her head and laid her back, somehow managing to strip her of her jeans and panties in record time in the close confines of the truck. Then he took hold of the buckle on his belt, and she heard the rasp of fabric and metal as he worked the leather strap through, as he undid the zipper on his jeans.

She jumped when he pressed his hand between her thighs, moved his fingers through her slickness, drawing the moisture up over that sensitized bundle of nerves, then slid his thumb expertly back and forth, creating a kind of tension inside her she wasn't sure she could withstand.

"I'll make it last longer later," he said gruffly. "Promise."

But she didn't really understand what he meant, and when she heard the tearing of a plastic packet, she only dimly registered what was about to happen. Then he was kissing her again, and she didn't think. Until the blunt head of his arousal was pushing into her body, until he thrust hard and deep, a fierce, burning sensation claiming any of the pleasure she had felt a moment before.

She cried out, digging her fingernails into his shoulders, trying to blot out the pain that was rolling through her like a storm.

"Faith…"

She tensed up, turning her head away, freezing for a moment. "Don't say anything," she whispered.

"Sorry," he said, sinking more deeply into her, a groan on his lips. "You feel so damn good."

And that tortured admission did something to her, ignited something deep inside her that went past pain. That went past fear. The scary part was over. It was done. And the pain was already beginning to roll itself back.

"Don't stop," she whispered, curling her fingers around his neck and holding on as she shifted beneath him.

It was strange, this feeling. His body inside hers. How had she not realized? How intimate something like this would be?

Everybody talked about sex at university. Gave great proclamations about what they liked and what they didn't, had endless discussions about the *when*, the *why* and the *with who*. But no one had ever said sex made you feel like someone hadn't just entered your body, but your whole soul. No one had said that you would want to run away and draw closer at the same time.

No one had said that it would be a great, wrenching pain followed by a deep, strange sense of connection that seemed to bloom into desire again as he shifted his hips and arched into her.

She tested what it might feel like if she moved against him, too, and found that she liked it. With each and every thrust that he made into her body, animalistic sounds coming from deep inside of him, she met him. Until her body was slick with sweat—his or hers, she didn't know. Until that fierce need she had felt the first time he had kissed her was back. Until she thought she might die if she didn't get more of him.

Until she no longer wanted to run at all.

He growled, his hardness pulsing inside her as he froze above her, slamming back into her one last time. And then, a release broke inside her like a wave, and she found herself drowning. In pleasure. In him.

And when he looked at her, she suddenly felt small and fragile. Any sense of being resolute crumbled.

And much to her horror, a tear slid down her cheek.

She was crying. God in heaven, the woman was crying.

No. He wasn't going to think about God. Not right now. Because God had nothing to do with this. No, this was straight from hell, and he was one of the devil's chosen. There was no other way to look at it.

Not only had he taken her in his truck like a beast— a fancy justification for sidestepping the word *monster* if ever there was one—but she had also been a virgin.

And he hadn't stopped.

When he had hit that resistance, when he had seen that flash of pain on her face, he had waited only a moment before he kept on going. She'd lifted her hips, and he hadn't been able to do anything but keep going. Because she was beautiful. And he wanted her. More than beautiful, she was soft and delicate, and an indulgence.

And he hadn't had any of that for more than five years.

Sinking into her tight body had been a revelation. As much as a damnation.

"Damn it to hell," he muttered, straightening and pulling his pants back into place. He chucked the condom out the window, not really giving a damn what happened to it later.

"What?" she asked, her petite frame shivering, shaking, her arms wrapped tightly around her body, as though she was trying to protect herself.

Too little, too late.

"You know."

"I don't," she said, shrinking more deeply into the far corner of the truck, her pale figure cast into a soft glow by the moonlight. "I don't… I thought it was good."

Her voice was trembling, watery, and he could hear the sigh that she breathed out becoming a sob.

"You didn't tell me you were a virgin," he said, trying to keep the accusation out of his voice, because dammit, he had known. On some level, he had known. And he hadn't been put off by it all.

No, he had *told* himself to be put off by it. By her obvious innocence and inexperience. He had commanded himself not to be interested in it. To chase after someone more like him. Someone a little bit dark. Someone a little bit craven. But his body didn't want that.

Because his soul was a destroyer. A consumer of everything good and sweet.

Hadn't Alicia been sweet when he'd met her? Hadn't she transformed into something else entirely over their time together? How could he ignore the fact that he was the common denominator at the center of so many twisted scenarios in his life.

Him.

The one thing he could never fully remove from the equation unless he removed himself from the world.

"So what?" she asked, shuffling around in the car, undoubtedly looking for her clothes. "I knew that."

"I damn well didn't."

"What does it have to do with anything?"

"You told me you knew what you were doing."

"I did," she said, her voice shrinking even smaller. "I knew exactly what we were going to do." She made a soft, breathy laugh. "I mean, I didn't know that we were going to do it in the truck. I expected it to take a little bit…longer. But I knew we were going to have sex."

"You're crying."

"That's my problem," she said.

"No," he said, reaching across the space and dragging her toward him. He gripped her chin between his thumb and forefinger and gazed into her eyes. It was dark, but he could see the glitter in her gaze. Like the stars had fallen down from the sky and centered themselves in her. "Now it's my problem."

"It doesn't have to be. I made a choice. My lack of experience doesn't make it less my choice."

"Yes, it does. Because you didn't really know. I hurt you. And because you didn't tell me, I hurt you worse than I would have."

"Again, that's on me. I wanted to have sex with an older guy. One who knew what he was doing. I'm way too old to be a virgin, Levi. I never found someone I wanted to change that with, and then I met you and I wanted you. It seems simple to me."

"Simple."

The top of his head had just about blown off. Nothing about this seemed simple to him.

"Yes," she said.

"Little girl, I haven't had sex in more than five years. You don't want a man like me in bed with you. You want a nice man who has the patience to take time with your body."

"But I like *your* body. And I like the way it made mine feel."

"I hurt you," he pointed out.

She lifted a pale shoulder. "It felt good at the end."

"Doesn't matter. That's all I have. Rough and selfish. That's what I am. It's all I want to be."

"Well, I want to be my own person. I want to be someone who makes her own choices and doesn't give a damn what anyone else thinks. So maybe we're about perfect for each other right now."

"Right now."

"Yes," she said. "I don't know why you find it so hard to believe, but I really do know what I want. Do you think I'm going to fall in love with you, Levi?"

She spoke the words with such disdainful incredulity, and if he was a different man, with a softer heart—with a heart at all—he might've been offended. As it was, he found her open scorn almost amusing.

"Virgins fall in love with all kinds of assholes, sweetheart."

"Have you deflowered a lot of them?"

"No. I haven't been with a damn virgin since I was one."

"Then maybe calm down with your pronouncements." She was wiggling back into her jeans now, then pulling her top over her head. She hadn't bothered to put her bra back on. And he was the perverse bastard who took an interest in that.

"I'm a lot more experienced than you. Maybe you should recognize that my pronouncements come from a place of education."

"It's done," she said. "And you know what? It was fine. It was fine until this."

"I'll take you home."

"Take me back to my car," she said.

"I'd rather not drop you back in the parking lot at this hour."

"Take me back to my damn car," she said. "I don't want to arrange a ride later. I don't need my car sitting in the parking lot all night, where people can draw conclusions."

"You didn't mind that earlier."

"Well, earlier I didn't feel bad or ashamed about my choices, but you've gone and made that…it's different now. It's different."

If he had a conscience, he would have felt guilt over that. But it wasn't guilt that wracked his body now. It was rage.

Rage that the monster had won.

The rage had nothing to do with her. Nothing about the way it might impact her life. It was about him.

Maybe that was selfish. He didn't really know. Didn't really care, either.

"If you'd like to withdraw from the job, I understand," he said when they pulled back into the parking lot of Ace's bar.

"Hell, no," she said, her tone defiant. "I'm not losing this job. You don't get to ruin that, too."

"I wouldn't figure you'd want to work with me anymore."

"You think you know a lot about me. For a man who knows basically nothing. The whole…intimacy-of-sex thing is a farce. You have no idea who I am. You have no idea what I want, what I need. I will finish this job because I took it on. And when I said that I wanted you, when I said I wanted this, I knew we were going to continue working together."

"Suit yourself."

"None of this suits me."

She tumbled out of the truck and went to her car, and he waited until she was inside, until she got it started and began to pull out of the space, before he started heading back toward his place.

But it wasn't until he parked in front of his house that he realized she had left her bra and panties behind.

The two scraps of fabric seemed to represent the final shreds of his humanity.

He reached out and touched her bra, ran his thumb over the lace.

And he asked himself why the hell he was bothering to pull away now. She had been…a revelation. Soft and perfect and everything he'd ever wanted.

He wondered why the hell he was pretending he cared about being a man, when being a monster was so much easier.

Chapter 8

One thought kept rolling through Faith's mind as she sat at her desk and tried to attend to her work.

She wasn't a virgin anymore.

She had lost her virginity. In the back of a pickup truck.

Of all the unexpected turns of events that had occurred in her life, this was inarguably the *most* unexpected. She surely had not thought she would do that, ever.

Not the virginity thing. She had been rather sanguine about that. She had known sex would happen eventually, and there was no point in worrying about it.

But the pickup truck. She had really not seen herself as a do-it-in-a-pickup-truck kind of girl.

With a man like that.

If she actually sat and broke down her thoughts on what kind of man she had imagined she might be with, it wasn't him. Not even a little bit. Not even at all.

She had imagined she would find a man quite a bit like herself. Someone who was young, maybe. And understood what it was like to be ambitious at an early age. Someone who could relate to her. Her particular struggles.

But then, she supposed, that was more relationship stuff. And sex didn't require that two people be similar. Only that they ignited when they touched.

She certainly hadn't imagined it would be an ex-convict accused of murder who would light her on fire.

Make her come.

Make her cry.

Then send her away.

It had been a strange twelve hours indeed.

"Faith?" She looked up and saw Isaiah standing in the doorway. "I need estimates from you."

"Which estimates?" She blinked.

"The ones you haven't sent me yet," he said, being maddeningly opaque and a pain in the ass. He could just tell her.

She cleared her throat, tapping her fingers together. Hoping to buy herself some time. Or a clue. "Is there a particular set of estimates that you're waiting on?"

"If you have any estimates put together that I don't have, I would like them."

She realized that she didn't have any for him. And if she should…

That meant she had dropped the ball.

She never dropped the ball.

She had been working, full tilt, at this job for enough years now that she had anticipated the moment when she might drop the ball, but she hadn't. And now she had taken on this extra project, this work her brothers didn't know about, and she was messing up.

That isn't why...

No, it wasn't.

She was messing up because she felt consumed. Utterly and completely consumed by everything that was happening with Levi.

Levi Tucker was so much more than just an interesting architecture project.

It was the structure of the man himself that had her so invested. Not what she might build for him.

She wanted to see him again. Wanted to talk to him. Wanted to lie down in a bed with him, with the lights on so she could look at all his tattoos and trace the lines of them.

So she could know him.

Right. That makes sense. He's nothing like you thought you wanted. Why are you fixating?

A good question.

She didn't want him to be right. Right about virgins and how they fell in love as easy as some people stumbled while walking down the street.

"Faith?"

Isaiah looked concerned now.

"I'm fine," she said.

"You don't look fine."

"I am." She shifted, feeling a particular soreness between her legs and trying to hide the blush that bled into her cheeks. It was weird to be conscious of that while she was talking to her brother.

"Faith, no one has ever accused me of being particularly perceptive when it comes to people's emotions. But I do know you. I know that you're never late with project work. If all of this has become too much for you..."

"It isn't," she insisted. "I love what we do. I'm so proud of what we've built, Isaiah. I'm not ever going to do anything to compromise that. I think I might have overextended myself a little bit with…extra stuff."

"What kind of extra stuff?"

"Just…community work."

Getting screwed senseless for the first time in my life…

"You don't need to do that. Joshua can handle all of that. It's part of his job. You should filter it all through him. He'll help you figure out what you should say yes to, what you can just send a signed letter to…"

"I know. I know you'll both help me. But at some point… Isaiah, this is *my* life." She took a breath. "We are partners. And I appreciate all that you do. If I had to calculate the finances like you, I would go insane. My brain would literally leak out of my ears."

"It would not literally leak out of your ears."

She squinted. "You don't know that."

"I'm pretty confident that I do."

She shook her head. "Just don't worry about me. You have a life now. A really good one. I'm so happy for you and Poppy. I'm so excited for your baby, and for…everything. You've spent too many years working like a crazy person."

"Like a robot," Isaiah said, lifting his brow. "At least, that's what I've been told more than once."

"You're not a robot. You came here to check on me. That makes it obvious that you aren't. But, you also can't carry everything for me. Not anymore. It's just not… I don't need you to. It's okay."

"You know we worry. We worry because you're right. If it weren't for us…then you wouldn't be in this position."

She made a scoffing sound. "Thanks. But if it weren't for me you wouldn't be in this position, either."

"I know," he returned. "I mean, I would still be work-

ing in finance somewhere else. Joshua would be doing
PR. And you would no doubt be working at a big firm
somewhere. But it's what we could do together that has
brought our business to this level. And I think Joshua
and I worry sometimes that it happened really quickly
for you and we enabled that. So, we don't want to leave
it all resting on your shoulders now."

She swallowed hard. "I appreciate that. I do. But I
can handle it."

Isaiah nodded slowly and then turned and walked out
of her office.

She could handle all of this.

Her job, which encouraged her to open up some files
for her various projects and collect those estimates Isaiah
was asking for, and this new turn of events with Levi.

She was determined to finish the project. The idea of
leaving it undone didn't work for her. Not at all. Even if
he was being terrible.

*And you think you can be in the same room with him
and not feel like you're dying?*

She didn't know. She had just lost her virginity twelve
hours ago, and she had no idea what she was supposed
to do next.

Sitting at her desk and basking in that achievement
was about all she could do. It was lunchtime when she
got into her car and began to drive.

She had spent the rest of the morning trying to catch
up, and as soon as she got on the road her thoughts began
to wander. Back to what Levi had said to her last night.
All the various warnings he had given. About how rough
he was. How broken. And in truth, he had not been gentle. But none of it had harmed her. It might have hurt her
momentarily, but that pain wasn't something she minded.

Maybe…

Maybe he had been right.

Maybe the whole thing was something she'd been ill-prepared for. Something she shouldn't have pushed for. Because, while physically she had been completely all right with everything that had happened, emotionally she wasn't okay with being pushed away.

And maybe that was the real caution in this story.

He had gone on and on about all that he believed she could handle and she had imagined he meant what she could handle from a sexual-sophistication standpoint. Moves and skills and the knowledge of how things went between men and women.

But that had been the easy part. Following his lead. Allowing his hands, his mouth, his… All of him, to take her on a journey.

But afterward…

She frowned, and it was only then that she realized which direction she was driving.

And she knew she had a choice.

She could keep on going, or she could turn back.

But even as she thought it, she knew the truth. It was too late.

She couldn't go back.

She might have a better understanding of things after last night, and with everything she knew now, she might have made a different decision in that bar.

But she had to go forward.

With that in mind, she turned onto the winding road that led up to Levi's house.

And she didn't look back.

When Levi heard the knock on his door, he was less than amused. He was not in the mood to be preached at, subjected to a sales pitch or offered Girl Scout cookies.

And he could legitimately think of no other reason why anyone would be knocking on his door. So he pulled it open on a growl, and then froze.

"You're not a Jehovah's Witness."

Faith cleared her throat. "Not last I checked." She lifted a shoulder. "I'm Baptist, but—"

"That's not really relevant."

Her lips twitched. "Well... I guess not to *this* conversation, no."

"What are you doing here?"

"I felt like I was owed a chance to have a conversation with you when I wasn't naked and waiting to be returned to my car."

When she put it like that... He felt like even more of a dick. He hadn't thought that was possible.

"Go ahead," he said, extending his hand out.

"Oh. I didn't think... Maybe you should invite me in?"

"Should I?"

"It would be the polite thing to do."

"Well, you'll have to forgive me. In all the excitement of the last few years of my life, I've forgotten what the polite thing is."

"Oh, that's BS." And she breezed past him, and stamped into the house. "I understand that's your excuse of choice when it comes to all of your behavior. But I don't buy it."

"My excuse?" he asked. "I'm glad to know you consider five years in prison to be an excuse."

"I'm just saying that if you know you're behaving badly you could probably behave *less badly.*"

He snorted. "You have a lot of unearned opinions."

"Well, maybe help me earn some of them. Stop making pronouncements at me about how I don't know what

I'm doing and help me figure out what I'm doing. We had sex. We can't change that. I don't want to change it."

"Faith…"

"I don't see why we can't…keep having sex. I'm designing a house for you. There's a natural end to our acquaintance. It's…" She laughed, shaking her head. "You know, when my brother Isaiah proposed to his wife he told her it made sense. That it was logical. And I was angry at him because it was the least romantic thing I'd ever heard."

"I'm not sure I follow you."

"They weren't dating. She was his assistant. He was looking for a wife, and because he thought she was such a good assistant it meant she would likely make a good wife."

"And that went well for him?"

"Well, not at first. And I was angry at him. I hated the fact that he was turning something personal into a rational numbers game. It didn't seem right. It didn't seem fair. But now it kind of makes sense to me. Not that we are talking about marriage, but…an arrangement. Being near each other is going to be difficult after what we shared."

"I'm fine," he lied, taking a step away from her and her far too earnest face.

If *fine* was existing in a bad mood with a persistent hard-on, yeah, he was fine.

"I'm not," she said softly.

She took a step toward him, just like she had done on those other occasions. Like a kid who kept reaching her hand toward the stove, even though she'd been burned.

That he thought of that metaphor should be the first clue he needed to take a step away. But he didn't.

It's too late.

The damage had already been done.

The time in prison had already changed him. Hell, maybe the damage had been done when he was born. His father's genes flowing through his veins were far too powerful for Levi to fight against.

"Until you're done designing the house," he said, his voice hard. "Just until then."

Her shoulders sagged in relief, and the look of vulnerability on her face would have made a better man rethink everything.

But Levi wasn't a better man. And he had no intention of attempting to be one at this point.

"I'm supposed to be at work," she said. "I really should get back."

He reached out and grabbed the handle on the front door, shutting it hard behind her. "No," he said. "Baby, you stepped into the lion's den. And you're not leaving until I'm good and ready for you to leave."

"But work," she said, her voice small.

"But this," he responded, wrapping his hand around her wrist and dragging her palm toward him. He pressed it against that hard-on making itself known in the front of his jeans.

"Oh," she said, pressing her palm more firmly down and rubbing against him.

"You want to do this, we're doing it my way," he said. "I didn't know you were a virgin the first time, but now it's done. Taken care of. I'm not going to go easy on you just because you're inexperienced, do you understand?"

And he wasn't sure she had any idea at all what she was agreeing to. She nodded again.

If he was a better man, that, too, might have given him pause.

But he wasn't. So it didn't.

"I like to be in charge. And I don't have patience for

inhibition. Do you understand me?" She looked up at him, those eyes wide. He didn't think she understood at all. "That means if you want to do it, you do it. If you want me to do it, you ask for it. Don't hide your body from me, and I won't hide mine from you. I want to see you. I want to touch you everywhere. And there's no limit to what I'm going to do. That means the same goes for you. You can do whatever you want to me."

"But you're in charge," she said faintly.

"And that's my rule. If you think it'll feel good, do it. For you, for me." He leaned in, cupping her head in his hand and looking at her intently. "Sex can be a chore. If you're in a relationship with someone for a long time and there's no spark between you anymore—which doesn't happen on accident, you have to stop caring—then it can be perfunctory. Lights off. Something you just do. Like eating dinner.

"Now, if there's no emotional divide I don't mind routine sex. There's a comfort in it. But I haven't had sex in five years. There is no routine for me. That means I want raw. I want dirty. Because it can be that, too. It can be wild and intense. It can be slow and easy. It can be deliciously filthy. Sex can make you agree to things, say things, do things that if you were in your right mind you would find…objectionable. But when you're turned on, a lot of things seem like a good idea when they wouldn't otherwise. And that's the space I want to go to with you. That means no thinking. Just feeling."

Then he lifted her up and slung her over his shoulder. She squeaked, but she didn't fight his hold as he carried her out of the entry and up the stairs.

"You don't have your custom orgy bed yet."

He chuckled as they made their way down the hall,

and he kicked open the door with his foot. "Well, we're not having an orgy, are we? This is a party for two."

"How pedestrian. It must be so boring for you."

"No talking, either."

He laid her down on the bed and she looked up at him, mutinous.

"Did you have a bra to wear today?"

"Yes."

"I have your other one."

She squinted. "I have more than one. I have more than *two*."

"Let me see this one."

She shifted, sat up and pulled her top over her head, exposing the red lace bra she had underneath. Then she reached behind herself, unzipped her pencil skirt and tugged it down, revealing her pair of matching panties.

"Damn," he said. "Last night, before we started, I'd planned on that side-of-the-road stuff being just the introduction."

"Yes, and then you got ridiculous."

"I *tried*," he said, his voice rough. "I tried not to be a monster, Faith. Because I might not have known you were a virgin, or at least I didn't admit it to myself, but I knew that…my hands are dirty. I'm just gonna get you dirty."

She looked up at him, and the confusion and hope in her eyes reached down inside him and twisted hard. "You said sex was fun when it was dirty."

"Different kinds of dirty, sweetheart."

She eased back, propping herself up on her forearms. It surprised him how bold she was, and suddenly, he wanted to know more. About this little enigma wrapped in red lace. An architectural genius. So advanced in so many ways, and so new in others.

"Take your bra and panties off," he commanded.

She reached back and unclipped her bra, pulling it off quickly. There was a slight hesitation when she hooked her thumbs in the waistband of her panties and started to pull them down. But only a slight one.

She wiggled out of them, throwing them onto the floor.

She kept the same position, lying back, not covering herself. Exposing her entire, gorgeous body.

Small, perfect breasts with pale pink nipples and a thatch of dark curls between her legs.

"I wanted to do the right thing. Just once. Even if I'd already done the wrong thing. But I give up, babe. I give the hell up."

He moved toward the edge of the bed, curved his arms up around her hips and dragged her toward him, pressing a kiss to her inner thigh. She made a small, kittenish sound as he moved farther down, nuzzled her center and then took a leisurely lick, like she was the finest dessert he'd ever encountered. She squirmed, squeaking as he held her more tightly, and he brought her fully against his face and began to devour her.

It had been so long. So long since he'd tasted a woman like this, and even then…

Faith was sweeter than anyone.

Faith wiped away the memory of any previous lover. Doing this for her was like a gift to himself.

He brought his hand between her legs and pressed two fingers deep inside her, working them in and out, in time with his tongue. He could feel her orgasm winding up tight inside of her. Could feel little shivers in her internal muscles, her body slippery with need. He drew out that slickness, rubbing two fingers over her sensitive core before bringing his lips back down and sucking that bundle of nerves into his mouth as he plunged his fingers back in. She screamed, going stiff and coming hard, those muscles like a vise around his fingers now as her climax poured through her.

By the time she was finished, he was so damn hard he thought he was going to break in two.

He stood up, stripped his shirt over his head and came back down on the bed beside her.

She was looking at him with a kind of clouded wonder in her eyes, delicate fingertips tracing over the lines on his arms. "These are beautiful," she said.

"You want to talk about my tattoos now?"

"That was great," she said, breathless. "But I was waiting to see these."

"Celtic knot," he said, speaking of the intricate designs on his arms. That wasn't terribly personal. He'd had it done when he was eighteen and kind of an idiot. He'd hated his father and had wanted to find some identity beyond being that man's son. Inking some of his Irish heritage on his skin, making it about some long-dead ancestors, had seemed like a way to do that at the time.

Or at least that's what he'd told himself.

Now Levi figured it was mostly an attempt at looking like a badass and impressing women.

"And the bird?" she pressed.

Freedom. Simple as that. Also not something he was going to talk about with a hard-on.

"I like bird-watching," he said, his lips twitching slightly. "Now, no talking."

He gripped her chin and pulled her forward, kissing her mouth and letting her taste her own arousal there.

He took her deeper, higher, playing between her legs while he reached into his bedside table to get a condom.

Her head was thrown back, her breasts arched up toward him. Her lips, swollen from kissing, parted in pleasure. She was his every dirty dream, this sweet little angel.

He kept on teasing her, tormenting her with his fingers while he lifted the condom packet to his lips with his free hand and tore it with his teeth. Then he rolled it onto his length, slowly, taking his position against the entrance of her body.

She was so hot. So slick and ready for him. He couldn't resist the chance to tease them both just a little bit more.

He held himself firmly at the base and arched his hips forward, sliding through those sweet folds of hers, pushing down against her sensitive bundle of nerves and reveling in her hoarse sound of pleasure.

He wasn't made for her. There was no doubt about that. He was hard, scarred and far too broken to ever be of any use to her. But as he pressed the thick head of his erection against her, as he slid into her tight heat, inch by agonizing inch, he wondered if she wasn't made for him.

She gasped, arching against him, this time not in pain. Not like the first time.

She held onto his shoulders, her fingertips digging into his skin as he thrust into her, pulling out slowly before pressing himself back home.

Again. And again.

Until they were both lost in the fog of pleasure. Until she was panting. Begging.

Until the only sound in the room was their bodies, slapping against each other, their breathing, harsh and broken. It was the middle of the day, and he hadn't taken her on a date. Hadn't given her anything but an orgasm. And he couldn't even feel guilty about it.

He had spent all those days in the dark. Counting the hours until nothing. Until the end. He had been given a life sentence. And with that there was almost no hope. Just a small possibility they'd find a body—as horrendous as that would be—and exonerate him. He had felt guilty hoping for that, even for a moment. But something. *Anything* to prove his innocence.

That had been his life. And he had been prepared for it to be the rest of his life.

And now, somehow, he was here. With her.

Inside Faith's body, the sunlight streaming in through the windows.

Blinded by the light, by his pleasure, by his need.

This was more than he had imagined having a chance to feel ever again. And he wasn't sure he'd ever felt anything like this. Like this heat and hunger that roared in his gut, through his veins.

He opened his eyes and looked at her, forced himself to continue watching her even as his orgasm burst through him like a flame.

It was like looking at hope.

Not just a sliver of it, but full and real. Possibilities he had never imagined could be there for him.

He had come from a jail cell and had intended to ask this woman to build a house for him, and instead...

They were screwing in the middle of the afternoon.

And something about it felt like the first real step toward freedom he'd taken since being released from prison.

She arched beneath him, gasping at her pleasure, her internal muscles gripping him as she came. He roared out his own release, grasping her tightly against his body as he slammed into her one last time.

And as he held her close against his chest, in a bed he should never have taken her to, he let go of the ideas of right and wrong. What she deserved. What he could give.

Because what had happened between them just now was like nothing he'd ever experienced on earth. And it wouldn't be forever. It couldn't be.

But if it was freedom for him, maybe it could be that for her, too.

Maybe...

Just for a little while, he could be something good for her.

And as he stared down at her lovely face, he ignored the hollow feeling in his chest that asked: even if he knew he were bad for her, would he be able to turn away now?

He knew the answer.

He held her close, pressed her cheek against his chest, against his thundering heartbeat.

And she pressed her hand over the knife wound on his midsection.

Oh, yes. He knew the answer.

Chapter 9

By the time Faith woke up, the sun was low in the sky, and she was wrapped around Levi, her hand splayed on his chest. He was not asleep.

"I was wondering when you might wake up."

She blinked sleepily. "What time is it?"

"About five o'clock."

"Shit!" She jerked, as if she was going to scramble out of bed, and then she fell back, laying down her head on his shoulder. "I'm supposed to have dinner with my parents tonight."

"What time?"

"Six. But Isaiah and Levi are going to pester me about where I was. Poppy probably won't let me off, either. My sister-in-law. She works in the office. She's the one who—"

"Former assistant," Levi said.

"Yes. Also, she's pregnant right now and you know

how pregnant women have a heightened sense of smell?" she asked.

"Um…"

"Well, she does. But I think more for shenanigans than anything else."

"Shenanigans?" he repeated, his tone incredulous. "Are we engaging in shenanigans?"

"You know what I mean," she huffed.

"When are you going to tell them?"

She blinked. "About…this?"

"Not this specifically," he said, waving his arm over the two of them to indicate their bodies. "But the design project. They're going to have to know eventually."

"Oh, do they?" She tapped her chin. "I was figuring I could engage in some kind of elaborate money-laundering situation and hide it from them forever."

"Well, that will impact on my ability to do a magazine spread with my new house. My new life as a non-convict. As a free man."

"Right. I forgot."

"The best revenge is living well. Mostly because any other kind of revenge is probably going to land me back in prison."

"Isn't that like…double jeopardy at this point?"

"Are you encouraging me to commit murder?"

"Not encouraging you. I just… On a technicality…"

"I'm not going to do anything that results in a body count," he said drily. "Don't worry. But I would really like my ex to see everything I'm buying with the money that she can't have. If she can't end up in prison, then she's going to end up sad and alone, and with nothing. That might sound harsh to you…"

"It doesn't," Faith said, her voice small. "I can't imagine caring about someone like that and being betrayed. I can't imagine being in prison for five days, much less five years. She deserves…" She looked down, at his beautiful body, at the scar that marred his skin. "She deserves to think about it. What she could have had. What she gave away. Endlessly. She deserves that. I am so…sorry."

"I don't need your pity," he said.

"Just my body?" She wiggled closer to him, experimenting with the idea that she, too, could maybe be a vixen.

"I do like your body," he said slowly. "When are you going to tell your brothers about the job?"

"You know what? I'll do it tonight."

"Sounds pretty good. Do it when you have your parents to act as a buffer."

She grinned. "Basically."

She didn't want to leave him. Didn't want to leave this. She hesitated, holding the words in until her heart was pounding in her ears. Until she felt light-headed.

"Levi… We have a limited amount of time together. It will only be until the design project is finished. And I don't want to go all clingy on you, but I would like to… Can I come back tonight?"

He sat up, swinging his legs over the side of the bed, his bare back facing her. Without thinking, she reached out, tracing the border of the bird's wing that stretched around to his spine.

"Sure," he said. "If you really want to."

"For sex," she said. "But it might be late when we're finished. So maybe I'll sleep here?"

"If you want to sleep here, Faith, that's fine. Just don't get any ideas about it."

"I won't. I'll bring an overnight bag and I won't unpack it. My toothbrush will stay in my bag. It won't touch your sink."

"Why the hell would I care about that?"

He looked almost comically confused. On that hard, sculpted face, confusion was a strange sight.

"I don't know. There were some girls in college who used to talk about how guys got weird about toothbrushes. I've never had a boyfriend. I mean… Not that you're my boyfriend. But… I'm sorry. I'm speaking figuratively."

"Calm down," he said, gripping her chin and staring her right in the eyes. He dropped a kiss on her mouth, and instantly, she settled. "You don't need to work this hard with me. What we have is simple. We both know the rules, right?"

"Yes," she said breathlessly.

"Then I don't want you to overthink it. Because I definitely don't want you overthinking things when we're in bed together."

She felt a weight roll off her shoulders, and her entire body sagged. "Sometimes I think I don't know how to…not overthink."

"Why is that?"

She shrugged. "I've been doing it for most of my life."

He looked at her. Not moving. Like a predator poised to pounce. Those blue eyes were far too insightful for her liking. "Does it ever feel like prison?"

She frowned. "Does what ever feel like prison?"

"The success you have. You couldn't have imagined that you would be experiencing this kind of demand at your age."

"I really don't know how to answer that. Nobody sentenced me to anything, Levi, and I can walk away from it at any time."

"Is your family rich, Faith?"

She laughed. "No. We didn't grow up with anything. I only went to private school because I got a scholarship.

Joshua didn't even get to go to college. He didn't have the grades to earn a scholarship or anything. My parents couldn't afford it—"

"All the money in your family—this entire company—it centers around you."

"Yes," she said softly.

He made a scoffing sound. "No wonder you were a virgin."

"What does my virginity have to do with anything?"

"Have you done something for yourself? Ever?"

"I mean, in fairness, Levi, it's my…gift. My talent. My dream, I guess, that made us successful. It centers around me. Isaiah and Joshua fill in the holes with what they do well, but they could do what they do well at any kind of company. The architectural aspect… That's me. They're enabling me to do what I love."

"And you're enabling everyone to benefit from your talents. That they're supporting your talent doesn't make them sacrificial. It makes them smart. I'm not putting your brothers down. In their position I would do the same. But what bears pointing out is that whether you realize it or not, you've gotten yourself stuck in the center of a spider's web, honey. No wonder you feel trapped sometimes."

They didn't speak about anything serious while she got ready. She dodged a whole lot of groping on his end while she tried to pull on her clothes, and ended up almost collapsing in a fit of giggles as she fought to get her skirt back on and cover her ass while he attempted to keep his hand on her body.

But she thought about what he said the entire time, and all the way over to her parents' house. His observation made it seem… Well, like she really should fight harder for the things she wanted. Should worry less about what

Joshua and Isaiah felt about her association with Levi. Personally or professionally.

Though, she wasn't going to bring up any of the personal stuff.

Levi was right. The business, her career—all of this had turned into a monster she hadn't seen coming. It was a great monster. One that funded a lifestyle she had never imagined could be hers. Though, it was a lifestyle she was almost too busy to enjoy. And if that was going to be the case...

Why shouldn't she take on projects that interested her?

That was the thing. Levi had interested her from the beginning, and the only reason she had hesitated was because Joshua and Isaiah were going to be dicks about her interest and she knew it.

She pulled up to her parents' small, yellow farmhouse and sat in the driveway for a moment.

She wished Levi was with her. Although she had no reason to bring him. And the very idea of that large, hard man in this place seemed...impossible. Like a god coming down from Mount Olympus to hang out at the mall.

She got out of the car and walked up to the front porch, opened the door and walked straight inside. A rush of familiarity hit her, that familiar scent of her mother's pot roast. That deep sense of home that could only ever be attached to this place. Where she had grown up. Where she'd longed to be while at boarding school, where she had ached to return for Christmases, spring breaks and summers.

Everyone was already there. Devlin and his wife, Mia. Joshua, Danielle and and their son Riley. Isaiah and Poppy.

Faith was the only one who stood alone. And suddenly, it didn't feel so familiar anymore.

Maybe because she was different.

Because she had left part of herself in that bed with Levi.

Or maybe because everyone else was a couple.

All she knew was that she felt like a half standing there and it was an entirely unpleasant feeling.

"Hi," Faith said.

"Where have you been?" Joshua asked. "You left the office around lunchtime the other day and I haven't seen you since."

"You say that like it's news to me," she said drily. "I had some things to take care of."

Her mom came out of the kitchen and wrapped Faith in a hug. "What things? What are you up to?" She pressed a kiss to Faith's cheek. "More brilliance?"

Her dad followed, giving Faith a hug and a kiss and moving to his favorite chair that put him at the head of the seating arrangement.

"I don't know." Faith rubbed her arm, suddenly feeling like she was fifteen and being asked to discuss her report card. "Not especially. Just… I picked up another project."

"What project?" Isaiah asked, frowning.

"You didn't consult me about the schedule first," Poppy said.

"I can handle it," Faith said. "It's fine."

"This is normally the kind of thing you consult us on," Joshua said, frowning.

"Yes. And I didn't this time. I took a job that interested me. And I had a feeling you wouldn't be very supportive about it. So I did it alone. And it's too late to quit, because I already have an agreement. I'm already working on the project, actually."

"Is that why you were behind on sending me those estimates?" Isaiah asked. As if this error was proof positive they were actually correct, and she couldn't handle all this on her own.

"Yes," she said. "Probably. But, you know, I'm the one who does the design. And I should be able to take on projects that interest me. And turn down things that don't."

"Are we making you do things you don't like?"

"No. It's just… The whole mass-production thing we're doing, that's fine. But I don't need to be as involved in that. I did some basic designs, but my role in that is done. At this point it's standardized, and what interests me is the weird stuff. The imaginative stuff."

"I'm glad you enjoy that part of it. It's what makes you good. It's what got us where we are."

"I know. I mean…" Everyone was staring at her and she felt strange admitting how secure she was in her talent. But she wasn't a fifteen-year-old explaining a report card. She was a grown woman explaining what she wanted to do with the hours in her day, confident in her area of expertise. "You can't get where I'm at without being confident. But what I'm less confident about is whether or not you two are going to listen to me when I say I know what I want to do."

"Of course we listen to you."

She sucked in a sharp breath and faced down Joshua and Isaiah. "I took a design job for Levi Tucker."

Isaiah frowned. "Why do I know that name?"

It was Devlin who stood up, and crossed large, tattooed arms over his broad chest. "Because he's a convict," he said. "He was accused of murdering his wife."

"Who isn't dead," Faith pointed out. "So, I would suggest that's a pretty solid case *against* him being a murderer."

"Still."

Mia spoke tentatively. "I mean, the whole situation

is so…suspicious, though," she said softly. "I mean… what woman would run from her husband if he was a good guy?"

"Yes," Faith said, sighing heavily, "I've heard that line of concern before. But the fact of the matter is, I've actually met him." She felt like she did a very valiant job of not choking on her tongue when she said that. "And he's…fine. I wouldn't say he's a nice guy, but certainly he's decent enough to work with."

"I don't like it," Devlin said. "I think you might be too young to fully understand all the implications."

Anger poured into her veins like a hot shot of whiskey, going straight to her head. "Do not give me that shit," she said, then looked quickly over at her mother and gave her an apologetic smile for the language. "Your wife is the same age as I am. So if I'm too young to make a business decision, your wife is certainly too young to be married to you."

Mia looked indignant for a moment, but then a little bit proud. The expression immediately melted into smugness.

"I like his ideas." Faith didn't say anything about his house being a sex palace. "And it's a project I'm happy to have my name on."

Joshua shook his head. "You want to be associated with a guy like that? A young, powerful woman like yourself entering into a business agreement with a man who quite possibly has a history of violence against women…"

She exploded from the table, flinging her arms wide. "He hasn't done anything to anyone. There have been no accusations of domestic violence. He didn't… As far as anyone knows, he never did anything to her. She disappeared and he was accused of all manner of things with no solid evidence at all. And I think there was bias against him because he comes from…modest beginnings."

"It's about the optics, Faith," Joshua pointed out. "You're a role model. And associating with him could damage that."

Optics. That word made her feel like a creature in a zoo instead of a human. It made her feel like someone who was being made to perform, no matter her feelings.

"I don't care about *optics*, Joshua. I'm twenty-five years old and I have many more years left in this career. If all I ever do is worry about optics and I don't take projects that interest me—if I don't follow my passion even a little bit—then I don't see the point of it."

"The point is that you are going to be doing this for a long time and when you're more well-established you can take risks. Until then, you need to be more cautious."

She looked around the room at her family, all of them gazing at her like she had grown a second head. Suddenly she did feel what Levi had described earlier.

This was, in its way, a prison.

This success had grown bigger than she was.

"I'm not a child," she said. "If I'm old enough to be at the center of all this success, don't you think I should follow my instincts? If I…burn out because I feel trapped then I won't be able to do my best work. If I burn out, I won't be able to give you all those years of labor, Joshua."

"Nobody wants that," her mother said. "Nobody expects you to work blindly, Faith. No one wants you to go until you grind yourself into the ground." She directed those words at Joshua and Isaiah.

"You think it's a good idea for her to work with an ex-con?" Joshua directed *that* question at their father.

"I think Faith's instincts have gotten all of you this

far and you shouldn't be so quick to dismiss them just because it doesn't make immediate sense to you," her father responded.

Right. This was why she had confessed in front of her parents. Because, while she wanted to please them, wanted all their sacrifices to feel worth it, she also knew they supported her no matter what. They were so good at that. So good at making her feel like her happiness mattered.

A lot of the pressure she felt was pressure she had put on herself.

But every year when there was stress about the scholarship money coming through for boarding school, every year when the cost of uniforms was an issue, when a school trip came up and her parents had to pay for part of it, and scraped and saved so Faith could have every opportunity... All of those things lived inside her.

She couldn't forget it.

They had done so much for her. They had set her out on a paved road to the future, rather than a dirt one, and it hadn't been a simple thing for them.

And she couldn't discount the ways her brothers had helped her passiona for architecture and design become a moneymaking venture, too.

But at the end of the day, she was still owed something that was *hers*.

She still deserved to be treated like an adult.

It was that simple.

She just wanted them to recognize that she was a grown woman who was responsible for her own time, for her own decisions.

"I took the project," she said again. "It's nonnegotiable. He's going to publicize it whether you do or not, Joshua. Because it's part of his plan for...reestablishing himself.

He's a businessman, and he was quite a famous one, for good reasons, prior to being wrongfully accused."

"Faith…" Joshua clearly sounded defeated now, but he seemed to be clinging to a last hope that he could redirect her.

"You don't know him," Faith said. "You just decided he was guilty. Which is what the public did to him. What the justice system did to him. And if he's innocent, then he's a man who lost everything over snap judgments and bias. You're in PR, maybe you can work with that when the news stories start coming out—"

"Dinner will be ready soon," her mother interrupted, her tone gentle but firm. "Why don't we table talk of business until after?"

They did that as best they could all through the meal, and afterward Faith was recruited to help put away dishes. She would complain, or perhaps grumble about the sexism of it, but her mother had only asked for her, and Faith had a feeling it was because her mother wanted a private word with her.

"How well do you know Levi Tucker?" her mother asked gently, taking a clean plate from the drying rack and stacking it in the cupboard.

"Well enough," Faith answered, feeling a twist of conviction in her chest as she plunged her hands into the warm dishwater.

"You have very strong feelings about his innocence."

"There's nothing about him that seems…bad to me."

Rough, yes. Wounded, yes. Stabbed through the rib cage because of his own wife, sure. But not bad.

"Be careful," her mother said gently. "You've seen more of the world than I ever will, sweetheart. You've done more, achieved more, than I could have ever hoped to. But there are some things you don't have experience with… And I fear that, to a degree, your advancement in other areas is the reason why. And it makes me worry for you."

"You don't have to worry for me."

"So your interest in him is entirely professional?"

Faith took a dish out of the soapy water and began to scrub it. "You don't have to worry about me."

"But I do," her mother said. "Just like I worry about your brothers sometimes. It's what parents do."

"Well, I'm fine," Faith said.

"It's okay to make mistakes," her mother said. "You know that, don't you?"

"What are you talking about?"

"Just, forget about Levi Tucker for a second. It's okay for you to make mistakes, Faith. You don't have to be perfect. You don't have to be everything to everyone. You don't have to make Isaiah happy. You don't have to make Joshua happy. You certainly don't have to make your father and I happy."

Faith shifted uncomfortably. "It's not a hardship to care about whether or not my family is happy. You did so much for me…"

"Look at everything you've done for *us*. Just having you as my daughter would have been enough, Faith. It would have always been enough."

Faith didn't know why that sat so uncomfortably with her. "I would rather not make mistakes."

"We would all rather not make them," her mother said. "But sometimes they're unavoidable. Sometimes you need to make them in order to grow into the person you were always supposed to be."

Faith wondered if Levi could be classified as a mistake. She was going into this—whatever it was—knowing exactly what kind of man he was and exactly when and how things were going to end. She wondered if that made her somehow more prepared. If that meant it was a calculated maneuver, rather than a mistake.

"I can see you, figuring out if you're still perfect."

Her mother's words were not spoken with any sort of unkindness, but they played at Faith's insides all the same. "I don't think I'm perfect," Faith mumbled, scrubbing more ferociously at the dish.

"You would like to be."

She made a sound that landed somewhere between a scoff and a laugh, aiming for cool and collected and achieving neither. "Who doesn't want to be?"

"I would venture to say your brothers don't worry very much about being perfect."

Sure. Because they operated in the background and worried about things like *her* optics, not their own. Isaiah somehow managed to go through life operating as if everything was a series of numbers and spreadsheets. Joshua treated everything like a PR opportunity. And Devlin... Well, Devlin was the one who had never cared what anyone thought. The one who hadn't gone into business with the rest of them. The one who had done absolutely everything on his own terms and somehow come out of it with Faith's best friend as a bonus.

"I like my life," Faith insisted. "Don't think that I don't."

"I don't think that," her mother said. "I just think you put an awful lot of pressure on yourself."

For the rest of the evening, Faith tried not to ruminate on that too much, but the words kept turning over and over in her head on the drive back to Levi's. She swung by her house and put together a toiletries bag, throwing in some pajamas and an outfit for the next day. And all the while she kept thinking...

You're too hard on yourself. You can make mistakes.

And her resistance to those words worried her more than she would like to admit.

Logically, she was completely all right with this thing with Levi being temporary. With it being a mistake, in many ways. But she was concerned that there was something deep inside her that believed it would become something different. That believed it might work out.

Beneath her practicality she was more of a dreamer than she wanted to acknowledge.

But how could she be anything but a dreamer? It was her job. To create things out of thin air. Even though another part of her always had to make those dreams a practical reality. It wasn't any good to be an architect if you couldn't figure out how to make your creations stand, make them structurally sound.

She didn't know how to reconcile those two halves of herself. Not right now. Not in this instance.

Now she had just confused herself. Because sex with Levi was not designing a house. Not even close.

She needed to stop trying to make sense of everything.

Maybe there were some things you couldn't make sense of.

She was having a just-physical relationship with the man. She nodded her head resolutely as she pulled up to the front of his house and put the car in Park. Then she shut off the engine decisively.

She knew exactly what was happening between them, and she was mature enough to cope with it.

He wasn't a mistake. He was an experience.

So there. She didn't need to make mistakes.

Satisfied with that, Faith grabbed her overnight bag, got out of her car and went to Levi's house.

Chapter 10

Faith had only left his house once in the past two days. On Friday she went to work. But on Friday evening she returned, and stayed the night again. Now it was deep into Saturday, a gloomy, rainy day, and she was loitering around his kitchen wearing nothing but a T-shirt and a smile.

He didn't mind.

"I've got some horses coming later today," he commented, looking over at her lithe, pale form.

She hauled herself up onto the counter, the T-shirt riding up, nearly exposing that heaven between her thighs. She crossed those long, lovely legs at the ankles, her expression innocent, her hair disheveled from their recent activities.

The woman managed to look angelic and completely wicked all at once, and it did things to him he couldn't quite explain.

She wasn't for him. He had to remind himself. Because the things he liked about her... They didn't say anything good about him.

He had practically been born jaded. His vision of the world had been blackened along with his mother's eye the first time he had seen his father take his fists to her when he had been... He must've been two or three. His earliest memory.

Not a Christmas tree or his mother's smile. But her bruises. Fists connecting against flesh and bone.

That was his world. The way he had known and understood it from the very start.

He had never been able to see the world with the kind of unspoiled wonder Faith seemed to.

He had introduced her to dirty, carnal things, and had watched her face transform with awe every time he'd made her come. Every time he'd shown her something new, something illicit. She touched his body, his tattoos, his scars, like they were gifts for her to discover and explore.

There was something intoxicating in that.

This woman who saw him as *new*.

He had never had that experience with a woman before.

His high-school girlfriend had been as jaded and damaged as he was, and they might have experienced sex for the first time together, but there was no real wonder in it. Just oblivion. Just escape. The same way they had used drugs and alcohol to forget what was happening in their homes.

Sex with Faith wasn't a foggy escape. It was sharp and crisp like crystal, and just as able to cut him open. He had never felt so present, so in his own body, as he was when he was inside her.

He didn't know what the hell to make of it, but he didn't have the strength to turn away from it, either.

"Horses?"

"There's a small stable, and some arenas and pastures on this property. Of course, when I move to the other one…"

"You didn't tell me you needed a riding facility."

"I figured that's pretty standard, isn't it?"

"It doesn't have to be. It can be whatever you want it to be."

"Well, maybe I'll have you sketch that out for me, too."

"Can I meet the horses?" She looked bright and happy at the idea.

"Sure," he said. "You like to ride?"

"I never did as much of it as my brothers. I did a little bit when I was away at school, but I didn't spend as much time doing the farm-life thing as they did. I know how to ride, obviously. We always had a couple horses. It's just been a while. That was actually one of my brothers' priorities, when we moved back here." She blinked. "You know, to get a ranching operation up and running."

He frowned. "Where do you live?"

She laughed. He realized that although the woman designed houses for a living, they had never discussed her own living situation. "Okay. You know how they say contractors are notorious for never finishing the work in their own houses? Or how mechanics always have jacked-up cars? I am an architect who lives above a coffeehouse."

"No shit."

"None at all. It's too much pressure. Think of designing a place for myself. I haven't done it. I was living in this great, modern, all-glass space up in Seattle. And I loved it. But I knew that I wasn't going to stay there, so I didn't do anything else. When we moved back to Copper

Ridge… I didn't really know what I wanted to do here, either. So I haven't designed a house. And the vacancy came up above The Grind in town and I figured an old building like that, all redbrick and right there in the center of things, was the perfect place for me to get inspiration. I was right. I love it. It works for me."

"That's disappointing. I thought you lived in some architectural marvel. Like something made entirely out of cement shaped like the inside of a conch shell."

"That's ridiculous."

"Is it?"

"Okay, it's not that insane. I've definitely seen weirder. How did you learn to ride?"

This was skating close to sharing. Close to subjects he didn't want to go into. He hesitated.

"I got a job on a ranch. I was a kid. Twelve. Thirteen. But it's what I did until I went away to school. Until I got into manufacturing. Until I made my fortune, I guess. There was an older guy, by the name of Bud. He owned a big ranching spread on the edge of Copper Ridge. He passed on a couple years ago now. He took me on, and let me work his land. He was getting old, he was downsizing, but he didn't have the heart to get rid of everything. So… I got to escape my house and spend my days outdoors. Earn a little money doing it. My grades suffered. But I was damn happy.

"Ranch work will always be that for me. Freedom. It's one of the things I hated most about being in prison. Being inside. Four walls around you all the time. And… Nothing smells like a ranch does. Like horses. Hay, wood chips. Even horse piss. It's its own thing. That stuff gets in your blood. Not being around it at all was like sensory deprivation. My assets were liquified when I went to prison. Not frozen, though, which was convenient for Alicia. Though, in the end less convenient."

"Of course," she said testily.

"So, my horses were taken and sold, and the money was put into an account. I was able to get two of them back. They're coming today."

"Levi… That's… I mean… I can't believe you lost your ranch? Your animals?"

"It doesn't matter."

"It does. She took… She took everything from you." Faith blinked. "Do you think she did it on purpose?"

"I think she did," he said, his voice rough.

"Why? Look, I don't think that you did anything to her. But I…"

"The life I gave her wasn't the life she wanted," he said.

"Well, what life did she think she would be getting?"

"She—she was just like me. Poor and hating every minute of it. I was twenty-one. She was eighteen. She thought I might be on my way to something, and I swore to her I was. I thought she had hearts in her eyes, but they were just dollar signs. I loved her. We forged a path together, I thought. Were working toward a future where we could both look down on everyone who'd ever looked down on us."

"From a house on a hill?" Faith asked, softly.

"Yeah. From a house on a hill. But Alicia wanted more than that. She wanted to be something other than country, and I was never going to be that. Galas and all that crap. Designer clothes and eating tiny portions of food standing up and pretending to care about what strangers have to say about anything—it wasn't me. But I thought we were weathering those differences, I really did."

He shook his head. "When she went missing, it was the

worst night of my life. She didn't take anything with her, not that I could see. I thought for sure something had happened to her. She had her purse, but that was it. It looked like she'd been snatched walking between a grocery store and her car. I lost sleep wondering what was happening to her. Dammit, I was picturing her being tortured. Violated. Terrified. I've never been so afraid, so sick to my stomach, in my whole life. We might not have been in the best space right then, but I didn't want anything to happen to my wife, Faith. Hell, I didn't even think it was so bad that we would get divorced. I figured we needed to work on some things, but we could get around to it."

Faith bit her lip. "I can't imagine. I can't imagine what you went through."

"It was awful. And then they came and arrested me. Said they had reason to believe I'd done something to her. And later…that there was evidence I'd killed her and made sure the body wouldn't be found. The body. My wife was a body at that point. And they were accusing me of being responsible for that." He shook his head. "And what an ass I was. I grieved for her."

"Do you—do you think she ever loved you?" Faith asked. "I can't imagine doing that to someone I hated, much less—"

"I think she did in the beginning. But everything got twisted. She thought wealth and success meant something to me that it didn't. I wanted a ranch, and I wanted to go to fewer parties. I was fine with her going by herself. She didn't like that. She wanted me to be on her arm. She wanted a very specific life, and it was one she didn't inform me she wanted until it was too late. And I"—

"You weren't willing to give it."

He felt like he'd been punched in the chest.

Faith shrugged. "It's still no excuse to go framing

you for murder," she said. "Or, whatever she intended to frame you for. But I just mean… There were maybe one or two things you could have given her to make her happier. If she weren't a psycho."

He chuckled hollowly. "I expect you're right. If she weren't a psycho. But that's why I don't ever intend to get married again."

"Honestly, I can't blame you." Faith looked down, a dark curl falling into her face.

"Do you want to go for a ride later today?"

She looked at him, her whole face bright, her expression totally different from the way it had been a moment before. "Yes."

"Well, cowgirl, I hope you brought your jeans."

Chapter 11

Faith sat on the top of the fence while she watched the horses circle the paddock. They seemed content in their new surroundings. Or maybe, it was the presence of Levi. Watching as he had greeted the horses, pressing his hand to their velvet soft noses, letting them take in his scent had been…

Her chest felt so full she thought it might burst.

He was such a hard man. And yet… It was that hardness that made the soft moments so very special. She didn't know why she was thinking about him in those terms. Why she wanted special moments. Why she cared.

But seeing him like that, even now, out in the paddock, as the horses moved around him, and he stood in that black Stetson, black T-shirt and tight jeans…

She ached.

She had been outside of so many things. There, but not quite a part of them.

The only single person at dinner last night. A prodigy in architecture, but so much younger than everyone else, seemingly someone people couldn't relate to. The poor girl at boarding school, there on a scholarship. The smart kid who would rather escape into books and her imagination than go to a party.

That had been fine. It had been fine for a long time.

But it wasn't fine now.

She wanted to meld herself with him. Mold herself into his life. Melt against him completely. She didn't know what that meant. But the urge tugged at her, strongly. Made it so she could hardly breathe.

She hopped down off the fence, her boots kicking up dust as she made her way across the arena and toward him.

"What are you doing?" he asked.

"I just… They're beautiful horses." And he was beautiful. With them, he was stunning. It was like watching him be right where he belonged. At ease for the first time since she'd met him.

Like a bird spreading his wings.

A smile tipped up the corners of his lips. "I'm glad to have them back."

"The others?"

"It's not possible to track all of them down. It's okay. For now, this is enough."

"And then what?"

"They'll make a great story," he said, his expression suddenly shuttered. "When we do that big magazine spread. Showing my new custom home, and the equestrian facility you're going to build me. A big picture of me with these horses that Alicia took from me."

"Is that what everything is about?"

"My entire life has been about her for seventeen years,

Faith. In the last five years of that all I could do was think about…" He gritted his teeth. "That is the worst part. I worried about her. All that time. And she was fine. Off sipping champagne and sitting on a yacht. Screwing who the hell knows. While I sat in prison like a monk. An entire life sentence ahead of me. And I was worried about her. She knew I was in prison. She knew. She didn't care. That's the worst part. How much emotional energy I wasted worrying about the fate of that woman when…"

She stepped forward, put her fingertips on his forearm. "This isn't emotional energy?"

He looked down at her. "How would you feel? How would you feel in my position?"

"I don't know. Possibly not any better. I don't know what I would do. You're right. I can't comment on it."

"Stick to what you do, honey. Comment on the design work you can do for me."

She took a step back, feeling like she had overstepped. That little bubble of fantasy she'd had earlier, that need to get closer to him, had changed on her now. "I will. Don't worry."

"How did you realize you were an architecture prodigy?" he asked suddenly.

"I don't know," she said, lifting a shoulder. "I mean, I drew buildings. I was attracted to the idea of doing city design in a slightly more…organic way. I was fascinated by that from the time I was a kid. As for realizing I was good… I was naturally good at art, but I've always been good at math and science as well. History. Art history."

"So you're one of those obnoxious people who doesn't have a weakness."

"Well, except for…social stuff?" She laughed. "Academically, no. Not so much. And that opened a lot of doors for me. For which I will always be grateful. It was really my brothers who helped me focus. Because, of course, Isaiah being a numbers guy, he wanted to help me figure out how I could take what I did and make money with it. My education was paid for because I was brilliant, but that comes to an end eventually. You have to figure out what to do in the real world. Architecture made sense."

"I guess so."

"Why...manufacturing? And what did you make?"

"Farm equipment," he said. "Little generic replacement parts for different things. A way to do it cheaper, without compromising on quality."

"And what made you do that?"

"Not because I'm an artist. Because there are a lot of hardworking men out there, pleased as hell to replace the parts themselves if they can. But often things are over-complicated and expensive. I wanted to find a way to simplify processes. So it started with the basic idea that we can get around some of the proprietary stuff some of the big companies did. And it went from there. Eventually I started manufacturing parts for those big companies. It's a tricky thing to accomplish, here in the United States, but we've managed. And it served me well to keep it here. It's become part of why my equipment is sought after."

She giggled. "There's a double entendre."

"It's boring. That was another thing my wife objected to. She wanted me to get into real-estate investing. Something more interesting for her to talk about with her friends. Something a little bit sexier than gaskets."

"A gasket is pretty sexy if it's paying you millions of dollars, I would think."

"Hell, that was my feeling." He sighed heavily. "It's not like you. Mine was a simple idea."

"Sometimes simplicity is the better solution," she said.

"People think you need to be complicated to be interesting. I don't always think that's true, in design, or in life. Obviously, in your case, the simple solution was the revolutionary one."

"I guess so. Are you ready to go for a ride?"

"I am," she said.

And somehow, she felt closer to him. Somehow she felt...part of this. Part of him.

She wanted to hold onto that feeling for as long as it would last, because she had a feeling it would be over a lot sooner than she would like.

But then, that was true of all of this. Of everything with him.

She was beginning to suspect that nothing short of a lifetime would be enough with Levi Tucker.

Chapter 12

Levi had missed this. He couldn't pretend otherwise. Couldn't pretend that it hadn't eaten at him, five years away from the ranch.

The animals were in his blood, in his bones. Had been ever since he had taken that job at Bud's ranch. That experience had changed him. Given him hope for the future. Allowed him to see things in a different way. Allowed him to see something other than a life filled with pain, fear.

The other kids at school had always avoided him. He was the boy who came to school with bruises on his face. The boy whose family was whispered about. Whose mother always looked sallow and unhappy, and whose father was only ever seen at night, being pulled drunkenly out of bars.

But the horses had never seen him that way. He had earned their trust. And he had never taken it for granted.

The back of a horse was the one place he had ever felt

like he truly belonged. And things hadn't changed much. Twenty-three years—five of them spent behind bars—later, and things hadn't changed much.

He looked back from his position on the horse, and the grin on Faith's face lit up all the dark places inside him. He hadn't expected to enjoy sharing this with her. But then, he hadn't expected to share so much with her at all.

There was something about her. It was that sense of innocence.

That sense of newness.

A sense that if he could be close enough to her he might be able to see the world the way she did. As a place full of possibility, rather than a place full of pain. Betrayal. Heartbreak.

Yes, with her, he could see the scope of so much more. And it made him want to reach out to her. It made him want to...

He wanted her to understand him.

He couldn't remember ever feeling that way before. He hadn't wanted Alicia to understand him.

He hadn't cared. He'd loved her. But that love had been wrapped up in the life he wanted to build. In the vision of what they could be. He'd been focused on forward motion, not existing in the moment.

And maybe, there, Faith was right. Maybe that was where he had failed as a husband.

Though, he still hadn't failed so spectacularly that he'd deserved to be sent to prison, but he could acknowledge that some of the unhappiness in his marriage had come down to him.

"It's beautiful out here," Faith said.

"This is actually part of the property for the new house," he said. He glanced up at the sky, where the dark gray clouds were beginning to gather, hanging low.

"It's starting to look stormy, but if you don't mind taking a chance on getting caught in the rain, I can show you where we might put the equestrian facility."

"I'd like that," she said.

He urged his horse on, marveling at how quickly he had readjusted to this thing, to horsemanship, to feeling a deep brightness in his bones. If that wasn't evidence this was where he belonged, in the woods on the back of a horse, he didn't know what was.

They came through a deep, dark copse of trees and out into a clearing. The clouds there were layers of patchwork gray, moving from silver to a kind of menacing charcoal, like a closed fist ready to rain down judgment on the world below.

And there was the clearing. Overlooking the valley below.

The exact positioning he wanted, so he could look down on everyone who had once looked down on him.

"You think you can work with this?" he asked.

"Definitely," she responded. She maneuvered her horse around so she was more fully facing the view before them. "I want to make it mirror your house somehow. Functional, obviously. But open. I know the horses weren't in prison for the last five years, but they had their lives stolen from them, too, in a way. I want it all connected. And I want you to feel free."

Interesting that she had used that word. A word that had meant so much to him. One he had yearned for so much he'd traded cigarettes to have a symbol of it tattooed on his body.

It was a symbol he was deeply protective of. He wasn't a sentimental man, and his tattoos were about the closest thing to sentiment he possessed.

"I like the way you think," he said.

He meant it. In many ways. And not just this instance.

She tilted her head, scrunching her nose and regarding him like he was something strange and fascinating. "Why do you like the way I think?"

"Because you see more than walls, Faith. You see what they can mean to people. Not just the structure. But what makes people feel. Four walls can be a prison sentence or they can be a refuge. That difference is something I never fully appreciated until I was sent away."

"Homes are interesting," she said. "I design a lot of buildings that aren't homes. And in those cases, I design the buildings based on the skyline of the city. The ways I want the structure to flow with the surroundings. But homes are different. My parents' house, small and simple as it is, could not feel more like home to me. Nothing else will ever feel like home in quite the same way it does. It's where I grew up. Where the essential pieces of myself were formed and made. That's what a home is. And every home you live in after those formative years…is not the same. So you have to try and take something from the life experience people have had since they left their parents and bring it all in and create a home from that."

He thought of his own childhood home. Of the way he had felt there. The fear. The stale scent of alcohol and sadness. The constant lingering threat of violence.

"Home to me was the back of a horse," he said. "The mountains. The trees. The sky. That's where I was made. It's where I became a person I could be proud of, or at the very least, a person I could live with. My parents' place was prison."

He urged his horse forward, moving farther down the trail, into the clearing, before he looped around and headed back toward the other property. Faith followed after him.

And the sky opened up. That angry fist released its hold.

He urged the horse into I canter, and he could hear Faith keeping pace behind him. As they rode, the rain soaked through his clothes. All the way through to his skin. It poured down his face, down his shirt collar.

Rain.

It had been five years since he had felt rain on his skin. *Hell.*

He hadn't even known he'd missed it until now. And now he realized he was so thirsty for it he thought he might have been on the brink of death.

He released his hold on the reins and let his arms fall to his sides, spread his hands wide, keeping his body movements in tune with the horse as the water washed over him.

For a moment. Then two.

He counted the raindrops at first. Until it all blended together, a baptism out there in the wilderness.

He finally took control of the animal again. By then, the barn was back in view.

The horse moved with him as Levi encouraged him into a gallop. The rain whipped into his eyes now, but he didn't care. He brought the horse into the stable and looped the lead rope around a hook, then moved back outside and stripped off his shirt, letting the rain fall on his skin there, too.

If Faith thought it was strange, she didn't say anything. She went into the barn behind him and disappeared for a few moments. Leaving him outside, with the water washing over him. When she returned she was without her horse, her chin-length dark hair wet and clinging to her face.

"Are you okay?" she asked.

"I just realized," he said, looking up above, letting

the water drops hit him square on the face. "I just realized that it's the first time I've felt the rain since before I was in jail."

Neither of them said anything. She simply closed the distance between them and curved her fingers around his forearm.

They stood there for a while, getting wet together.

"Tell me about your family," she said softly.

"You don't want to hear the story."

"I do," she said.

"Maybe I don't feel like telling it," he responded, turning to face her.

She looked all around them, back up at the sky, and then back at him. "We're home," she said. "It's the best place to tell hard stories."

And he knew exactly what she meant. They were home. They were free. Outside and with no walls around them. In the exact kind of place he had found freedom for himself the first time.

"My very first memory is of my father hitting my mother in the face," he said. "I remember a bruise blooming there almost instantly. Blood. Tears. My home never felt safe. I never had that image of my father as a protector. My father was the enemy. He was a brutal man. He lived mean, and he died mean, and I've never mourned him. Not one day."

"How did he die?" she asked softly.

"Liver failure," he said. "Which is kind of a mundane way to die for a man like him. In some ways, it would've been better if he'd died in violence. But sometimes I take comfort in the fact that disease doesn't just come for good people. Sometimes it gets the right ones."

"Your mother?"

"Packed up and left Oregon the minute he died. I send her money sometimes. At least, I did before…"

"Obviously you couldn't send money when you were in prison."

He shook his head. "No. I don't think you understand. She didn't want anything from me after that. She didn't believe me. That I didn't have something to do with Alicia's disappearance. She figured I was cut from the same cloth as my old man."

"How could she think that?" Faith asked. "She was your mother."

"In the end, she was a woman standing with another woman. And part of me can't blame her for that. I think it was easier for her to believe that her worst nightmare had come true. That I had fully become the creation of my genetics. You can understand why she would have feared that."

He had feared it, too. Sometimes he still did.

Because that hate—that hard, heavy fist of rage living in his chest—felt far too evil to have been put there recently. It felt born into him. As much a part of him as that first memory.

He swept her up into his arms then and carried her toward the house, holding her tightly against his chest. She clung to him, her fingers slick against his skin, greedy as they trailed over him.

"That's who I am," he said, taking her hand and pressing it against the scar left by the knife. "And that's why I told you I wasn't the right man for you. That's why I told you to stay away from me."

She shifted her hand, moving her fingertips along the scarred, raised flesh. The evidence of the day he'd been cut open and left to bleed. He'd considered lying down and dying. A damn low moment. He had been sentenced to life in prison, he'd thought. Why not let that sentence be a little shorter?

But his instincts, his body, hadn't let him give up. No. He'd gotten back up. And hit the man who'd come after him. And then hit him again, and again.

No one had come for Levi after that.

She made a soft sound as she shifted, letting her fingers glide over to the edge of the bird's wing. She traced the shape, its whole wingspan.

"No," she said, shaking her head. "*This* is who you are. This," she said. "This scar… You didn't choose that. You didn't choose to be born into a life of violence. You didn't choose your father. You didn't choose that time in prison. Didn't choose to get in a fight that day and have your body cut open. You chose *this*. These wings. This design. Whatever it means to you, you chose that. And it's more real than anything that was inflicted on you could ever be."

He stopped her from talking then, captured her mouth with his and silenced her with the fierceness of his kiss.

He wanted everything she said to be real. He wanted her words to matter, as much as everything that had come before them. As much as every blow he'd witnessed, every blow he'd been subjected to, every vile insult.

He wanted her kiss to mean more than his past.

He smoothed his hands down her body, his touch filled with reverence, filled with awe.

This woman, so beautiful and sweet, would touch *him*. Would give herself to *him*.

Yes, he wanted to believe what she said. He did. But he could see no way to do that. Couldn't find it in himself.

He could only be glad that somehow, he had found her.

He wanted to drown in her, as much as he had wanted to drown in the rain. To feel renewed. Clean. If only for a moment. She was like that spring rain. Restorative. Redemptive. More than he deserved, and essential in ways he wouldn't let himself think about.

She moved her hands over his body, over his face, pressing kisses to the scar on his ribs, to the tattoo, lower. Until she took him into her mouth, her tongue swirling in a torturous pattern over the swollen head of his erection. He bucked up, gripping her hair even as a protest escaped his lips.

"Let me," she said softly.

And then she returned her attention to him, this beautiful woman who had never done this for a man before. She lavished him with the kind of attention he didn't deserve, not from anyone, least of all her.

But he wanted it, wanted her. He wanted this in a way he hadn't wanted anything for longer than he could remember. He *wanted*, and it was because of her.

He *wanted*, and he would never forget her for it.

He *wanted*, and he would never forgive her for it.

She was hope. She was a promise of redemption he could never truly have.

She was *faith*, that's what she was. Believing in something you couldn't see or control. Until now, he had never wanted any part of something like that.

But here he was, drowning in it. In her.

A missing piece. To his life.

To his heart.

His vision began to blur, his body shaking, wracked with the need for release as Faith used her hands and her mouth on him. As she tempted him far beyond what he could handle.

He looked down at her, and their eyes met. He saw desire. Need.

And trust.

She trusted him. This beautiful angel trusted him like no one ever had.

And it pushed him right over the edge.

He didn't pull away from her, and she didn't stop, swallowing down his release before moving up to his mouth again, scattering kisses over his abs and his chest as she went. He claimed her lips, pressing his hands between her thighs, smoothing his fingers over her and pushing two deep inside her as he brought her to her own climax.

She clung to him, looking dazed, filled with wonder.

Yet again, because of him. She was a gift. Possibly the only gift he'd ever been given in all his life.

But Faith should have been a gift for another man. A man who knew how to treasure her.

Levi didn't know how to do that.

But he knew how to hold on.

She clung to him, breathing hard, her fingernails digging into his shoulders. "I don't want to go home," she said softly.

"Then stay with me."

She looked up at him, her face questioning.

"Yes," he confirmed. "Stay with me."

Chapter 13

It was easy to let time slowly slip by, spending it in a bubble with Levi. It was a lot less easy for Faith to hide where she was spending all her nights and, frankly, half her days. If her brothers weren't suspicious of her behavior, Poppy certainly was.

There was no way she could get her unusual comings and goings past the eagle eye of her sister-in-law, and Poppy was starting to give Faith some serious side eye whenever Faith came into the office late, or left a little early.

Faith knew the reckoning was coming. She was going to have to deal with whatever was between her and Levi, and soon. Because the fact of the matter was, whatever they had agreed on in the beginning, she no longer wanted this relationship to be temporary.

The two of them had lapsed into a perfect routine over the past few weeks. When she wasn't at work, she was at his house, and often sketching.

Working sometimes late into the night while she watched him sleep, more and more ideas flowing through her mind.

She had begun to think of his new house like a bird's nest.

To go with the bird that he'd tattooed on his body. A place for that soaring creature to call home. A home that rested effortlessly in the natural environment around it, and seemed to be made from the materials of the earth.

Of course, maybe she was pondering all of that to the detriment of her other work. And that was a problem. She felt…so removed from her life right now. From everything she was supposed to care about.

She cared about Levi.

About what lay on the other side of all of this. About the changes taking place inside of her.

She should care more about her upcoming interview with *Architectural Digest*. She should care more about a television spot she was soon going to be filming in the office. One that was intended as a way to boost the participation of young girls in male-dominated fields, like architecture.

Instead, Faith was fixating on her boyfriend.

Immediately, her heart fell.

He wasn't her boyfriend. He was a man she had a temporary arrangement with, and she was becoming obsessed. She was becoming preoccupied.

Even so, she wasn't sure she cared. Because she had never been preoccupied in her life. She had always been focused, on task. Maybe it was her turn to go off the trail for a little while.

Maybe it was okay.

You don't have to be perfect.

Her mother's words rang in her ears, even as Faith

sat there at her desk. She wasn't sure what perfect even looked like for her anymore and the realization left her feeling rocked.

Poppy was going to appear in a moment to film the television spot they were sending in, and Faith knew she needed to pull herself together.

She wasn't sure if she could.

The door cracked open and Poppy came in, a smile on her perfectly made-up face, her figure—and her growing baby bump—highlighted by the adorable retro wiggle dress she was wearing.

Poppy was always immaculate. The only time she had ever seemed frazzled in any regard was when she had been dealing with issues in her relationship with Isaiah. So maybe—*maybe*—Poppy would be the ally Faith needed.

Or at the very least, maybe she would be the person Faith could confide in. For all that they had married older men with their own issues, Hayley and Mia did not seem like they would be sympathetic to Faith's situation.

It was all very "do as I say and do" not "do the kind of man that I do."

"Are you ready?" Poppy asked.

Her skeptical expression said that Faith was not ready. Though, Faith wasn't sure why Poppy felt that way.

"I was going to say yes," Faith said slowly. "But you clearly don't think so."

Poppy frowned. "You look very pale."

"I *am* pale," Faith said drily.

"Well," Poppy said, patting her own glowing, decidedly *not* pale complexion, "compared to some, yes. But that isn't what I meant. You need some blush. And lipstick with a color. I don't support this millennial pink nonsense that makes your lips blend into the rest of your skin."

"I'm *not* wearing lipstick."

"Well, there's your problem."

Poppy opened the drawer where Faith normally kept her makeup, and that was when Faith realized her mistake. The makeup wasn't there. Because she had taken the bag over to Levi's.

Poppy narrowed her eyes. "Where is your makeup?"

Faith tapped her fingers on her desk. "Somewhere?"

"Honestly, Faith, I wouldn't have been suspicious, except that was a dumb-ass answer."

"It's at Levi Tucker's," Faith said, deciding right in that moment that bold and brazen was what she would go for.

Everything was muddled inside her in part because she hadn't been sure if she wanted to go all in here. Cash her chips in on this one, big terrible thing that might be the mistake to end all mistakes.

But she did. She wanted to.

She wanted to go all in on Levi.

That horrible ex-wife of his had done that. She had cashed in all her chips on a moment when she could take his money and have the life she wanted with absolutely no care about what it did to him.

Well, why couldn't Faith do the opposite? Blow her life up for him. Why couldn't she risk herself for him?

No one in his life ever had. Not his father, who was drunk and useless and evil. Not his mother, who had allowed the scars and pains from her past to blind her to her own son's innocence.

Not his wife, who had been so poisoned by selfishness.

And Faith... What would she be protecting if she didn't?

Her own sense of perfection. Of not having let anyone down.

None of that mattered. None of it was *him*.

"Because you were…working on a job?" Poppy asked, her expression skeptical, but a little hopeful.

Faith's lips twitched.

"Some kind of job," she responded, intentionally digging into the double entendre, intentionally meeting Poppy's gaze. "So, there you have it."

"Faith…" Poppy said. "I don't… With a *client*?"

"I know," Faith said. "I didn't plan for it to go that way. But it did. And… I only meant for it to be temporary. That's all. But… I love him."

The moment she said it, she knew it was true. All her life she had been apart. All her life she had been separate. But in his arms, she belonged. With him, she had found something in herself she had never even known was missing.

"Your brothers…"

"They're going to be mad. And they're going to be afraid I'll get hurt. I know. I'm afraid I'll get hurt. Which is actually why I said something to you. Isaiah is not an easy man."

Poppy at least laughed at that. "No," she said. "He isn't."

"He's worth it, isn't he?"

Poppy breathed out slowly, then took a few steps toward Faith's desk, sympathy and understanding crinkling her forehead. "Faith, I've loved your brother for more than ten years. And he was worth it all that time, even when he was in love with someone else."

"Levi's not in love with anyone else. But he's…angry. I'm not sure if there's any room inside him for any other emotion. I don't know if he can let it go."

"Have you told him that you love him?"

"No. You're the first person I've told."

"Why me?" Poppy asked.

"Well, first of all," Faith said, "Isaiah won't kill you."

"No," Poppy said.

"Second of all... I need to know what I should do. Because I've never loved anyone before and I'm terrified. And I don't want him to be a mistake, and that has nothing to do with wanting to be perfect. And everything to do with wanting him. I'm not hiding it anymore. I'm not."

"You never had to hide it. No one needed you to be perfect."

"Maybe I needed it. I can't let them down." Faith shook her head. "I can't let them down, Poppy. Isaiah and Joshua have poured everything into our business. I can't... I can't mess up."

"They would never look at it that way," Poppy said. "Isaiah loves you. So much. I know it's hard for him to show it."

"It's easy for me to forget that he struggles, too. He seems confident."

"He is," Poppy said. "To his detriment sometime. But he's also just human. A man who fell in love. When he didn't see it coming. So, he's not going to throw stones at you for doing the same."

"They're going to be angry about who it is. Levi's older than they are."

Poppy shook her head. "And Isaiah is my foster sister's ex-fiancé. We all have reasons things shouldn't be. But they are. And sometimes you can't fight it. Love doesn't ask permission. Love gets in the cracks. And it expands. And it finds us sometimes when we least expect it."

"So, you don't judge me?"

"I'm going to judge you if you don't put on a better lipstick color for the video. But I'm not going to judge you for falling in love with a difficult man who may or may not have the capacity to love you. Because I've been there."

"And it worked out."

"Yes," Poppy said, putting her hand on her stomach. "It worked out."

"And if it hadn't?" Faith asked.

Poppy seemed to consider that for a while, her flawlessly lipsticked mouth contorting. "If it hadn't, it would have still been worth it. In my case, I would still have the baby. And she would be worth it. But also… No matter what Isaiah was able to feel for me in the end, I never would have regretted loving him. In a perfect world, he would have always loved me. But the world isn't perfect. It's broken. I suspect it's that way for your Levi, too."

Faith nodded. "I guess the only question is…whether or not he's too broken to heal."

"And you won't know that unless you try."

"That sounds an awful lot like risk."

"It is. But love is like that. It's big, Faith. And you can't hold on to fear. Not if you expect to carry around something so big and important as love. Now get some lipstick on."

Chapter 14

She was finished designing the house.

That day had been inevitable from the beginning. It was what they had been moving toward. It was, in fact, the point. But still, now that the day had arrived, Levi found himself reluctant to let go. He found himself trying to figure out ways he might convince her to stay. And then he questioned why he wanted that.

The entire point of hiring her, building this house, had been to establish himself in a new life. To put himself on a new path. The point had not been to get attached to his little architect.

He was on the verge of getting everything he wanted. Everything he needed.

She should have nothing to do with that.

And yet, he found himself fantasizing about bringing her into his home. Laying her down on that custom bed he didn't really want or need.

He hadn't seen the designs yet. In fact, part of him wanted to delay because after he approved the designs, Jonathan Bear would begin work on the construction aspects of the job. Likely, any further communications on the design would be between her and Jonathan.

Levi should be grateful that once this ended, it would end cold like that. For her sake.

He wasn't.

It was a Sunday afternoon, and he knew that meant she had dinner with her parents later. But she hadn't left yet. In fact, she was currently lying across the end of his bed, completely naked. She was on her stomach, with her legs bent at the knees and crossed at the ankles, held up in the air, kicking back and forth. Her hair had fallen in her face as she sketched earnestly, full lips pursed into a delicious O that made him think of how she'd wrapped them around his body only an hour or so earlier.

"Don't you have to be at your parents' place soon?" he asked.

She looked over at him, her expression enigmatic. "Yes."

"But?" he pressed.

"I didn't say 'but.'"

"You didn't have to," he said, moving closer to the bed and bringing his hands down on her actual butt with a smack. "I heard it all the same."

"Your concern is touching," she said, shooting him the evil eye and rolling away from him. "It's complicated."

"I understand complicated family." He just didn't want to talk about complicated family. He wanted to get his hands all over her body again. But he could listen to her. For a few minutes.

"No," she corrected. "You understand irredeemable, horrendous families. Mine is just complicated."

"Are you going to skip this week?"

"Why do you care?"

It was a good question. Whether or not she went to her family's weekly gathering was only his concern if it impacted his ability to make love with her.

Right. Because making love was what she's been doing all day, every day at your house.

Not living together. Not playing at domesticity.

Going out and riding on the trails. Cooking dinner. Eating dinner. Going to sleep, waking up, showering.

Hell, they had ended up brushing their teeth together.

He could suddenly see why—per her earlier concern—men got weird about toothbrushes.

There was something intimate about a toothbrush.

There was also something about knowing her so intimately that made the sex better. Everything that made the sex unique to her, made it better. Living with her, being near her, was foreplay.

He didn't have to understand it to feel it.

Faith cleared her throat. "I told Poppy about us."

He sat down on the edge of the bed. "Why?" He had never met Poppy, but he knew all about her. Knew that she had pretty recently become Faith's sister-in-law. But he hadn't gotten the impression they were friends in particular.

"It just kind of…came out." She shrugged, her bare breasts rising and falling. For the moment, he was too distracted to think about what she was saying. "And I didn't see the point in hiding it anymore."

"I thought you really didn't want your brothers to know."

"I didn't. But now…"

"You finished designing the house. We both know that." She ducked her head. "I haven't shown it to you yet."

"That doesn't change the fact that you're done. Does it?"

"I guess not. It's not a coincidence that I went ahead and told her now. I needed to talk to her about some things."

"Don't you think that if it's about—" he hesitated over saying the word *us* "—this, that you should have talked to me?"

"Yes, I do need to talk to you." She folded her knees upward, pushing herself into a sitting position. "I just... I needed to get my head on straight."

"And?"

"I failed. So, this is the thing." She frowned, her eyebrows drawing tightly together. "I don't want us to be over."

Her words hit him with all the force of a blade slipping into his rib cage.

"Is that so?"

He didn't want it to be over, either.

That was the thing. *Not being over* was what he had been pondering just a few moments ago. They didn't have to be over yet.

He almost felt as if everything else was on pause. His revenge, his triumphant return back into Alicia's circles. His determination to make sure that she went to prison by proving what she had done to him.

All of that ugliness could wait. It would have to. It was going to start once the house was finished. And until then...

What was the harm of staying with Faith?

Right. Her brothers know. Soon, her parents will know. And you really want all of that to come down on you?

That's not simple. That's not casual.

That's complicated.

But still. The idea that he could have her, for a little while longer. That he could keep her, locked away with him…

It was intoxicating.

"You want more of this?" he asked, trailing his finger along her collarbone, down her rib cage, then skimming over her sensitized nipple.

"Yes," she said, her voice a husky whisper. "But not just more of this. Levi, you have to know… You have to know."

Her eyes shone with emotion, with conviction. His chest froze, his heart a block of ice. He couldn't breathe around it.

"I have to know what, little girl?" he asked, locking his jaw tight.

"How much I love you."

That wasn't just a single knife blade. That was an outright attack. Stabbing straight through to his heart and leaving him to bleed.

"What?"

"I love you," she said. She shook her head. "I didn't want it to be like this. I didn't want to be a cliché. I didn't want to be who you were afraid I would be. The virgin who fell for the first man she slept with. But I realized something. I'm not a cliché. I'm not a virgin who fell for the first man she slept with. I'm a woman who waited until she found something powerful enough to act on. Our connection came before sex. And I have to trust that. I have to trust myself. Until now, everything I've done has been safe."

"You went away to boarding school. You have excelled in your profession before the age of thirty. How can you call any of that safe?"

She clasped her hands in front of her, picking at her fingernails. "Because it made everyone happy. Not only that—for the most part, it made me happy. It was the path of least resistance. And it still is. I could walk away from you, and I could continue on with my plan. No love. No marriage. Until I'm thirty-five maybe. Until I've had more of a career than many people have in a lifetime. Until I've done everything in the perfect order. Until I'm a triumph to my brothers and an achievement to my parents. It will make me feel proud, but it will never make me...*feel.* Not really.

"A career isn't who you are. It can't be. You know that. Everything you accomplished turned to dust because of what your ex did to you. She destroyed it, because those things are so easily destroyed. When everything burns there's one thing that's left, Levi. And that's the love of other people."

"You're wrong about that," he said, his chest tightening into a knot. "There is something else that remains through the fire. That's hatred. Blinding, burning hatred, and I have enough of that for two men. I have too much of it, Faith. Sometimes I think I might have been born with it. And until I make that bitch pay for what she did to me, that's how it's going to be."

"I don't understand what that has to do with anything."

Of course she didn't understand. Because she couldn't fathom the kind of rage and darkness that lived inside him. She had never touched a fire that burned so hot. Had never been exposed to something so ugly.

Until now. Until him.

"Then choose something else," she said. "Choose a different way."

"I've never had a choice," he said. "Ever. My fate was decided for me before I ever took a breath in this world."

"I don't believe that. If people can't chose, what does

that mean for me? Have I worked hard at any of this, or was it just handed to me? Did I ever have a choice?"

"That's different."

"Why?" she pressed. "Because it's about you, so that means you can see it however you want? You can't see how hypocritical that is?"

"Hypocrisy is the least of my concerns," he said.

"What *is* your concern then? Because it certainly isn't me."

"That's where you're wrong. I warned you. I told you what this could be and what it couldn't be. You didn't listen."

"It wasn't a matter of listening. I fell in love with you by being with you. Your beauty is in everything you do, Levi. The way you touch me. The way you look at me."

"What's love to you?" he asked. "Do you think it's living here in this house with me? Do you think it's the two of us making love and laughing, and not dealing with the real world at all?"

"Don't," she said, her voice small. "Don't make it like that."

He interrupted her, not letting her finish, ignoring the hurt on her face. "Let me tell you what love is to me. A continual slog of violence. Blind optimism that propels you down the aisle of a church and then into making vows to people who are never going to do right by you. And I don't even mean just my wife. I mean *me*. You said it yourself. I was a bad husband."

"Not on the same level as your father," she argued. "Not like your wife was a bad wife."

He shrugged. "What did she get from me? Nothing but my money, clearly. And what about in your family? They're normal, and I think they might even be good people, and they still kind of mess you up."

"I guess you're right. Loving other people is never going to be simple, or easy. It's not a constant parade of happiness. Love moves. It shifts. It changes. Sometimes you give more, and sometimes you take more. Sometimes love hurts. And there's not a whole lot anyone can do about that. *But it's worth it*. That's what it comes down to for me. I know this might be a tough road, a hard one. But I also know that love is important. It matters."

"Why?" he asked, the question torn from the depths of his soul.

He wanted to understand.

On some level, he was desperate to figure out why she thought he was worth all this. This risk—sitting before him, literally naked, confessing her feelings, tearing her chest open and showing those vulnerable parts of herself. He wanted to understand why he merited such a risk.

When no one else in his life had ever felt the same.

"All my life I've had my sketchpad between myself and the world," she said. "And when it hasn't been my sketchbook it's been my accomplishments. What I've done for my family. I can hold out all these things and use them to justify my existence. But I don't have to do that with you. I don't think I really have to do it with my family, but it makes me feel safe. Makes me feel secure. I don't have to share all that much of myself, or risk all that much of myself. I can stand on higher ground and be impressive, perfect even. It's easy for people to be proud of me. The idea of doing something just for myself, the idea of doing something that might make someone judge me, or make someone reject me, is terrifying. When you live like I have, the great unknown is failure. You were never impressed with me. You wanted my architecture because it was a status symbol, and for no other reason."

"That isn't true. If I didn't like what you designed, I would never have contacted you."

"Still. It was different with you. At first, I thought it was because you were a stranger. I told myself being with you was like taking a class. Getting good at sex, I guess, with a qualified teacher. But it wasn't that. Ever. It was just you. Real chemistry with no explanation for it."

"Chemistry still isn't love, Faith," he said, his voice rough.

She ignored him. "I want to quit needing explanations about something magical happening. I wanted to be close to you without barriers. Without borders. No sketchbook, no accomplishments. You made me want something flawed and human inside myself that scared me before."

"The idea of some flawed existence is only a fantasy for people who've had it easy."

She frowned. "It's not a fantasy. The idea that there is such a thing as perfect is the fantasy. Maybe it's the fantasy you have. But there is no perfect. And I've been scared to admit that."

Tucking her hair behind her ear, Faith moved to the edge of the bed and stood before continuing. "My life has been easy compared to yours. You made me realize how strong a person can be. I've never met someone like you. Someone who had to push through so much pain. You made yourself out of nothing. My family might come from humble beginnings, but it isn't the same. We had each other. We had support. You didn't have any of that.

"I don't want you to walk alone anymore, Levi. I want to walk with you. From where I'm sitting right now, that's the greatest accomplishment I could ever hope to have. To love and be loved by someone like you. To choose to walk our own path together."

"My path is set," he said. "It has been set from the beginning."

He looked down at her, at her luminous face. Her eyes, which were full of so much hope.

So much foolish hope.

She didn't understand what she was begging him to do. He had thought of it earlier. That he could pull her inside and lock her in this cage with him.

And he might be content enough with that for a while, but eventually… Eventually she wouldn't be.

Because this hatred, this rage that lived inside him, was a life sentence.

Something he had been born with. Something he feared he would never be able to escape.

And asking Faith to live with him, asking Faith to live with what he was—that would be letting her serve a life sentence with him. And if anyone on this earth was innocent, it was her.

Even so, it was tempting.

He could embrace the monster completely and hold this woman captive. This woman who had gripped him, body and soul, and stolen his sense of self-preservation, stolen his sense of just *why* vengeance was so important.

It was all he had. It consumed him. It drove him.

Justice was the only thing that had gotten him through five years in prison. At first, wanting justice for his wife, and then, wanting it for himself.

Somewhere, in all of that, wanting justice had twisted into wanting revenge, but in his case it amounted to more or less the same. And he would not bring Faith into that world.

She stood there, a beacon of all he could not have. And still he wanted her. With all of him. With his every breath.

But he knew he could not have her.

Knew that he couldn't take what she would so freely give, because she had no idea what the repercussions would be.

He knew what it was to live in captivity.

And he would not wish the same on her.

He had to let her go.

"No," he said. "I don't love you."

"You don't love me?" The question was almost skeptical, and he certainly hadn't cowed her.

He had to make her understand what he was.

"No."

It was easy to say the word, because what was love? What did it mean? What did it mean beyond violence and betrayal, broken vows and everything else that had happened in his life? He had no evidence that love was real. That there was any value in it. And the closest he had ever come to believing was seeing Faith's bright, hopeful eyes as she looked up at him.

And he knew he didn't deserve that version of love.

No. If there was love, real love, and it was that pure, it didn't belong with him.

Faith should give that love to someone who deserved it. A man who had earned the right to have those eyes look at him like he was a man who actually had the hope of becoming new, better.

Levi was not that man.

"I can't love you. You or anyone."

"That isn't true. You have loved me for weeks now. In your every action, your every touch."

"I haven't."

"Levi…" She pressed her hand to his chest and he wanted to hold it there. "You changed me. How can you look at me and say that what we have isn't love?"

He moved her hand away. And took a step back.

"If there is love in this whole godforsaken world, little girl, it isn't for me. You'll go on and you'll find a man who's capable of it. Me? I've chosen vengeance. And maybe you're right. Maybe there is another path I could walk on, but I'm not willing to do it."

She stared at him, and suddenly, a deep understanding filled her brown eyes. He was the one who felt naked now, though he was dressed and she was not. He felt like she could see him, straight to his soul, maybe deeper even than he had ever looked inside himself.

It was terrifying to be known like that.

The knowledge in Faith's eyes was deep and terrible. He wanted to turn away from it. Standing there, feeling like she was staring into the darkness in him, was a horror he had never experienced before.

"The bird is freedom. That's what it means," she said suddenly, like the sun had just risen and she could see clearly for the first time. She turned away from him, grabbing her sketchbook off the bed and holding it up in front of his face. "Look at this," she said. "I have the real plans on my computer, but look at these."

He flipped through the journal, until he found exactly what she was talking about. And he knew. The moment he saw it. He didn't need her to tell him.

It was a drawing of a house. An aerial view. And the way it was laid out it looked like folded wings. It wasn't shaped like a bird, not in the literal sense, but he felt it. Exactly what she had intended him to feel.

"I knew it was important to you, but I didn't know why. Freedom, Levi. You put it on your body, but you haven't accepted it with your soul."

"Faith…"

"You never left that prison," she said softly.

"I did," he said, his voice hard. "I left it and I'm standing right here."

"No," she responded. "You didn't. You're still in there." She curled her fingers into fists, angry tears filling her eyes. "That woman got you a life sentence, Levi. But it was a wrongful sentence. The judge released you, but you haven't released yourself. You don't deserve to be in prison forever because of her."

"It's not just her," he said, his voice rough. "I imagined that if I changed my life, if I earned enough money, if I got married and got myself the right kind of house, that I would be free of the fate everyone in my life thought I was headed for. Don't you think every teacher I ever had thought I was going to be like my father? Don't you think every woman in Copper Ridge who agreed to go on a date with me was afraid I was secretly a wifebeater in training? They did. They all thought that's how I would end up. The one way people could never have imagined I would end up was rich. I did it to defy them. To define my own fate, but it was impossible. I still ended up in prison, Faith. That was my fate, no matter what I did. Was it her? Or was it me?"

"It's not you," she said. "It isn't."

"I can't say the same with such authority," he said.

"You're not a bad man," she said, her voice trembling. "You aren't. You're the best man I've ever known. But you can tattoo symbols of freedom on your skin all you want, it won't make a difference. Revenge is not going to set you free, Levi. Only hope can do that. Only love can do that. You have to let it. You have to let me."

He couldn't argue, because he knew it was true. Because he had known that if he brought her into his life then he would be consigning her to a prison sentence, too.

And if it was true for her, it was true for him.

He was in prison. But for him there would be no escape. She could escape.

"For my part," he said, his voice flat, as flat as the beating of his heart and his ears, "I've chosen vengeance. And there's nothing you can do to stop it."

"Levi…" She blinked. "Can you just give us a chance? You don't have to tell me that you love me now. But can't you just—"

"No. We're done. The house is done, and so are we. It's already gone on too long, Faith, and the fact that I've made you cry is evidence of that."

"Please," she said. "I'll beg. I don't have any pride. I'm more than willing to fall into that virgin stereotype you are so afraid of," she reiterated. "Happily. Because there is no point to pride if I haven't got you."

He gritted his teeth, and took a step forward, gripping her chin between his thumb and forefinger. "Now you listen to me," he said. "There is every reason for you to have pride, Faith Grayson. Your life is going to go on without me. And when you meet the man who loves you the way you deserve to be loved, who can give you the life you should have, you'll understand. And you'll be grateful for your pride."

"I refuse to take a lecture on my feelings from a man who doesn't even believe in what I feel." She turned and began to collect her clothes. "I still want you to have my design. My house. Because when you're walking around in it, I want you to feel my love in those walls. And I want you to remember what you could have had." She blinked her eyes. "I designed it with so much care, Levi. To be sure that you never felt like you were locked in again. But you're going to feel like you're in prison. Whether you're inside or outside. Whether you're alone or with me or whether you're on the back of a horse or not. And it's a prison of your own making. You have to let go. You have to let go of all the hate you're carrying around. And then you might be surprised to find out how much love you can hold. If you decide to do that, please come and find me."

She dressed quietly, slowly, and without another word. Then she grabbed her sketchbook and turned and walked out of the bedroom.

He didn't go after her. He didn't move at all until he heard the front door shut, until he heard the engine of her car fire up.

He walked into the bathroom, bracing himself on the sink before looking up slowly at his reflection. The man he saw there…was a criminal.

A man who might not have committed a crime, but who had been hardened by years in jail. A man who had arguably been destined for that fate no matter which way he had walked in the world, because of his beginnings.

The man he saw there…was a man he hated more than he hated anyone.

His father. His ex-wife.

Anyone.

Levi looked down at the countertop again, and saw the cup by the sink where his toothbrush was. Where Faith's still was.

That damn toothbrush.

He picked up the cup and threw it across the bathroom, the glass shattering decisively, the toothbrushes scattering.

It was just a damn toothbrush. She was just a woman.

In the end, he would have exactly what he had set out to get.

And that was all a man like him could ever hope for.

Chapter 15

Faith had no idea how she managed to walk into her parents' house. Had no idea how she managed to sit and eat dinner and look like a normal person. Force a smile. Carry on a conversation.

She had no idea how she managed to do any of it, and yet, she did.

She felt broken. Splintered and shattered inside, and like she might get cut on her own damaged pieces. But somehow, she had managed to sit there and smile and nod at appropriate times. Somehow, she had managed not to pick up her dinner plate and smash it on the table, to make it as broken as the rest of her.

She had managed not to yell at Joshua and Danielle, Poppy and Isaiah, Devlin and Mia, and even her own parents for being happy, functional couples.

She felt she deserved a medal for all those things, and yet she knew one wasn't coming.

When the meal was finished, her mother and Danielle and Poppy stayed in the kitchen, working on a cake recipe Danielle had been interested in learning how to bake for Joshua's birthday, while Devlin and her father went out to the garage so that Devlin could take a look under the hood of their father's truck.

And that left Faith corralled in the living room with Joshua and Isaiah.

"Poppy told me," Isaiah said, his voice firm and hard.

"She's a turncoat," Faith said, shaking her head. Of course, she had known her sister-in-law would tell. Faith had never expected confidentiality there, and she would never have asked for it. "Well, there's nothing to tell. Not anymore."

"What does that mean?" Joshua asked.

"Just what it sounds like. My personal relationship with Mr. Tucker is no more, the design phase has moved on to construction and he is now Jonathan Bear's problem, not mine. It's not a big deal." She waved a hand. "So now your optics should be a little clearer."

"I don't care about my optics, Faith," Joshua said, his expression contorted with anger. "I care about you. I care about you getting hurt."

"Well," she said, "I'm hurt. Oh, well. Everybody goes through it, I guess."

"That bastard," Joshua said. "He took advantage of you."

"Why do you think he took advantage of me? Because I'm young?" She stared at her brother, her expression pointed. "Because I was a virgin?" She glared at them both a little bit harder, and watched as both expressions paled slightly, and they exchanged glances. "People who live in glass towers cannot be throwing stones. And I think the two of you did a pretty phenomenal job of breaking your wives' hearts before things all worked out."

"That was different," Isaiah said.

"Oh, really?"

"Yes," Joshua said. "Different."

"Why?"

"Because," Joshua said simply, "we ended up with them."

"But they didn't know that you would end up together. Not when you broke things off with them."

"Do you think you're going to end up with him?" Isaiah asked.

"No," she said, feeling deflated as the words left her lips. "I don't. But you can't go posturing about me not knowing what I want, not knowing what I'm doing, when you both married women closer to my age than yours."

"Poppy is kind of in the middle," Isaiah said. "In fairness."

"No," Faith said, pointing a finger at him. "No *in fairness*. She was in love with you for a decade and you ignored her, and then you proposed a convenient marriage to her with absolutely no emotion involved at all. You don't get any kind of exception here."

He shrugged. "It was worth a shot."

"I don't need a lecture," she said softly. "And I don't need you to go beat him up."

"Are you still going ahead with the project?" Joshua asked. "Because you know, you don't have to do that."

"I do," she said. "I want to. I want to give him the house. I mean, for money, but I want him to have it."

"Well, he's the asshole who has to live in the house designed by his ex, I guess," Joshua said.

She sighed heavily. "I know what you're thinking— you're thinking that you were right, and you warned me. But you *weren't* right. Whatever you think happened between Levi and I, you're wrong."

"So he didn't defile you?" Joshua asked.

"No," Faith said, not backing down from the challenge in her brother's eyes. "He definitely did. But I love him. And I don't regret what happened. I can't. It was a mistake. But it was my mistake. And I needed to make it."

"Faith," Joshua said, "I know it seems like it sometimes, but I promise, you don't have to justify yourself to me. Tell us. I know what I said about optics, but that was before I realized... Hell," he said, "it was before I realized what was going on. I'm sorry that you got hurt."

"I'll survive," she said, feeling sadly like she might not.

"Faith," Isaiah said, her older brother looking uncharacteristically sympathetic. "Whatever happens," he said, "sometimes a person is too foolish to see what's right in front of them. Sometimes a man needs to be left on his own to fully understand what it was he had. Sometimes men who don't deserve love need it the most."

"Do you mean you?" she asked.

He looked at her, his eyes clear and focused. And full of more emotion than she was used to seeing on him. "Yes. And it would be hypocritical of me to accept the love I get from Poppy and think Levi doesn't deserve the chance to have it with you. Or maybe *deserve* is the wrong word. It's not about deserving. I don't deserve what I have. But I love her. With everything. And it took me a while to sort through that. The past gets in the way."

"That's our problem," she said. "There's just too much of the past."

"There's nothing you can do about that," Isaiah said. "The choice is his. The only question is...are you going to wait for him to figure it out?"

"I vote you don't," Joshua said. "Because you're too good for him."

"I vote you decide," Isaiah added, shooting a pointed look at Joshua. "Because you probably are too good for him. But sometimes when a woman is too good for a man, that means he'll love her a hell of a lot more than anyone else will." He cleared his throat. "From experience, I can tell you, that if you're hard to love, when someone finally does love you, it's worth everything. Absolutely everything."

"You're not hard to love," she said.

"That's awfully nice of you to say, but I definitely have my moments. I bet he does, too. And when he realizes what it is you're giving him? He'll know what a damn fool he was to have thrown it away."

"I still disagree," Joshua said.

"And who are you going to listen to about interpersonal relationships? Him or me?"

Faith looked over at Isaiah, her serious brother, her brother who had difficulty understanding people, connecting with people, but no difficulty at all loving his wife. She smiled, but didn't say anything. She felt broken. But Isaiah had given her hope. And she would hold onto that with everything she had.

Because without it… All that stretched before her was a future without Levi. And that made all her previous perfection seem like nothing much at all.

Chapter 16

It had been two weeks since Levi had last seen Faith.

And in that time, ground had been broken on the new house, he'd had several intensive conversations with Jonathan Bear and he'd done one well-placed interview he knew would filter into his ex-wife's circles. He'd had the reporter come out to the house he was currently staying in, and the man had followed him on a trail ride while Levi had given his version of the story.

It had all gone well, the headline making national news easily, and possibly international news thanks to the internet, with several pictures of Levi and his horses. The animals somehow made him seem softer and more approachable.

And, of course, his alliance with Faith had only helped matters. Because she was a young woman and because the assumption was that she would have vetted him before working with him. What surprised him the most was the quote that had been included in the story from GrayBear

Construction. Which, considering what Levi knew about the company, meant Faith's brother Joshua. It surprised him, because Joshua had spoken of Levi's character and their excitement about working on the project with him. On this chance for a new start.

For redemption.

Levi wasn't sure what the hell Faith had told her brother, but he was sure he didn't deserve the quote. Still, he was grateful for it.

Grateful was perhaps the wrong word.

He looked at the article, running his thumb over the part about his redemption.

And in his mind, he heard Faith's voice.

You never walked out of that prison.

She didn't understand. She couldn't.

But that didn't change the fact that he felt like he'd been breathing around a knife for the past two weeks. Faith—*his* Faith—had left a hole in his life he couldn't imagine would ever be filled. But that was…how it had to be.

He had his path, she had hers.

There was nothing to be done about it. His fate had been set long before he'd ever met her. And there was no changing it now.

He had gone out to the building site today, just to look around at everything. The groundwork was going well, as was the excavation over where he wanted to put the stables. She had been right about Jonathan Bear. He was the best.

Jonathan had assembled a crew in what seemed to be record time, especially considering that this particular project was so large. It looked like a small army working on the property. Jonathan was also quick and efficient at acquiring materials, and speeding through permits and inspections. He also seemed to know every subcontractor in the state, and had gotten them out to bid right away.

Levi had already built on a property where money was no object, but this was somewhere beyond that.

He turned in a circle, watching all the commotion around him, then stopped and frowned when he saw a Mercedes coming up the drive. Bright red, sporty. Not a car that he recognized.

The car stopped, and he saw a woman inside, large sunglasses on her face, hair long and loose.

Flames licked at the edge of his gut as a sense of understanding began to dawn on him.

The blonde got out of the car, and that was when recognition hit him with full force.

Alicia.

His ex-wife.

She was wearing a tight, black dress that looked ludicrous out here, and she at least had the good sense to wear a pair of pointed flats, rather than the spiked stilettos she usually favored. Still, the dress was tight, and it forced her entire body into a shimmy with each and every step as she walked over to meet him.

He'd loved her. For so many years. And then he'd hated her.

And now… His whole chest was full of Faith. His whole body. His whole soul. And he looked at Alicia and he didn't feel much of anything anymore.

"Are you really here?" he asked, not quite sure why those were the words that had come out of his mouth. But… It was damn incredulous. That she would dare show her face.

"I am," she said, looking down and back up at him, her blue eyes innocent and bright. "I wasn't sure you would be willing to see me if I called ahead. I took a chance, hoping I would find you here. All that publicity for your new build… It wasn't hard to find out where it was happening."

"You're either a very brave woman or a very stupid one."

She tilted her chin upward. "Or a woman with a concealed-carry permit."

Suddenly, the little black handbag she was carrying seemed a lot less innocuous.

"Did you come to shoot me?"

She lifted a shoulder. "No. But I'm not opposed to it."

"Why the hell do you have the right to be angry at me?"

"I'm not here to be angry at you," she said. "But I didn't know how you would receive me, so self-defense was definitely on my mind."

He shook his head. "I never laid a hand on you. I never gave you a reason to think you would have to protect yourself around me. Any fear you feel standing in front of me? That's all on you."

"Maybe," she said. "I didn't really mean for them to think you killed me."

"Didn't you? You knew I went to prison. Hell, babe, you siphoned money off me for a couple of years to fund the lifestyle you knew you wanted to live out in the French Riviera, and you only got back on police radar when you had to dip into my funds. So I'd say you knew exactly what you were doing."

"Yes, Levi, I meant to steal money from you. But I didn't want you to go to jail. I wanted to disappear. And I needed the money to live how I wanted. When you got arrested, I didn't know what to do. At that point, there was such a circus around my disappearance that I couldn't come back."

"Oh, no, of course not."

"People like us, we have to look out for ourselves."

"I looked out for you," he said. "You were mine for twelve years, and even when I was in prison it was only you, so, for me, it was seventeen years of you being mine, Alicia. I worried about you. Cared for you. Loved you."

"I'm sorry," she said.

"You're sorry? I spent five years in prison and had my entire reputation destroyed, and you're sorry."

"I want you back." She shook her head. "I know it sounds insane. But I… I'm miserable."

"You're broke," he spat. "And you're afraid of what I'm going to do."

The way she looked up at him, the slight flash of anger in her eyes before it was replaced by that dewy innocence, told him he was definitely on the right track. "I don't have money, I'm not going to lie to you."

"And yet, that's a nice car."

She shrugged. "I have what I have. I can hardly be left without a vehicle. And I was your wife for all that time, you're right. And that's basically all I was, Levi. I enhanced your image, but being your wife didn't help me figure out a way to earn the kind of money you did, and now no one will touch me with a ten-foot pole. My reputation is completely destroyed."

"Forgive me for not being overly concerned that you faking your death has left you without a lot of options."

"In fairness, I didn't fake my death. I disappeared. That the police thought I was dead is hardly my fault."

"Alicia, are you honestly telling me you thought I would say I wanted you back?"

"Why not? You want a redemption story, and getting back with me would benefit us both. I don't think either of us were ever head over heels in love with each other.

We both wanted things from the other. And you know it. Don't go getting on your high horse now. We can come back. You don't need to be vindictive," she said.

"I don't need to be vindictive?" He shook his head. "This, from you?"

She was standing in front of him, imploring him to rescue her. That was what she wanted. For him to reach down to lift her out of this hell of her own making.

It was this exact moment when he knew he had her under his heel. He could take her in, make her think he was going along with her plan, and maybe get some information about what exactly she had done that was illegal, and get the exact kind of revenge he wanted. Or, if not that, he could finish it now, devastate her.

And then what?

That question echoed inside him, hollow and miserable.

Then what?

What was on the other side of it? What was feeding all that anger, all that hatred?

Where was the freedom? Where was the reward? Nothing but an empty house filled with reminders of Faith, but without the woman herself inside it.

Somehow, he had a vision of himself standing by a jail cell holding a key. And he knew that whatever he decided to do next was the deciding factor. Did he unlock the door and walk out, or did he throw the keys so far away from himself he would never be able to reach them again?

Faith was right.

He had been given a life sentence, but he didn't have to submit to it.

Faith.

He had been looking for satisfaction in this. Had been looking for satisfaction in revenge. In hatred.

And maybe there was satisfaction there. Something twisted and dirty, the kind of satisfaction his father would have certainly enjoyed.

But there was another choice. There was another path.

It was hope.

It was love.

But a man couldn't straddle two paths.

He had to choose. He had to choose hope over darkness, love over hate.

And right now, with dark satisfaction so close at hand, it was difficult. But on the other side...

Faith could be on the other side.

If he was strong enough to turn away from this now, Faith was on the other side.

"Go away," he said, his heart thundering heavily, adrenaline pulsing through his veins.

"What?"

"I don't ever want to see you again. I'm going to write you a check. Not for a whole lot of money, but for some. Trade in your car, for God's sake. Don't be an idiot. I'm not giving you money for *you*, I'm doing it for me. To clear this. Let it go. Whatever you think I did to you... Whatever you really wanted to do to me... It doesn't matter. Not anymore. We are done. And after you cash that check I want you to never even speak my name again. Do you understand me?"

"I don't want a check," she said, taking a step forward, wrapping her hands around his shirt. "I want you."

He jerked her hands off him, his lip curling. "You don't. You don't want me. And I sure as hell don't want you. But I'm also not going to let you suffer for the rest of your life. Do you know why not? Because everything in me, every natural thing in me, *wants* to. Wants to make you regret everything you've ever done, wants to make you regret you ever heard my name. But I won't do it. I won't let that part of myself with. Because I met a woman. And I love her. I love her, Alicia. You don't even know about the kind of love I found with her. The kind of love she has for me. I don't deserve it. Dammit, I have to try to be the kind of man that deserves it. So I want you to walk away from me. Because I'm choosing to let you go. I'm choosing to get on a different road.

"Don't you dare follow me."

"Levi..."

"Leave now, and you get your money. But if you don't..."

She stared at him. For a long time. As if he might change his mind. As if she had some kind of power over him. She didn't. Not over any part of him. Not his anger. Not his love. Not his future.

It was over, all of it. Her hold on him. The hold his childhood had over him.

Because love was stronger.

Faith was stronger.

"Okay," she said, finally. "I'll go."

"Good."

He watched her, unmoving, as she got back in her Mercedes and drove away. And as she did, he looked up into the sky and saw a bird flying overhead.

Free.

He was free.

Whatever happened next, Faith had given him that freedom.

But he wanted her to share it with him. More than his next breath, more than anything else.

He'd lived a life marked by anger. A life marked by

greed. He'd been saddled with the consequences of the poison that lived inside other people, and he'd taken that same poison and let it grow and fester inside him.

But he was done with that now.

He was through letting the darkness win.

He was ready. He was finally ready to walk out of that cell and into freedom.

With Faith.

Chapter 17

It was Sunday again. It had a tendency to roll around with alarming regularity. Which was massively annoying for Faith because it was getting harder and harder to put on a brave face in front of her family.

Although, how brave her face was—that was up for debate.

Her brothers already knew exactly what had happened, and by extension so did their wives. And even though she hadn't spoken to her parents about it at all, she suspected they knew. Well, her mother had picked up on her attachment to Levi right away, so why wouldn't she have this figured out as well?

Faith sighed heavily and looked down at her pot roast. She just wasn't feeling up to it. You would think that after two weeks things would start to feel better. Instead, if anything, they were getting worse.

How was that supposed to work? Shouldn't time be healing?

Instead she was reminded that she had a lot more time without him stretching in front of her. And she didn't want that. No. She didn't.

She wished she could have him. She wished it more than anything.

The problem was, Joshua was right. She was kind of secretly hoping things would work out. That he would come back to her.

But he hadn't.

That was the problem, she supposed, about never having had a real heartbreak before.

She hadn't had all that hope knocked out of her yet.

Well, maybe this would be the thing that did it.

Not at all a cheering thought.

There was a knock on the door, and her parents looked around the table, as if counting everybody in attendance. Everyone was there. From Devlin on down to baby Riley.

"I wonder who that could be," her mother said.

"I'll check," said her father as he stood and walked out of the dining room, heading toward the entryway.

For some reason, Faith kept watch after him. For some reason, she couldn't look away, her entire body filled with tension.

Because she knew. Part of her knew.

When her father returned a moment later, Faith knew.

Because there he was.

Levi.

Levi Tucker, large and hard and absurd, standing in the middle of her parents' cozy dining room. It seemed… beyond belief. And yet, there he was.

"This young man says he's here to see you, Faith," her father said.

As if on cue, all three of her brothers stood, their

height matching Levi's. And none of them looked very happy.

"If he wants to see Faith, he might need to talk to us first," Devlin said.

Those rat bastards. She hadn't told Devlin. That meant clearly they'd had some kind of older-brother summit and had come to an agreement on whether or not they would smash Levi's face if he showed up. And obviously, they had decided that they would.

"I can talk to him," Faith said.

Their father now looked completely concerned, like maybe he should be standing with his sons on this one.

But her mother stood also, her tone soft but firm. "If Faith would like to a chance to speak to this gentleman, then I expect we should allow it."

Her sons, large, burly alpha males themselves, did exactly as their mother asked.

"I'll just be a minute," Faith said, as she slipped around the table, worked her way behind all the chairs and met Levi in the doorway.

"Hi," she said.

"Why don't we go into the living room?" he asked.

"Okay."

They walked out into the living room, where his presence was no less absurd. Where, in fact, he looked even more ridiculous standing on the hand-braided rug that her grandmother had made years ago, next to the threadbare sofa where she had grown up watching cartoons.

She had known she wouldn't be able to bring this man home with her.

He had followed her home anyway.

"Is everything all right with the design?" she asked, crossing her arms to make a shield over her heart. As if she could ever hope to protect it from him.

As if there were any unbroken pieces that remained.

He tipped back his hat, his mouth set into a grim line. "If I needed to talk to you about your design work I would have come to the office."

"Well, you might have made less of a scene if you would have come to the office."

"I also would have had to wait. Until Monday. And I couldn't wait." He took off his hat and set it on the side table by the couch. And now she'd think of his hat there every time she looked at it.

This was the real reason he should never have come to her parents' house.

She'd never be in it again without thinking of him, and how fair was that? She'd grown up in this house. And Levi had erased eighteen years of memories without him here in one fell swoop.

He sighed heavily. "It took some time, but I got my thoughts sorted out. And I needed to see you right away."

"Yes?" She tightened her crossed arms and looked up at him. But this time she didn't let herself get blinded by all that rugged beauty. This time she looked at him. Really looked.

He looked…exhausted. His handsome face seemed to have deeper lines etched into the grooves by his mouth, by his eyes, and he looked like he hadn't been sleeping.

"Alicia came to see me," he said.

Her stomach hollowed out, sinking down to her toes. "What?"

"Alicia. She came to see me. She wanted us to get back together."

Faith's response was quick and unexpected. "How dare she? What was she thinking?" Even angry at him, that enraged her. The idea of that woman daring to show her face filled Faith with righteous fury. How dare Alicia speak to him with anything other than a humble apology as she walked across broken glass to get to him?

And if there had been broken glass he would have mentioned it.

"It was a perfect opportunity to find a way to make her pay for what she did to me, Faith. She handed herself to me. Told me her troubles. Told me she needed me to fix them. I wanted to destroy her, and she handed herself to me. Gave me all the tools to do that."

Ice seemed to fill her veins as he spoke those words. Those cold, terrifying words.

What had he done? What would he do?

"But you're right," he continued, his voice rough. "You were right all this time."

"About?" She pressed her hand to her chest, trying to calm her heart.

"I do have a choice. I have a choice about what kind of man I want to be, and about whether or not I choose to live my life in prison. I have a choice about what path I want to walk. I was worried I was on the same road as my father. That his kind of end was inevitable for me, but it was only ever inevitable if I embraced the hatred inside myself instead of the love. You showed me that. You taught me that. You gave me…something I didn't deserve, Faith. You believed in me when no one else did. When no one else ever had. You gave me a reason to believe I can have a different future. You gave me a reason to want a different future."

"I don't know how," she said. "I don't know how I could—"

"Sometimes looking at someone and seeing trust in their eyes changes everything. You looked at me and saw someone completely different than anyone else saw.

I want to be that man. For you. The man you see. The man you care about. That you want."

"Levi, you are. You always were."

"No," he said, the denial rough on his lips. "No, I wasn't. Because I was too consumed with other things. You are right. To take hold of something as valuable as love there are other things that need to be set down. Because love is too precious to handle without care. It's far too precious to carry in the same arms as hate, as anger. I couldn't hate Alicia with the passion that I did and also give you the love you deserve. It would have been like locking you in a prison cell with me, and you don't deserve that, Faith. You deserve so much more. You deserve everything." He took a deep breath. "I love you. I gave Alicia money. And it took the past couple of days to get that squared away. But I also drafted some legal documents. And she is not going to ever approach us. She's not speaking about me in the media. Nothing. If she does, she's going to have to return what I gave her."

"Why?" Faith asked. "Why did you…give her money?"

"To make sure she stayed out of our lives. I don't ever want her touching you."

"You didn't have to do that, Levi…"

"I would do anything to protect you," he said. "And I don't trust her. I needed to at least hold some kind of card to keep her away from us. And I knew that if she was just out there, desperate and grasping, she could become a problem later."

"But to give money to a woman you hate…"

He shook his head. "You know, suddenly it didn't matter as much. Not when there is a woman I love. A woman I would die for. Laying all my anger down was a small thing when I realized I'd lay my life down for you just as easily."

"Levi…"

"That feeling, *this* feeling," he said, taking a step toward her and grabbing her hand, placing her palm flat on his chest. "It is so much bigger than hate. That's what I want. I don't want to be my father's son. I don't want to be my ex-wife's victim. I want to be your husband."

"Yes," Faith said, her heart soaring. Her arms went around his neck and she kissed him. Kissed him like she wasn't in her parents' living room. Like he wasn't absurd, and they weren't a ridiculous couple.

She kissed him like he was everything.

Because he was.

"What about your plan? I didn't think you were going to get married until you were at least thirty-five? And to be clear, Faith, I would wait for you. I would. I will. Whatever you need."

She shook her head. "I don't want to wait. I don't see why I can't have all my dreams. I'm an overachiever, after all."

"Yes, you are." He laughed and picked her up off the floor. "Yes, you are."

She heard a throat clear, and she turned, seeing her dad standing in the doorway. "I expected that the man who would ask my daughter to marry him would ask for my permission first."

Levi squared his shoulders, moved forward and extended his hand. "I'm Levi Tucker," he said. "I would like to marry your daughter. But, no disrespect, sir, she's already said yes. And strictly speaking, hers is the answer I need."

Her father smiled slowly, and shook Levi's hand. "That is correct. And I think…you just might be the one who can handle her."

"Handle me?" Faith said, "I'm not *that* hard to handle."

"Not hard to handle," her dad said. "You are precious cargo. And I think he knows that."

"I do," Levi said. "She's the most important thing in my life."

"I'm not that important," she said.

"No, you only saved me. That's all."

"That's all," Faith said, smiling up at him.

"It's good he proposed," her father said. "Now I probably won't have to stop my sons from killing you. Probably."

Her dad turned and walked back into the dining room, leaving Levi and Faith alone together.

"How badly do I really have to worry about your brothers?"

She waved a hand. "You're probably fine."

"Probably?"

"Probably," she confirmed.

She looked up into his eyes, and her heart felt like it took flight. Like a bird.

Like freedom.

And as he gathered her up in his arms, held her close, she knew that for them that was love.

Redemption. Hope. Freedom.

Always.

Epilogue

When the house was finished, he carried her over the threshold.

"You're only supposed to do that with your wife," she pointed out.

"You're going to be my wife soon enough," Levi said, leaning in and kissing her, emotion flooding his chest.

"Just a couple of months now."

"It's going to be different," he said.

"What is?"

"Marriage. For me. When I got married the first time... It wasn't that I didn't care. I did. But I thought I could prove something with that marriage. She wasn't the important thing—I was. No matter what I told myself, it was more about proving something to me than it was about being a good husband to her. And that isn't what I want with you. I love you. I don't want to prove anything. I just want to be with you. I just want to make you happy."

"And I want to make you happy. I think if both of us are coming at our relationship from that angle, we're going to be okay."

He set her down in the empty space, and the two of them looked around. The joy in her eyes was unmistakable. The wonder.

"We're standing in a place you created. Does that amaze you?"

It amazed him. She amazed him. He'd thought of her as too innocent for him. Too young. Too a lot of things. But Faith Grayson was a force. Powerful, creative. Beautiful.

Perfect for him.

She ducked her head, color flooding her cheeks. "It kind of does. Even though I've made a lot of buildings now. I've never…made one for me."

"You did this for *me*. I never asked you if that bothered you."

"Why would it bother me?"

"We talked about this. You haven't had a chance to design your own house yet."

She looked down at her hands, and then back up at him, sincerity shining from her brown eyes. "You know, I've always thought a lot about homes. Of course I did. How could I not, in my line of work? But I always felt like home was the place where you grew up. I never thought any place could feel like home to me more than my parents' house. I took my first steps there. I cried over tests, I was stressed about college admissions in my little bed. I had every holiday, endless family discussions around the dinner table. I never thought any place, even if it was custom-built for me, could ever feel more like home than there. I was wrong, though."

"Oh?"

She took a step toward him, pressing her fingers to his chest. "This is home."

"We don't even have any furniture."

"Not the house." She stretched up on her toes and kissed him on the lips. "You. You're my home. Wherever you are. That's my home."

* * * * *

Get 4 FREE REWARDS!

We'll send you 2 FREE Books <u>plus</u> 2 FREE Mystery Gifts.

FREE
Value Over
$20

Both the **Harlequin® Desire** and **Harlequin Presents®** series feature compelling novels filled with passion, sensuality and intriguing scandals.

YES! Please send me 2 FREE novels from the Harlequin Desire or Harlequin Presents series and my 2 FREE gifts (gifts are worth about $10 retail). After receiving them, if I don't wish to receive any more books, I can return the shipping statement marked "cancel." If I don't cancel, I will receive 6 brand-new Harlequin Presents Larger-Print books every month and be billed just $6.30 each in the U.S. or $6.49 each in Canada, a savings of at least 10% off the cover price, or 6 Harlequin Desire books every month and be billed just $5.05 each in the U.S. or $5.74 each in Canada, a savings of at least 12% off the cover price. It's quite a bargain! Shipping and handling is just 50¢ per book in the U.S. and $1.25 per book in Canada.* I understand that accepting the 2 free books and gifts places me under no obligation to buy anything. I can always return a shipment and cancel at any time by calling the number below. The free books and gifts are mine to keep no matter what I decide.

Choose one: ☐ **Harlequin Desire**   ☐ **Harlequin Presents Larger-Print**
                  (225/326 HDN GRJ7)   (176/376 HDN GRJ7)

Name (please print)

Address   Apt. #

City   State/Province   Zip/Postal Code

Email: Please check this box ☐ if you would like to receive newsletters and promotional emails from Harlequin Enterprises ULC and its affiliates. You can unsubscribe anytime.

Mail to the **Harlequin Reader Service:**
IN U.S.A.: P.O. Box 1341, Buffalo, NY 14240-8531
IN CANADA: P.O. Box 603, Fort Erie, Ontario L2A 5X3

Want to try 2 free books from another series! Call 1-800-873-8635 or visit www.ReaderService.com.

*Terms and prices subject to change without notice. Prices do not include sales taxes, which will be charged (if applicable) based on your state or country of residence. Canadian residents will be charged applicable taxes. Offer not valid in Quebec. This offer is limited to one order per household. Books received may not be as shown. Not valid for current subscribers to the Harlequin Presents or Harlequin Desire series. All orders subject to approval. Credit or debit balances in a customer's account(s) may be offset by any other outstanding balance owed by or to the customer. Please allow 4 to 6 weeks for delivery. Offer available while quantities last.

Your Privacy—Your information is being collected by Harlequin Enterprises ULC, operating as Harlequin Reader Service. For a complete summary of the information we collect, how we use this information and to whom it is disclosed, please visit our privacy notice located at corporate.harlequin.com/privacy-notice. From time to time we may also exchange your personal information with reputable third parties. If you wish to opt out of this sharing of your personal information, please visit readerservice.com/consumerschoice or call 1-800-873-8635. **Notice to California Residents**—Under California law, you have specific rights to control and access your data. For more information on these rights and how to exercise them, visit corporate.harlequin.com/california-privacy.

HDHP22R3

HARLEQUIN
PLUS

Try the best multimedia subscription service for romance readers like you!

Read, Watch and Play.

Experience the easiest way to get the romance content you crave.

Start your **FREE TRIAL** at
<u>www.harlequinplus.com/freetrial</u>.